Longtree was as tense as a guitar string, and he stared at the Japanese soldier's eyes. He knew that the Japanese soldier wanted to get away, and he could see the panic in the Jap's eyes. The Japanese soldier shouted, feinted with the knife in his left hand, then tossed the knife to his right hand and pushed forward to Longtree's stomach.

Longtree tucked his stomach in and dodged to the side, as graceful as a matador, while slicing down with his knife. His razor-sharp blade caught the Jap on the neck...

Hot Lead and Cold Steel

by
John Mackie

A JOVE BOOK

Excepting basic historical events, places, and personages, this series of books is fictional, and anything that appears otherwise is coincidental and unintentional.

The principal characters are imaginary, although they might remind veterans of specific men whom they knew. The Twenty-third Infantry Regiment, in which the characters serve, is used fictitiously—it doesn't represent the real historical Twenty-third Infantry, which has distinguished itself in so many battles from the Civil War to Vietnam—but it could have been any American line regiment that fought and bled during World War II.

These novels are dedicated to the men who were there. May their deeds and gallantry never be forgotten.

HOT LEAD AND COLD STEEL

A Jove book / published by arrangement with
the author

PRINTING HISTORY
Jove edition / September 1984

ISBN: 0-515-07747-X

Jove books are published by The Berkley Publishing Group,
200 Madison Avenue, New York, N.Y. 10016. The words
"A JOVE BOOK" and the "J" with sunburst are trademarks
belonging to Jove Publications, Inc.

PRINTED IN THE UNITED STATES OF AMERICA

ONE . . .

It was the first of August, 1943, and the Twenty-third Infantry Regiment moved west through the jungle of New Georgia, heading for the main military objective on the island, the Japanese airfield on Munda Point.

It had rained all night, and the leaves of the jungle were coated with water. The ground had become muck and the GIs slogged through it, their rifles in their hands, ready to fire. They knew the Japs would defend their airfield with the same fanaticism with which they defended everything else, and the final showdown would be bloody and grim.

The recon platoon was on the left flank of the advance, and it had taken heavy casualties since the landing in mid-July. Always in the thick of the fighting, now it was forty percent of strength, and many of its soldiers wore red bandages as they made their way through the steaming, stinking jungle.

It was morning and the sun was bright and hot, but its rays couldn't pierce the gloom of the thick jungle. The heat radiated through, and the men felt as if they were in a steambath.

Pfc. Sam Longtree, a full-blooded Apache Indian from a reservation in Arizona, was the point man for the recon platoon, and he slipped through the jungle twenty yards ahead of the platoon's main advance. He was tall and lanky, with weathered skin and sharp eyes. His helmet was festooned with leaves and his shirt was unbuttoned to his waist, with the sleeves rolled up over his sinewy biceps. A bandage was tied around his left thigh and bulged out underneath his fatigue pants. He'd been slashed by a bayonet in the vicious hand-to-hand fighting near Zanana, but the wound wasn't deep and he walked with only a slight limp.

The jungle was so thick, Longtree could see only a few yards in front of him. An entire battalion of Japs could be within hand-grenade–throwing distance and Longtree wouldn't be able to spot them. But no Jap ever would get close enough to knife him. Longtree was too clever for that. His M 1 rifle had a round in the chamber and a bayonet affixed to its end. If a Jap tried to jump him, the Jap would wind up skewered on the end of an American bayonet.

The jungle was silent, its animals and birds made apprehensive by the movement of so many men through their territory. Monkeys sat on branches with their arms around each other, looking down at the strange biped creatures with leaves growing out of their heads. Birds hopped from tree to tree, making low clucking sounds. On the ground, lizards and wild pigs lay in the bushes and tried not to draw attention to themselves. Most of the creatures were shocked and traumatized by the constant shelling and gunfire, and the war had forced many of them to leave their usual haunts.

It was eight o'clock, and the recon platoon had been on the move since six. It had met no enemy resistance, and Longtree was getting bored. His mind wandered back to the reservation in Arizona, to the pretty girls he had left behind, to the poverty and misery, and sometimes he wondered what he was doing fighting on the same side as the people who had cheated and slaughtered Apaches for more than a hundred years.

Machine-gun fire erupted behind him, shattering the silence of the jungle. Birds shrieked and flew into the air, flapping their wings hysterically, and Longtree dived toward the ground. He turned in the direction of the fire, trying to home in on it, when suddenly it stopped and the jungle became silent again. He heard shouting behind him as American officers and noncoms issued orders.

Longtree had been in the Pacific war for nearly a year, long enough to know that the machine gun he'd heard was Japanese, probably the water-cooled Type 92, a heavy machine gun used in fixed fortifications. That meant it was most likely firing from a bunker. It was possible that he'd passed within sight of the bunker, but the Japs didn't fire at him because he was only one man. Their firing discipline was always excellent, and they didn't open up until they had a lot of targets directly in front of them. They stopped firing when the targets took cover, so they wouldn't give their position away.

Longtree wondered if anybody in the recon platoon had been hit. He decided to circle back and try to find the bunker.

Master Sergeant John Butsko, the platoon sergeant of the recon platoon, knelt over Private Michael Reiner of Green Bay, Wisconsin, who had stopped a machine-gun bullet with his lower abdomen. Reiner's shirt and pants were soaked with blood and his face was ashen as he lay unconscious on the ground. Private Joe Gundy, the medic, had just jammed an ampule of morphine into Reiner's ass and now was reaching into his haversack for sulfa powder to disinfect the wound.

"Whataya think?" Butsko asked Gundy.

"They'll probably have to take out about half his stomach, but he'll live."

Butsko grit his teeth and looked around. Private Watson, Pfc. Futterman, and Private Borak had also been hit by those Japanese machine-gun bursts, which had been so sudden that nobody saw where they came from. The other men lay behind trees and underneath bushes, waiting for somebody to tell them what to do.

Butsko crawled past them, heading toward First Lieutenant Dale Breckenridge, the platoon leader. He saw Breckenridge crouching in a little glen, a stream two feet wide running past him, and the air was thick with mosquitoes and other flying insects that lived on blood.

Breckenridge held a walkie-talkie against his face and was listening to it; Butsko surmised he was talking with Captain Ilecki, the CO of Company A, to which the recon platoon was temporarily attached. Next to Breckenridge was Private Craig Delane, the rich guy from New York, who was Lieutenant Breckenridge's runner.

Butsko slithered into the glen, cradling his M 1 rifle in his arms. He was six feet tall, built like a tank, and wore a filthy bandage on his left cheek. Lieutenant Breckenridge was six feet five inches tall, weighed 265 pounds, and his face and neck were pitted with acne. His helmet sat high on his head because a bandage covered a large portion of his scalp.

"Yes, sir," he said into the mouthpiece of the walkie-talkie. "Over and out." He handed the walkie-talkie to Craig Delane, and looked at Butsko. "What's the story?"

"Watson is dead; Futterman, Borak, and Reiner are wounded."

Lieutenant Breckenridge scratched a mosquito bite on his pug nose. "Captain Ilecki wants us to find that machine gun. Anybody see where it was?"

"No."

"Have the men fan out squad by squad and look for it. Has Longtree reported anything?"

"No."

"Get him back here. Maybe he saw something."

Butsko cupped his hands around his mouth. *"Longtree!"*

There was no answer.

"Longtree, get the fuck back here!"

Still no answer.

Lieutenant Breckenridge wrinkled his brow. "Maybe something happened to him."

"Maybe," Butsko replied, "but I don't think so."

Longtree had heard Butsko calling for him, but he didn't want to reply because he didn't know how close he was to the Jap machine gun. He was crawling through the thick underbrush in the direction of the fire that he'd heard, and it might be only a few yards away.

He stopped to reorient himself, glancing around, taking note of terrain details, not wanting to get lost in the jungle. The wind shifted and brought him a faint whiff of something awful, the unmistakable odor of a latrine.

Longtree knew the Americans hadn't been in the area long enough to build a latrine, so it had to belong to the Japs. Maybe it was the latrine used by the Japs in that bunker. He sniffed the air and determined the direction of the wind, then shifted direction and crawled toward the stink.

He was as silent as a snake and nearly as fast as he moved

4

over the muck and gunk that was the jungle floor. The bandage on his leg rubbed against the ground, but Longtree had been trained since early childhood to disregard pain. The smell of the latrine became stronger and Longtree smiled. The Japs wouldn't dig the latrine too far from their bunker. They'd want to get back in a hurry in case of trouble. But it would be far enough away so that the latrine wouldn't stink up the bunker.

Longtree heard a footstep in front of him, perhaps ten or twenty yards away. He knew he might be mistaken; it might be an animal rustling in the leaves or a dead branch falling to the ground, but it sounded like a footstep to him. He paused and listened closely, hearing the same sound again. Somebody was walking out there, and Longtree wondered whose side he was on.

The footsteps stopped. The jungle became silent again. Longtree wondered what the person out there was doing, when suddenly he heard the comical sound of a big burbling fart. Longtree grinned and crept silently toward the sound. He made his way around a tree and underneath a network of vines, then stopped. Parting the leaves in front of him, he saw the back of a Japanese soldier with his pants down, squatting over a hole in the ground. The stench was horrible in the heat of the jungle, and swarms of flies buzzed loudly around the hole and the Jap's bottom.

The Jap was a sitting duck, motionless except for a big turd being squeezed out of his rear end. Longtree gripped his rifle tightly, took a deep breath, and leaped up, running toward the Jap, aiming his bayonet at the Jap's back.

The Jap heard him coming and turned his head around, but Longtree was already on top of him. Longtree rammed his rifle forward and his bayonet went into the Jap's right kidney up to the hilt. The Jap opened his mouth and shrieked for a second, but the Longtree's big hand covered the Jap's mouth. The odor from the latrine nearly knocked Longtree out, and the mud at the rim of the hole was still slippery from the previous night's rain.

Longtree nearly lost his footing and fell in the shit. He let go of the Jap and lurched back, yanking his bayonet out of the Jap's kidney. The Jap had gone into shock, and blood spurted out of the hole in his back. He toppled backward and fell headfirst into the pool of shit and piss in the hole. Longtree

5

watched in fascination as the Jap sank down to his waist, his legs bent over as if he were sitting upside down. The flies, disturbed by the sudden action, returned with a vengeance, covering the Jap's legs and bottom and the surface of the shit.

They also swarmed around Longtree's face, trying to fly into his nose and mouth, brushing their wings and legs against his eyeballs. Longtree waved them away and retreated into the jungle, crouching behind a bush. The flies left him and returned to the latrine.

Longtree wondered if the Japs in the bunker had heard the death cry of their comrade and, if they did, what would they do about it. Would they venture out of the bunker to investigate, when they knew American soldiers were moving into the area? Longtree decided they probably wouldn't. They'd want to stay at their posts and contend with the real danger in front of them.

He raised himself on his toes and moved through the jungle again, circling around the latrine, looking for the path that led from the latrine to the bunker.

Meanwhile the recon platoon was combing the jungle, searching for the Japanese bunker. Sergeant Charles Bannon from Pecos, Texas, the leader of the First Squad, had his men spread ten feet apart and moved them cautiously through the thick foliage.

"Keep your heads down," he said, "and keep your eyes open!"

Bannon was tall and lean, with blond hair and blue-green eyes. Before the war he'd been a cowboy, and he'd enlisted on the day after Pearl Harbor on a patriotic impulse that he'd since regretted many times.

His eyes roved back and forth through the jungle, searching for the bunker, hoping to spot it before the Japs inside saw him and his men. It was scary business, because the bunker would be well camouflaged. The Japs excelled in the art and science of camouflage. Bannon wouldn't see the bunker until he was right on top of it, and then it might be too late.

He kept himself loose, ready to drop to the ground at the least sign of danger. His body was covered with sweat, which soaked his uniform and plastered it against his skin. He smelled like a pig wallowing in shit and he itched all over from rashes and mosquito bites. He wished he could be anyplace exccpt in the hothouse jungle of New Georgia.

The Japanese machine gun opened fire, and Bannon hit the dirt, rolling to the side once so that he'd make a difficult target. The machine gun sounded like it was to the right of his squad. It stopped firing and Bannon heard Sergeant Cameron of the Third Squad asking if anybody was hurt. The thick jungle made it difficult for Bannon to hear distinctly, but it was his impression that at least one man was wounded. *How many people are we going to lose before we find that bunker?* he wondered.

"All right, swing to the right!" he shouted. "Watch your step because we're getting close!"

He and his men arose and moved, hunched over, in the direction of the machine-gun fire that they'd heard. Bannon hoped they'd run into the bunker on its flank, instead of walking into the mouth of the machine gun. "Fucking Japs," he said to himself. "Fucking bastards."

The First Squad stepped cautiously through the jungle as the sun rose in the sky and the day grew hotter. Bannon had a stomach ache and his feet alternately itched and ached from the trench foot that had been afflicting him ever since he had landed on New Georgia. His eyes stung from peering intently through the leaves ahead. Reaching into his shirt pocket, he took out a pack of Chesterfield cigarettes and poked one into his mouth. He lit it with his Zippo and dropped the Zippo into his pant pocket. The smoke in his lungs made him slightly dizzy for a moment, but it was better than what he'd been feeling. *I really ought to stop smoking,* he thought. *It cuts my wind.*

To the left of Bannon was Private Frankie La Barbara from New York City, husky and swarthy, with wavy jet black hair and handsome Mediterranean features. Frankie chewed gum frantically and was as tense as a guitar string because he'd dreamed the previous night that he'd be shot by a Jap today, and he was superstitious enough to believe that dreams could predict the future.

He was afraid that the Jap machine gunners would see him first and shoot him down, so he tried to lag behind the skirmish line, hoping the Japs would shoot somebody else.

"Move it up, Frankie!" shouted Bannon. "Get the lead out!"

Shit, Frankie thought, *he saw me.* Pinching his lips together, he moved forward and lined himself up with the others. Sweat poured down his face and he'd been constipated for three days; His stomach was bloated and he felt awful. *I can't take this*

7

war anymore, he thought. *I'm gonna go nuts if I have to keep this up.*

Suddenly a figure rose out of the bushes three feet in front of Frankie, and he nearly jumped out of his skin. His eyes bulged, his tongue stuck out, and he raised his rifle to shoot the man down.

"Relax," said Longtree. "It's me."

Frankie wheezed. "You scared the shit out of me!"

Longtree stepped forward. "Where's Bannon?"

"I'm over here," Bannon replied. "Where the fuck you been?"

Longtree trudged toward Bannon and pointed west. "Back there."

"Didn't you hear Butsko calling you?"

"Yeah, I heard him. Where is he? I found the Jap bunker."

"No shit?"

"No shit."

"Hey, Butsko!" Bannon yelled.

"Whataya want?" replied Butsko from somewhere in the jungle ahead of them and slightly to the right.

"Longtree's here and he's found the bunker!"

"Longtree!" Butsko bellowed.

"Hup, Sarge!" Longtree replied.

"Get your ass over here!"

"Yo!"

Longtree turned and headed toward Butsko's voice. Everybody in the platoon had heard the conversation and stopped where they were, because they figured new orders would be coming down soon. They dropped to the ground and took swigs from their canteens or lit cigarettes. They wiped the grit and perspiration from their faces and wished they were someplace else.

Longtree found Butsko with Lieutenant Breckenridge and Craig Delane sitting around in the jungle. Lieutenant Breckenridge had his map out and was trying to figure out where he was, relative to the Japanese airfield. Delane was listening to his walkie-walkie, trying to pick up some news, and Butsko puffed a cigarette, a pissed-off expression on his face.

"Where is it?" Butsko asked.

Longtree pointed in a westerly direction. "Over that way. Maybe it'd be better if I showed you."

"Okay," Butsko said, pushing himself up off the ground.

8

"I'll be right back," he said to Lieutenant Breckenridge.

"Don't get shot," Lieutenant Breckenridge replied.

Butsko grunted something that could have meant anything as he joined Longtree. Together they disappeared into the green sweltering sea that was the New Georgia jungle.

"Delane," said Lieutenant Breckenridge. "Get me Captain Ilecki."

"Yes, sir."

Delane pressed the button on the walkie-talkie. "Red Rover calling Boomer. Red Rover calling Boomer. Can you read me, Boomer? Can you read me, Boomer? Over."

Lieutenant Breckenridge looked at his map as Craig Delane tried to make the connection with Captain Ilecki's command post. Lieutenant Breckenridge was as tired and miserable as the others, but he was their officer and he had to set an example. The men could complain, and even Master Sergeant Butsko could piss and moan, but not Lieutenant Breckenridge. Although he was an OCS graduate, a ninety-day wonder instead of a West Pointer, he was from an old Virginia family that traced itself back to the Revolutionary War, and he had a keen sense of honor and obligation. Butsko could bully the men and push them around, but Lieutenant Breckenridge had to inspire them even when he didn't feel very inspired himself.

"I've got Captain Ilecki, sir," Craig Delane said.

Lieutenant Breckenridge took the walkie-talkie. "I've found that bunker, sir."

"You think you can take it out yourself?"

"It's only got one machine gun, as far as we know. We should be able to handle it."

"Call me if you need anything."

"Yes, sir."

Lieutenant Breckenridge handed the walkie-talkie back to Craig Delane, then pulled out an Old Gold cigarette and lit it up. He took off his helmet and ran his fingers through his close-cropped light-brown hair. Putting his helmet back on, he puffed his cigarette and lay on his back, stretching out, closing his eyes. He'd learned to rest whenever he could, because rest renewed his energy, and energy was the key to survival.

Craig Delane sat cross-legged a few feet away and looked Lieutenant Breckenridge over. Like Lieutenant Breckenridge, Craig Delane was from an old patrician family whose roots

9

extended back to colonial days, but Delane was from New York City, and he had no leadership ability that he was aware of. One of the smallest men in the recon platoon, he was only five feet eight inches tall, built on the slender side, and was amazed at how well Lieutenant Breckenridge ran the platoon, keeping even Master Sergeant Butsko in line.

Delane used to think that Lieutenant Breckenridge was an effective leader because he was so big and his size intimidated everyone, but after a while he'd been forced to admit that it wasn't just size. Lieutenant Breckenridge had a special quality that made people respect him. It was a certain inner strength and confidence, a quality of self-assurance that Craig Delane had never had in his life. Whenever the war quieted down and Delane had time to reflect on the differences between Lieutenant Breckenridge and himself, he became depressed. He felt inadequate, as if he'd missed the boat someplace in his life. Disgusted with himself, he lit a cigarette and held the walkie-talkie against his face in case somebody tried to reach the recon platoon.

TWO . . .

It was hotter inside the bunker than in the steaming, sweltering jungle. Constructed of logs and sandbags, its only ventilation came from the narrow slit provided for the barrel of the machine gun, and the heat of the firing made the confined space as hot as an oven.

The Japanese soldiers sat around their machine gun, stripped to their waists, their bodies glistening with sweat. They knew that American soldiers were trying to locate them and sooner or later their position would become known. Then the Americans would attack in overwhelming numbers and eventually kill them all.

The Japanese soldiers tried to be brave and think lofty thoughts of joining their ancestors in heaven and dying for the glory of their Emperor, but they also couldn't help thinking that they'd soon be shot down like dogs, or blown to bits by American hand grenades, or burned alive by American flame-throwers.

Sergeant Koji Ryufuku was in charge of the machine-gun section. He was a small wiry man with a thin mustache and a head that had been shaved smooth ten days earlier but was now covered with stubble a quarter of an inch long. He was wondering about Private Ono, who'd left to move his bowels fifteen minutes before and never returned. Some of his men thought they'd heard Private Ono shout something, but they couldn't be sure because the jungle was full of strange sounds, and they couldn't hear much anyway inside the thick-walled bunker.

Under normal circumstances they kept the rear door open, but it was closed and sandbagged now that the American soldiers were so close. Two Japanese soldiers peered out the narrow slit through binoculars, hoping to spot American soldiers. Another sat behind the gun, ready to fire. And Sergeant Ryufuku squatted on his heels in a corner, wishing he could smoke a cigarette, but the air was foul enough as it was.

They were all farmers, as were most of the ordinary soldiers in the Imperial Army. They were accustomed to hardship and were at home in the wilderness. This is what made them such outstanding jungle fighters. Colonel Hirata, who commanded the 229th Infantry Regiment, had ordered them to kill ten American soldiers each and to fight to the death.

All the Japanese soldiers in the bunker were determined to do just that. Their families would be proud of them when they learned that they'd died in battle, defending the glory of their Emperor.

Longtree crawled over the jungle floor with Butsko a few feet behind him. Branches scraped over their helmets and backs, and bugs bit their necks. It was nearly noon and the sun was at its peak in the bright blue sky. Steam wafted up from the floor of the jungle, along with the fetid odor of rotting vegetation. The fronts of their uniforms were covered with mud, and Butsko was getting a headache. He wished he'd brought his APC pills with him, but they were in his pack and his pack was back with Lieutenant Breckenridge.

Longtree stopped, twisted toward Butsko, and motioned with his finger for Butsko to come forward. Butsko dug his elbows and knees into the ground and advanced until he was beside Longtree, who pressed his forefinger against his lips, then pointed straight ahead through the bushes.

At first Butsko couldn't see anything, but then, among the leaves and branches, he picked out the unnatural lines of logs and sandbags. It was the usual Japanese bunker, solidly constructed, difficult to destroy without a howitzer, and howitzers couldn't be moved through thick jungle.

"You stay here and keep an eye on it," Butsko told Longtree.

Longtree nodded. Butsko slithered around and made his way back to Lieutenant Breckenridge.

"When will they come?" asked Private Ebara, sitting behind the machine gun inside the bunker.

"Soon enough," replied Sergeant Ryufuku. "Change places with Ishikura and be alert."

"Yes, Sergeant."

Private Ebara moved from behind the machine gun and accepted the binoculars from the hands of Pfc. Ishikura, who took Ebara's place behind the gun. Pfc. Ishikura worked the bolt one time and looked through the sights at the jungle ahead. The suspense was becoming unbearable. Even Sergeant Ryufuku, the old battle-hardened veteran, felt the rise of panic inside his heart.

"Let's settle down," said Sergeant Ryufuku. "Dying for the Emperor is the greatest glory that can come to any man."

"I feel hungry," said Private Kanda from the left side of the machine gun, his binoculars held to his eyes.

"Eat something," said Sergeant Ryufuku. "I'll take your place."

"No, I'll stay at my post," Private Kanda said. "It's all right."

"I said eat something." Sergeant Ryufuku leaned forward and gently took the binoculars from Private Kanda's hands. "It's time for lunch anyway. We can take turns eating until the Americans come."

"Maybe they won't come," said Private Ebara. "Maybe they'll go around us."

"I don't think we can count on that," Sergeant Ryufuku said.

Private Kanda unscrewed his metal container of cold cooked rice and picked some up with his chopsticks, placing the rice on his tongue. It was silent inside the bunker, except for the heavy breathing of the men and the sound of Private Kanda eating. The Japanese soldiers had expressions of grim resignation on their faces. Each knew that the bunker soon would become his tomb.

The recon platoon's Second Squad, under Corporal Lupe Gomez, the ex-pachuco from Los Angeles, crawled forward on a line perpendicular to the front of the bunker. They moved

13

slowly and cautiously, because they wanted to see the Japs before the Japs saw them. Their mission would be to occupy the center of the recon platoon line and lay down a heavy base of fire from fixed positions, pinning the Japs down, attracting their fire, and distracting them from the recon platoon's main effort, which would come from the First Squad.

Bannon led the First Squad forward on the left flank. Beside him was Private Tommy Shaw, a former heavyweight boxer, who carried the recon platoon's flamethrower. Shaw would be the key to victory over the bunker. All efforts were geared to getting him close to the opening of the bunker so he could pour the fire in and roast the Japs alive.

On the right flank of the recon platoon line the Third Squad moved forward under Sergeant Larry Cameron, a dirt farmer from Louisiana. The Third Squad's mission was to attack in tandem with the First Squad and then swing around to make sure no Japs escaped from the rear of the bunker.

After the Second Squad was on its way, Lieutenant Breckenridge moved his right hand forward, and the two sixty-millimeter sections from the weapons squad advanced. They'd set up their tubes to the rear of the Second Squad and lob mortar rounds at the bunker. Their mortar rounds wouldn't do any serious harm, but they'd make it difficult for the Japs to see clearly and think straight with explosions taking place all around them.

The two machine-gun sections from the heavy-weapons squad was with Corporal Gomez's Second Squad and would pepper the Japanese bunker, helping to keep the Japs pinned down.

The tactics were tried and true, used successfully against bunkers ever since the recon platoon had landed on New Georgia. But the recon platoon had never yet assaulted a bunker without taking at least one casualty, and everybody wondered if this time it would be him.

"I hear them!" said Private Ebara inside the bunker.

"Ssshhh," replied Sergeant Ryufuku.

They listened, and sure enough the sound of a large number of men coming through the jungle could be heard. The Americans were attacking, and it sounded like a whole army of them.

"Don't fire until I give the order," Sergeant Ryufuku whispered as he scanned the jungle ahead through his binoculars. His nerve endings tingled and his pores oozed with fresh per-

14

spiration. He knew that the last act in the story of his life was about to be played.

Private Ridgefield was the first man in the Second Squad to see the bunker. "There it is!" he muttered.

"Where?" asked Gomez.

Ridgefield pointed. "There."

Gomez followed his finger and saw the sandbags and logs in the thick jungle ahead. "Ah," he said. "*Excelente*. The rest of you guys move up until you see it, but for Chrissakes, don't let them see you."

His men crawled forward stealthily while Gomez raised his walkie-talkie to his face. "Red Dog One calling Red Rover. Red Dog One calling Red Rover. Do you read me? Over."

"It's Corporal Gomez," said Craig Delane. "He's in position."

Lieutenant Breckenridge looked at his watch; it was nearly high noon. He, Delane, and Sergeant Butsko were moving forward behind the Second Squad, and the excitement was building inside them. They'd done this many times already, but when your life is on the line, every time is like the first time.

"I think this is about far enough," Lieutenant Breckenridge said, dropping to his knees on the ground. "The Second Squad's just ahead."

Craig Delane wrinkled his brow as Sergeant Cameron reported in on the walkie-talkie. "The Third Squad is in position," he said.

Lieutenant Breckenridge took a deep breath. "Good."

"I'll leave for the First Squad now," Butsko said.

"Okay."

Butsko angled off to the side, walked several paces crouched over, and then lowered himself onto his belly, crawling toward the First Squad, the crucial place to be in the attack.

As he was moving up, Bannon's voice came in over Craig Delane's walkie-talkie. "First Squad in place," he said.

"I read you loud and clear," Delane replied.

The jungle was silent. Inside the bunker Sergeant Ryufuku sat behind the machine gun, swinging it from side to side, peering through its sights at the jungle in front of him. He

15

knew that the Americans were in position and that their attack would come any moment now.

Private Ebara sat to his left, feeding the belt into the chamber of the machine gun. Private Kanda was to the right of the gun, aiming his Arisaka rifle out the slit. Pfc. Ishikura was to the left of Private Ebara, and he also had his Arisaka rifle ready to fire.

"It won't be long now," Sergeant Ryufuku said, perspiration streaming down his face. "I shall give the order to fire, and remember that our orders are for each of us to kill ten American soldiers."

Lieutenant Breckenridge grunted as he crawled beside Gomez, who pointed straight ahead. Lieutenant Breckenridge focused his eyes and picked out the details of the bunker. "Well, well, well," he said. "So that's the place. Corporal Gomez, direct your squad to open fire."

"Open fire!" screamed Gomez.

The silence of the jungle was torn apart by the sound of rifles, Browning automatic rifles, and .30 caliber machine guns. Bullets slammed into the bunker, splintering the logs, ricocheting off rocks, and kicking up dirt in front of the narrow slit. Nearly simultaneously the First and Third squads also opened fire, and then mortar rounds landed behind the bunker.

"Tell the mortar sections to readjust their fire twenty yards forward!" Lieutenant Breckenridge shouted to Craig Delane.

"Yes, sir!"

Flashes of light leaped out of the hole in front of the bunker as the Japs opened fire. The Japanese bullets slashed through the jungle over the heads of the GIs or around them. The GIs had only a tiny target, the opening in front of the bunker, while the Japs had the whole jungle.

"Yooowwwwww!" shouted Pfc. Vitagliano, going limp on the ground, a bullet hole in his face. His cry was brief because he went unconscious immediately.

Private Gundy crawled toward him, rolled him over, and looked at the wound. It was big and ugly and in a bad place. He felt for Pfc. Vitagliano's pulse and found that there was none at all.

The battle for the bunker had claimed its first victim.

• • •

16

Inside the bunker the Japanese soldiers fired their weapons in a frenzy. Sergeant Ryufuku swung the machine gun from side to side, keeping the trigger depressed, but it was difficult for him to see through the tumult in front of his eyes. Dirt and spent American bullets flew in all directions, mortar rounds shook the bunker, and American lead sprayed through the narrow hole.

"Stay calm and keep firing!" Lieutenant Ryufuku yelled, shaking up and down with every recoil of the machine gun. "Make every shot count!"

Butsko lay next to Bannon on the left flank of the recon platoon line. All the soldiers pumped bullets into the bunker except for Shaw, who was behind them, fingering the nozzle of the flamethrower, a little jumpy because men with flamethrowers usually didn't live long.

"Okay!" Butsko shouted. "Move it out!"

The men from the First Squad gritted their teeth and began their long, slow crawl toward the Japanese bunker's right side.

Private Kanda's finger froze on the trigger of his rifle. "Look!" he said, pointing with his rifle. "They're attacking from over there!"

Sergeant Ryufuku swung his machine gun to the side, but it wouldn't go far enough. He fired a few bursts in that direction anyway, then turned to his front again.

"Don't worry!" he said. "The only way they can get us is from the front! Keep firing!"

Pfc. Ishikura flew backward as if he'd been shot out of a cannon. He smashed against the rear wall of the bunker and slid to the floor, a huge bloody wound on his forehead. Private Kanda stared at him in horror.

"Face front!" Sergeant Ryufuku ordered. "Maintain your fire!"

The First Squad worked itself around until it was on the blind left side of the bunker.

"Everybody okay?" Butsko asked, looking around.

Nobody said anything.

Butsko looked at Pfc. Hart, who carried the walkie-talkie. "Tell the lieutenant we're ready to roll."

Pfc. Hart pressed the button and called Craig Delane, transmitting the message. He waited, listened, and then turned to Butsko.

"The lieutenant says roll."

"Everybody ready?" Butsko asked.

The men nodded.

"You know what you gotta do?" Butsko asked Shaw.

"Yup."

"Okay," Butsko said. "This is it. One—two—three—*go!*"

The men jumped up and charged the side of the bunker; meanwhile the Third Squad was charging the other side. The Japs inside the bunker heard the pounding of feet, but there wasn't anything they could do about it. Each Jap felt like running out the back door, but there were too many sandbags to take out of the way and their honor wouldn't let them do it anyway. The Second Squad blasted them with bullets, and mortars exploded everywhere.

The First Squad sped through the jungle and approached the side of the bunker. Butsko spun around and landed with his back against the wall of the bunker, and the others crouched on both sides of him. Shaw was the last one to arrive, the seventy-pound flamethrower apparatus bouncing up and down on his back.

Bannon looked behind the bunker and saw the Third Squad rushing through the woods to cover the door.

"Cameron's here!" he yelled to Butsko above the roar of gunfire.

From in front of the bunker Lieutenant Breckenridge was watching everything through his binoculars. He'd ordered his mortar sections to stop firing as soon as the First Squad was near the bunker, and now everything was up to Butsko.

"Keep your fire tight on the front of the bunker!" Lieutenant Breckenridge told the men from the Second Squad. "I'll tell you when to stop!"

At the side of the bunker Butsko took a deep breath. "Everybody set?"

They all said that they were.

Butsko looked at Shaw. "Stay behind me."

Shaw nodded, his lips pale.

"Go!" yelled Butsko.

The First Squad charged around the corner and shot at the

tiny opening in front of the bunker. Butsko pulled a hand grenade from his lapel, yanked the pin, and let the handle fly away. He counted to three, then lobbed the grenade into the hole.

All the Japanese soldiers in the bunker saw the hand grenade fly through the opening. Private Kanda and Private Ebara tried to catch it, but they collided with each other while Sergeant Ryufuku looked on in horror. The grenade dropped to the ground and the two Japanese soldiers fell on top of it.

The grenade exploded violently, but its full blast was muffled by the bodies of the two soldiers, who were blown to bits. The concussion burst Sergeant Ryufuku's eardrums, and he was covered with the blood and guts of the two soldiers. Dazed, he stood behind the machine gun and pressed the palms of his hands against his ears. All thoughts of the Emperor and the glory of a soldier's death were submerged in the terrible head pain, and then he turned around to see a black tube intruding into the opening of the bunker. The tube roared and spat flame, and Sergeant Ryufuku was on fire. Shrieking, he fell to the floor and rolled around, trying to smother the flames that cooked him alive. His skin sizzled and blistered as the gobs of burning petroleum jelly ate him up.

He went into shock and the pain was gone. The flames continued to cook him, burning away his skin and charring his bones. His brains boiled inside his head, and the air inside the bunker smelled like charred meat.

Meanwhile the First and Third squads were at the rear of the bunker, and Butsko aimed his M 1 at the door. He pulled the trigger three times in rapid succession, blowing away the lock. Then he and Bannon rammed their shoulders against the door, pushing it open slightly, but sandbags prevented the door from being opened more.

"Nobody's alive in there," Bannon said. "Fuck 'em."

"We gotta make sure," Butsko said. "Everybody stand back."

The men retreated into the jungle as Butsko pulled another grenade from his lapel. He looked around to make sure everybody was safe, pulled the pin, and lay the grenade against the door. Releasing his grip, the lever popped off the grenade, and Butsko ran toward the jungle. He dived into the foliage and got behind a tree.

The grenade blew, shattering the door and ripping up the sandbags. The First and Third squads charged the rear of the bunker, and everybody had his rifle ready just in case. Smoke trailed into the sky from openings in the door, and Butsko kicked down the slats. The odor of burnt flesh from inside almost knocked him out. He kicked down the sandbags and jumped into the bunker with Bannon behind him and the rest of the men following.

Butsko landed on Sergeant Ryufuku's stomach, broke through the crispy charred skin, and went up to his ankles in steaming guts. Choking with revulsion, he leaped away, the gory mess clinging to his boots.

The others looked around at the shattered bodies. There were no escape hatches, no hidden trapdoors. The bunker had been put out of action. Butsko found some Japanese clothing in a corner and wiped off his boots.

"Hart," he said, "call the lieutenant and tell him we've got the bunker."

THREE . . .

The Twenty-third Infantry Regiment's command post was set up in the jungle about three-quarters of a mile from the bunker that the recon platoon had put out of the war. Colonel Stockton sat underneath a tree, his maps spread out on the ground around him. He made marks on the overlay with a pencil, indicating where his companies were and where he wanted them to go.

Next to him sat Private Levinson, carrying the backpack radio, and Private Nick Bombasino, the colonel's jeep driver and gofer. Nearby were Lieutenant Harper, the colonel's aide, and Major Cobb, the regimental operations officer. In the distance they could hear shells bursting and bullets being fired. American airplanes bombed the Japanese airfield on Munda Point, and Japanese fighter planes from Rabaul tried to force the American planes to return to Guadalcanal.

"Sir," said Private Levinson, "Captain Unger reports that he can see the outer runways of the Jap airfield from his position!"

Colonel Stockton's ears perked up, because this was the first contact his regiment made with the airfield. "Get me his coordinates."

"Yes, sir." Private Levinson obtained them from Captain

21

Unger and relayed them to Colonel Stockton, who marked the position on his map.

"Get me General Hawkins," Colonel Stockton said.

Private Levinson pressed the buttons and spoke the code words for the headquarters of General Clyde Hawkins, commanding officer of the Eighty-first Division. It took a few minutes to get through, and then he handed the headset to Colonel Stockton.

"Sir," said Colonel Stockton, "we've made contact with the Jap airfield. Should I keep going or stop?"

General Hawkins thought for a few moments. "Bring your regiment up to the airfield and hold them in place. I'll tell you when and how to attack. Is that clear?"

"Yes, sir."

"Over and out."

Colonel Stockton handed the headset back to Private Levinson and then looked at his map, planning the ways he could bring all of his units to the airfield. "Levinson," he said, "tell all the commanders to stop and dig in as soon as they can see the airfield."

"Yes, sir."

Private Levinson called the commander of the First Battalion. Meanwhile Colonel Stockton continued to draw lines on his map.

"Lieutenant Harper!" Colonel Stockton said.

"Yes, sir."

"Have my tent set up over here."

"Yes, sir."

The recon platoon had stopped for chow, while nearby the destroyed Japanese bunker continued to reek. Lieutenant Breckenridge had sent out listening posts to make sure no Japs would sneak up on them, and they dug into their cans of cold C rations.

They ate silently, because they were too tired to talk. They didn't think much, either, because their minds were numb. Insufficient sleep, constant anxiety, and a steady diet of greasy C rations was taking its toll. When they finished eating they took out cigarettes and lit up, hoping they could have a long rest but knowing they'd have to move out again soon.

Lieutenant Breckenridge's helmet was off, and the bandage

22

on his head was caked with muck and dried blood. He lay on the ground and puffed his cigarette, looking up at the sunlight peeking through openings in the leaves and branches of the trees.

Private Gundy, the medic, walked toward him. "Sir, why don't you let me change that bandage."

"Go ahead."

Private Gundy peeled the old bandage away as Lieutenant Breckenridge took a deep drag on his cigarette. He thought Gundy was one of the more interesting men in the recon platoon, since Gundy was a conscientious objector who'd refused to carry a gun but consented to be a combat medic. Gundy evidently was no coward; he just didn't want to kill anybody.

"How's it look?" Lieutenant Breckenridge asked.

Gundy wrinkled his short freckled nose as he examined the wound. "It's coming along okay. If it was someplace else you could let the air get at it, but since your helmet would chafe against it, I'd better put another bandage on."

"Anything you say, Doc."

Gundy opened his haversack and took out a pack of gauze. He tore off a piece, covered it with antiseptic, and cleaned the wound.

"Ouch," said Lieutenant Breckenridge.

"Got to do it," said Gundy.

"Go ahead and do it." Lieutenant Breckenridge sucked smoke into his lungs and looked at his cigarette. Only an inch was left, and he wondered whether he should light up another one right away. "Hey, Gundy," he said, "what would you do if a Jap with a bayonet attacked you and you saw a rifle lying on the ground. Would you pick up the rifle and kill the Jap?"

Gundy looked thoughtful as he applied the fresh bandage. "I really don't know. I hope I never have to find out."

"I hope so, too, but tell me something: Wouldn't you rather fight for your life than get killed?"

"Like I said, sir, I don't know. All I can tell you is that I don't want to kill anybody. I think I'd rather die myself than kill somebody. I think the pain of getting killed would be easier for me than the pain of killing somebody else."

"Even if the somebody else was evil."

"It's for God to decide who's evil and who isn't. Christ said that we're not supposed to judge other people."

Lieutenant Breckenridge recalled that Gundy had been in a Trappist monastery before he'd joined the Army. The war broke out before he'd taken his solemn vows, and he had left the monastery to become a combat medic.

"Do you ever miss the monastery, Gundy?"

Gundy smiled. "All the time."

"Ever wish you'd stayed there?"

"Every day."

"You mean you're sorry you joined the Army?"

"No."

"Well, you can't be in both places at once, Gundy."

"I know," Gundy replied, applying the adhesive tape to the area of Lieutenant Breckenridge's skull that had been shaved. "I think this is where I'm supposed to be, but I wish I could be back at the monastery."

"You'll go back after the war is over?"

"If I'm alive." Gundy looked at the bandage. "Well, that ought to hold you for a while, sir."

Gundy slung his haversack over his shoulder and walked away. Lieutenant Breckenridge lit a new cigarette with the butt of his old one and watched Gundy kneel down next to Bannon, whose hands had been cut by a Japanese sword in the bitter hand-to-hand fighting that had followed the initial landings on New Georgia.

Lieutenant Breckenridge watched Gundy through narrow eyes. Gundy had ended up in the recon platoon because his antiwar attitudes had grated on the nerves of officers and men in the other outfits he'd been in. He was considered an eight ball, and all the eight balls were transferred to the recon platoon sooner or later. *Maybe that's why I'm here*, Lieutenant Breckenridge thought. *The eight-ball platoon needed an eight-ball officer, and I guess I'm it.*

In the evening a meeting was held in the Eighty-first Division CP tent. General Hawkins presided, along with his staff officers, and all the regimental commanders, with their staff officers, attended.

They gathered around a topographical map of the Japanese airfield on Munda Point. Wooden markers indicated the positions of the division's units near the field and in the jungles nearby.

"You can see where we stand," General Hawkins said in his Arkansas drawl. "We're on top of our objective and we're going to hit it hard. I want to get this campaign finished so we can all take a rest." He took a deep breath and pointed at the map with his swagger stick, a varnished rod of oak with a .30-caliber bullet on its point and a cartridge case on its rear end. "We can't bring everything we have to bear on the airfield, because there are too many Japs in the vicinity who can hit us from the rear. That means part of the regiment will have to protect the troops who actually assault the airfield."

Colonel Stockton stood among the officers in the shadows of the tent, hoping the Twenty-third Regiment would be one of the units to attack the airfield. He didn't like holding actions and rearguard maneuvers. Everybody expected you to do those jobs right, so nobody paid much attention. The commander who took the objective was the one who got the recognition and maybe the promotion.

Colonel Stockton's dream was to become a general. He'd been passed over for his general's stars a few times already, because he was considered erratic and a hothead and because his wife had disgraced him by running off with another man. Sometimes he became resigned to being a colonel and a regimental commander for the rest of his career, but then the old ambitions would stir in his heart again, and he'd imagine those stars on his collar. He'd see himself commanding not a regiment but a division, six thousand men instead of two thousand, and conducting largescale operations. He had to admit to himself that that was what he really wanted, and he became hungrier than ever for those stars.

"The Twenty-third will attack the airfield from the southeast here," General Hawkins said, and Colonel Stockton's heart soared. "The Fifteenth will designate one battalion to move north and set up a roadblock, in case the Japs try to land reinforcements at Bairoko Harbor. The rest of the Fifteenth will come down on the airfield from the northeast, coordinated with the Twenty-third's drive. The Thirty-eighth will be in reserve, split into two combat units, ready to exploit any breakthroughs that occur. We'll have artillery support and about forty Marine tanks to help out. That's the basic plan in the rough. Any questions?"

Colonel Adrianson, the commander of the Fifteenth Regiment, asked about the route his blocking battalion would take, and Colonel Scott, the commander of the Thirty-eighth, said that his men were scattered throughout the jungle and asked how much time he would have to assemble them on the line of attack.

Colonel Stockton asked no questions. He always liked his orders to be as loose as possible so that he could have maximum freedom of movement. Afterward he'd find out what kind of reinforcements he could get, because he always needed more men.

"Very well," said General Hawkins, after fielding the questions. "Let's move along." He pointed to two bumps on the topographical map. "The airfield is protected by the usual Jap bunker-and-trench system with mutually supporting fields of fire, but our main problems will be these two hills, where the Japs have artillery, supplies, and everything they need for a protracted last-ditch defense. They'll fight to the last man, and we'll probably wind up prying them out with bayonets; but if that's the way they want it, that's the way they'll get it. The Fifteenth will take care of Biblio Hill to the north, and the Twenty-third's zone of operations will include the old missionary station on Kokengolo Hill to the south." General Hawkins tapped his swagger stick on each of the hills. "These are the keys to victory on this goddamned island. This is where we place our emphasis. Getting into these defense systems will be like crawling into a hornets nest, but we've got to do it and we will. Any questions?"

Nobody said anything.

"All right," said General Hawkins. "Let's get down to the particulars of the attack."

The next day the units of the Eighty-first Division moved into position around the Japanese airfield. Tanks from the Ninth Marine Defense Battalion moved up on the line, and a battalion from the Thirty-eighth Regiment deployed itself across the Munda-Bairoko Road. Ammunition was trucked to the front, and artillery moved into position. In the late afternoon Colonel Stockton took an airplane ride over the area to get a firsthand look at enemy defenses. He scribbled maps of their trench-and-bunker system around the airfield, but the fortress atop Kokengolo Hill was a mystery to him. He didn't know how many men were in there or what their armaments were. He hoped there'd be no nasty surprises.

The Japanese didn't interfere with the buildup around them, and the American commanders felt it was because they didn't have much left to fight with. The Americans controlled the air and had cut off the Japanese from their sources of supply. The Japanese were evidently saving whatever they had for the final showdown.

As the sun set on New Georgia the GIs ate hot C rations. Tomorrow would be no ordinary day for them. Tomorrow would be a major assault. Fighting in the jungle had been bad enough, but the big attacks against fixed fortifications were the ones that raised the casualty rates the most. A soldier behind sandbags and rocks was in a much better position than the one charging through open terrain, and the terrain around the airfield was wide open. Bombing and shelling had knocked down all the trees and blown away the foliage. The GIs and their tanks would be easy targets until they got inside the fortifications.

After dinner the GIs sacked out. But not all GIs could be asleep all the time. Some had to pull guard duty, others had to sit at telephone switchboards, and some drove truckloads of supplies to the front throughout the night.

Even officers had to stay awake, and one of these was Lieutenant Breckenridge, whose turn it was to be officer of the day. He had to sit at regimental headquarters and deal with any problems that came up.

He arrived a few minutes before 1800 hours, the time his tour of duty would begin. He relieved the previous OD, sat in the orderly room, and looked around. He was in a big walled tent, and during the day the regimental sergeant major sat there. A telephone was on the desk, a list of instructions lay in front of it, and beside it were two *Life* magazines.

The *Life* magazine on top was dated March 22, 1943, only four and a half months old, and its cover showed an officer with two stars on his epaulettes. The caption said: VICTOR OF BISMARCK SEA.

What's this about? Lieutenant Breckenridge wondered. He turned to the table of contents, and the first thing he saw was an ad for Cannon towels. It showed a color photograph of a beautiful young redhead taking a bath, and Lieutenant Breck-

27

enridge stared at her, mesmerized. Her cheeks were rosy red, her hair was piled high on her head, and she had an Irish smile, absolutely captivating.

He hadn't had a woman for nearly six months, and that had been a whore in Honolulu. The whore had been middle-aged and fat, but this girl was young and pure, just the sort of girl a man would like to be married to for his entire life.

Lieutenant Breckenridge couldn't tear his eyes away from the girl. Her nose was turned up and she looked like a saucy little bitch, the kind who would screw her husband until he was weak in the knees and then go outside and behave like a lady all day long.

Lieutenant Breckenridge wished he had a woman like that waiting for him someplace, but he had no one. He was twenty-five years old and had had many girlfriends in his life, but he had never thought he could go the distance with any of them. He didn't want to settle for just anything, but why was it that he could look at a picture of a model and decide he could spend the rest of his life with her?

A stiff cock has no judgment, he thought, shifting uncomfortably in his chair. He looked at the advertising copy next to the ad.

> *"Now that all household articles are getting scarce, it's up to me to see how I can make my family comfortable on as little as possible. I'm not going to buy any new towels unless I really have to. Instead, I'm going to make the ones I have last 'for the duration' by following Cannon's suggestions for taking care of them."*

Next came a list of suggestions for how to make towels last. Lieutenant Breckenridge felt weird to be sitting just behind the front lines of New Georgia, reading about the care of towels on the home front. How strange it must be back in the States, the people conserving their towels and buying food with ration stamps.

He turned to the next page and found himself staring at a drawing of a woman's curvaceous legs. It was an ad for rayon stockings and it told women how important it was for them to make their stockings last. Lieutenant Breckenridge looked at the legs and felt himself getting warmer. He'd been so busy

28

with the war that he'd forgotten how really alluring a pair of women's legs could be. He felt a deep longing in his stomach and quickly flipped the page.

He saw an ad for the North American Aviation Company, showing B-25s bombing a German truck convoy in North Africa. The ad confused him: What was it doing in a magazine for ordinary people? Nobody could buy a B-25 bomber, but then Lieutenant Breckenridge realized that the aviation company was trying to make itself appear patriotic, as if it weren't just interested in making millions out of the war. The ad also made war look exciting and adventurous, which Lieutenant Breckenridge knew wasn't so, but maybe it would make the civilians work harder in the war plants, and maybe some dopey young kid would join the Air Cops because of it.

On the facing page was a one-column ad for a Western movie starring Roy Rogers, Smiley Burnette, Bob Nolan, and the Sons of the Pioneers. At the bottom of the ad was a line that said: BUY WAR BONDS AND STAMPS.

Why aren't Roy Rogers and Smiley Burnette in the Army? Lieutenant Breckenridge wondered. Could they be too old? Roy Rogers didn't look too old, but maybe he was a 4-F with bad eyes, a bum heart, or a trick knee.

He spotted the table of contents and found the cover article about the victory in the Bismarck Sea. Turning to the page, he read that the Army Air Corps had sunk twelve Japanese transport ships and ten warships off the coast of New Guinea. The officer on the cover was Lieutenant General George C. Kenney, in charge of the operation, who had been called to Washington to describe his victory. Lieutenant Breckenridge was amazed that no one had ever told him about this great victory. Evidently the war was going better than he thought.

He found in the same magazine an article about a Marine named Al Schmid, who had killed two hundred Japs on Guadalcanal and had been blinded in the process. He was shown on the porch of his home in Philadelphia with his girl friend, both smiling grimly at the photographer who took the picture. Schmid had been awarded the Navy Cross.

Lieutenant Breckenridge closed the magazine, a frown on his face. He took out a cigarette and lit it up. He was disturbed but didn't know why. Was it the pictures of the girls he couldn't have, or the great victory he hadn't known about, or poor Al

29

Schmid, who had killed two hundred Japs and lost his eyesight?

Lieutenant Breckenridge scratched his head and thought about it. No, it wasn't any of those things. It was the magazine's attitude that was pissing him off. It made the war seem like something that was exciting and wonderful. It missed the point of all the suffering, of men lying in foxholes, afraid to sleep because Japs might creep up on them and slit their throats. It made the war seem like a great, noble adventure, and Lieutenant Breckenridge really didn't really think it was. He'd studied enough history at the University of Virginia to know that wars never settled anything. The First World War was supposed to be the war to end all wars, but only twenty years later the Second World War had broken out, and who knew how many more wars there'd be.

The Bible said there'd always be wars, and maybe that was so, but Lieutenant Breckenridge just wanted to get through the one he was in. He was fighting for his side because he didn't want Hitler or Tojo strutting through the streets of Richmond. He didn't want his family and friends living under military occupation.

He leafed through the magazine, looking for pictures of more girls. Sure enough, a few pages later he saw a big spread of chorus girls in a show called "Folies des Femmes," which was playing at the Roxy Theatre in Atlanta. The girls all wore big smiles and brief costumes that showed just about everything they had.

Lieutenant Breckenridge stared at the girls and puffed his cigarette. *Now* that's *something worth fighting for,* he thought.

"I hear something," said Sam Longtree, who was on guard duty ahead of the main American lines.

"Huh?" asked Frankie La Barbara, who was asleep.

"I said I heard something."

They were lying in a shallow foxhole. Frankie shook his head and tried to wake himself up. He wasn't supposed to sleep on guard duty, but he knew Longtree would stay awake for both of them.

"Go back to Butsko and tell him somebody's out here," Longtree said.

Frankie looked at Longtree as if he were insane. "Fuck you—I ain't going back there alone!"

30

"Then I'll go."

Longtree moved to climb out of the foxhole, but Frankie grabbed his legs and pulled him back in.

"You ain't leaving *me* alone in here!"

"Keep your voice down!" Longtree said.

"My voice is down! You keep your voice down!"

Longtree looked at Frankie and wanted to strangle him. Frankie was such a pain in the ass. Never did anything right. Never did what you told him to do. Always gave you an argument.

A twig snapped in front of them, and both GIs turned toward the sound.

"Uh-oh," said Frankie. "Maybe we'd better both go back."

"We can't do that. It'll leave an opening out here."

"What'll we do?"

"If you won't go back, and you won't let me go back, I guess we'll have to stay here and take what comes."

"We can fire a few shots in the air to alert the sergeant of the guard."

"If we do, those Japs will know where to lob their hand grenades."

Frankie chewed his lips. He didn't like the idea of fighting Japs hand-to-hand in the dark, and there might be a dozen Japs out there for all he knew. "I think we should get out of here."

"Nobody's stopping you."

"I'm not going alone."

"Then shut up."

"Who are you telling to shut up?"

"Ssshhhhh!"

Frankie heard more rustling in the jungle straight ahead. It was a cloudy night and the moon couldn't shine through. Frankie couldn't see more than a few yards in front of him.

"They shoulda give us a walkie-talkie," Frankie whispered.

"Ssshhhh."

"Fuck you."

"Uh-oh," said Longtree, leveling his rifle.

"Whatsa matter?"

Four Japanese soldiers exploded out of the jungle, screaming at the tops of their lungs. Longtree fired from the waist, and the flash of his shot lit up the jungle for a split second. A Jap fell to the ground on the rim of the foxhole and the other three

31

jumped in, holding their trench knives in their hands.

One landed in front of Frankie, who bashed him in the face with his rifle butt. The Jap fell down and Frankie turned to Longtree, when suddenly he felt something sharp and terrible enter his stomach. The pain was so severe that he screamed at the top of his lungs and then dropped onto the Jap he'd just bashed. Black curtains covered him.

Longtree was alone, facing two Japs. He'd dropped his rifle and held his Ka-bar knife in his hands. The two Japs bumped into each other and stumbled over the bodies of their comrade and Frankie La Barbara. Longtree whipped around with his knife and slashed open the throat of the Jap on his right, then sprang backward in time to avoid a thrust to his belly from the other Jap.

Longtree jumped out of the foxhole and stood on its edge, looking down at the Jap. "Sergeant of the Guard!" he yelled. "Jap infiltrators!"

The Japanese soldier heard him call for help and looked around fearfully. He didn't know whether to run or fight it out with Longtree. Something told the Jap that if he ran Longtree would shoot him down, so he'd have to fight it out.

The Jap leaped out of the foxhole and faced Longtree. Both men held their knives in their fists with the blades pointing up in the air. The Jap lunged at Longtree, and Longtree dodged to the side, slashing at the Jap's throat; but the Jap angled backward in time, and Longtree's knife whistled harmlessly through the air.

The two soldiers circled each other in the dark jungle. In the distance they could hear American soldiers. The Japanese soldier realized he'd better make his move quickly if he wanted to get away. He became anxious, and that was the worst frame of mind he could be in. Feinting, trying to catch Longtree off-guard, he was dismayed to see that Longtree wasn't falling for any of his tricks. He shifted direction and feinted again, but Longtree never opened himself up for a stab.

Longtree was as tense as a guitar string, and he stared at the Japanese soldier's eyes. He knew that the Japanese soldier wanted to get away, and he could see the panic in the Jap's eyes. The Japanese soldier shouted, feinted with the knife in his left hand, then tossed the knife to his right hand and pushed toward Longtree's stomach.

Longtree tucked his stomach in and dodged to the side, as

graceful as a matador, while slicing down with his knife. His razor-sharp blade caught the Jap on the neck and ripped through his throat, severing his jugular vein. Blood spurted out onto Longtree's uniform, and the Japanese soldier collapsed at Longtree's feet.

Longtree looked down at him, feeling no elation, only a sense of relief. Bending over, he wiped his knife on the Japanese soldier's pants, then tucked it into his scabbard and returned to the foxhole. He threw out the Jap he'd previously stabbed, picked up the Jap Frankie had bashed in the face, and heard him moan. Longtree realized the Jap was semiconscious, his face bloody and perhaps his skull fractured, but he didn't want to take any chances, so he took out his Ka-bar and slit the Jap's throat. Then he tossed him out of the foxhole.

Frankie La Barbara lay at the bottom all crumpled up, his knees close to his chest. Longtree felt his pulse: There was a faint beat. He rolled Frankie onto his back and gazed down at Frankie's blood-soaked shirt.

"This would not have happened if you had been quiet," Longtree said to Frankie.

Frankie's eyes were closed and his face was pale. Longtree unbuttoned Frankie's shirt but could not see the wound easily because there was so much blood. It was drying all over his chest, stomach, and pants, forming a muddy goo.

The sound of footsteps came closer, and a bunch of GIs crashed through the jungle behind the foxhole.

"What happened?" Butsko asked, holding his M 1 ready to fire, glancing around for trouble.

"Japs," Longtree said. "One of them got Frankie."

"All the Jap's gone?"

"They're all dead."

Butsko jumped into the foxhole and looked at Frankie. He picked up Frankie's wrist and felt the pulse. "He's alive, but not by much. We'd better get him out of here. Shaw—Shilansky—take him back."

Shaw, the ex-prizefighter, and Shilansky, the former bank robber from Boston, lifted Frankie by his arms and legs and carried him back to the main lines. Butsko kicked the Japs onto their backs to see what they looked like.

"I couldn't keep Frankie quiet, and the Japs just followed his voice," Longtree said.

Butsko scowled. "Frankie's been digging his grave with his

mouth ever since he was born. All right: Groves, you man this post with Longtree, and keep your mouth shut, got it?"

"Got it," replied Groves, who had been a furniture salesman in New York City before the war.

"Good. Everybody else follow me."

Butsko trudged back toward the American lines, followed by the men from the recon platoon.

Ahead of the rest, Tommy Shaw and Morris Shilansky carried Frankie La Barbara to safety.

"Jesus, he's heavy," said Shilansky, holding Frankie by the armpits.

"He's not that heavy," replied Shaw, who prided himself on his physical strength. Each of his big hands held one of Frankie's legs, and Frankie's body swayed from side to side with every step they took.

The jungle was dark and gloomy. Twigs crackled and leaves rustled underneath the GIs' feet.

"I hope he lives," said Shilansky. "Frankie's been with us since basic training at Fort Ord."

"It'll take more than a stomach wound to kill this rotten son of a bitch."

"What's that?" asked Shilansky.

"What's what?"

Two Japanese soldiers burst out of the underbrush next to them, knives in their hands. Shilansky and Shaw dropped Frankie La Barbara on the ground and stepped back, but they didn't have time to draw their Kabars because the Japanese soldiers were right on top of them. The one on the left made a pass at Shaw's throat, and Shaw grabbed the Japanese soldier's wrist, pivoted, and threw the Jap over his shoulder. The Jap fell onto the ground, his knife still in his hand, and Shaw planted one foot on his wrist and the other with all his might in the middle of the Jap's face. The Jap groaned and let go of the knife. Shaw picked it up and stabbed it into the Jap's throat, then withdrew it and spun around to see Shilansky rolling over and over on the ground with the other Jap, both of Shilansky's hands holding the Jap's wrist.

"Hold the bastard still!" Shaw said, dancing around, trying to stick the Jap.

"I . . . can't!" replied Shilansky.

"Kick him in the balls."

Shilansky tried to knee the Jap but hit the Jap's hip instead. However, the Jap got the idea, pushed Shilansky to the side, and kneed him in the balls. Shilansky went *"Oof"* and doubled up, and the Jap swung his knife down, but Shaw grabbed the Jap's wrist when the knife was only inches from Shilansky's throat and simultaneously jammed his own knife into the Jap's back.

The Jap shrieked and arched backward, reaching around to the wound in his back, and Shaw yanked out the knife, took aim, and ripped the blade across the Jap's throat. The Jap gurgled and closed his eyes, sagging to the side.

Shaw stepped back. The action had taken only a few seconds, but the adrenaline still pumped through his veins. Shilansky rolled over on the ground, cupping his groin in his hands.

"That fucking Jap! He kicked me in the balls!"

Shaw didn't know what to do first. Two dead Japs were on the ground, Frankie was dying, and now Shilansky had two mashed balls.

"Help!" Shaw shouted. *"Jap infiltrators!"*

"Ow, my balls!" Shilansky moaned. "Oh, that fucking son of a bitch!"

Shaw checked the two Japs to make sure they were dead. He stood and was walking toward Frankie to see how he was, when Butsko and the men with him came chugging through the jungle.

"Now what?" Butsko asked.

"More Japs!" Shaw replied.

Shilansky cupped his balls and squinched his eyes shut. "The motherfucker kicked me in the balls!"

Butsko ordered two men to carry Frankie and two to carry Shilansky, and they set out again for their lines.

"Watch out for more Japs," Butsko cautioned them. "They seem to be out in full force tonight.

At regimental headquarters Lieutenant Breckenridge was receiving reports about Japanese infiltrators from the listening posts. He wrote down the location of each incident to see if there was a pattern, but there wasn't; the Japs were just up to their usual harassing tactics.

The front door of the orderly room opened and Colonel

35

Stockton walked in, followed by Lieutenant Harper and Major Cobb. All of them carried briefcases and canvas tubes containing maps.

"Oh, hello there, Breckenridge," Colonel Stockton said. "How's it going?"

"Lots of Jap infiltrators, sir."

"I heard the shots... figured that must be what it was. Where are they?"

Lieutenant Breckenridge showed him the marks he'd made on his map overlay.

"Ah," said Colonel Stockton. "Looks like you've had some action in your recon platoon area."

"Two of my men were wounded."

"It could have been worse." Colonel Stockton straightened up and walked toward the door of his office. "Carry on."

"Yes, sir."

Lieutenant Harper rushed ahead to open the door of the office, and Colonel Stockton marched inside. Major Cobb followed, and finally Lieutenant Harper walked in, closing the door behind him. Lieutenant Breckenridge opened up the other *Life* magazine, this one dated February 22, 1943. The cover showed a flyboy looking through a bombsight, and the first page showed a jeep in a jungle, next to crates of ammunition. It was an ad for B. F. Goodrich tires, and the headline said: HOW THEY PASS THE AMMUNITION IN NEW GUINEA.

Lieutenant Breckenridge blinked, fascinated by the photograph. It could have been taken on Guadalcanal, New Georgia, or any other fucked-up island in the South Pacific, and it was being used to sell tires. *Jesus,* he thought, *they've turned the war into a sales-promotion gimmick.*

He closed the magazine and pushed it away. He had to stop looking at the magazines, because they were pissing him off. Everything in them was money, money, money, and there was no recognition of what the war was really about. *It's just business as usual back in the states,* he thought. *Even a world war can't stop that.*

The door to Colonel Stockton's office opened and Major Cobb walked out, followed by Lieutenant Harper. Both officers smiled at Lieutenant Breckenridge as they passed him by, and he smiled back. They left the office and Lieutenant Breckenridge stared out the window at the black night. He wished he had a book to read, but there were no bookstores near the front on New Georgia. They probably had books in the rear areas, but that was no good to him.

The telephone on his desk rang and he picked it up. "Lieutenant Breckenridge speaking, sir."

"This is Colonel Stockton," said the voice on the other end. "Come in a moment, will you?"

"Yes, sir."

Lieutenant Breckenridge stood, strapped on his Colt .45, and tucked his helmet under his arm. He walked toward the door, opened it, and entered Colonel Stockton's office, advancing to his desk and saluting.

"Lieutenant Breckenridge reporting, sir."

"At ease, Lieutenant. Have a seat."

"Yes, sir."

Lieutenant Breckenridge sat, leaned back, and crossed his legs. Colonel Stockton's white hair shone in the light of the kerosene lamp on his desk, and he puffed a pipe, filling the air with the earthy fragrance of Briggs tobacco.

"Have a smoke if you want to," Colonel Stockton said.

"Thank you, sir."

Lieutenant Breckenridge took out a cigarette and lit it up with his old battered Zippo, blowing smoke into the air over his head. The office filled up with smoke so fast that it might have appeared to an outsider as if a fire were burning someplace in there.

"Who was wounded in the recon platoon tonight?" Colonel Stockton asked.

Lieutenant Breckenridge was tempted to smile, because the recon platoon was Colonel Stockton's pet project and the colonel was interested in everything that happened to it. "Frankie La Barbara was knifed in the stomach, and Morris Shilansky was kicked in the groin."

Colonel Stockton wrinkled his forehead in pain. "Ouch," he said. "How serious?"

"I don't know yet, sir. They're back at the battalion aid station, last thing I heard."

"Let me know when you find out."

"Yes, sir."

Colonel Stockton puffed his briar. "How's everything else in the recon platoon?"

"Okay, sir."

"Ready for the big offensive tomorrow?"

"As ready as we'll ever be."

"How're you getting along with the men?"

"Not bad. We're getting used to each other." Lieutenant Breckenridge was the first officer the recon platoon had ever had, and he'd held the job for only a few months.

"Get along okay with Butsko?"

"No problem."

"Good. Glad to hear it. I promised you when you took over the recon platoon that if you did a good job, I'd give you a company to command and you'd get your captaincy shortly thereafter. I meant what I said. After the campaign on New Georgia is over, you'll get your company. So think about it. Get yourself ready."

Lieutenant Breckenridge shrugged. "I don't know, sir. I might want to stay in the recon platoon for a while longer."

Colonel Stockton grinned. "They kind of grow on you after a while, don't they?"

"I guess they do, sir."

"You can learn a lot from Butsko."

"I already have."

"Well, what should I do about your company?"

"Can you hold off on that for a while, sir?"

"I thought you wanted to be a company commander."

"I did, but now I'm not so sure. I'm not a career officer, you know. When the war's over, I'm going back to civilian life. It might not be a bad idea for me to spend the war with the recon platoon."

"The war might go on for a long time. They say that the road to Tokyo will be paved with young lieutenants like you. The more rank you have, the safer you'll be."

"I don't know, sir. A lot of company commanders have been getting killed lately."

"That's true," Colonel Stockton said, frowning. "Some colonels have bit the dust too. Nobody's safe, but young platoon leaders like you are in the most dangerous positions."

"Depends on who you're with. I'll take my chances with the recon platoon for a while."

"It's up to you, Lieutenant." Colonel Stockton looked at his watch. "Well, I guess it's time for me to turn in. If you change your mind, let me know, okay?"

"Yes, sir."

"You may return to your desk now, and don't bother saluting. It's a little late at night for that."

"Yes, sir."

Lieutenant Breckenridge stood, tucked his helmet under his arm, and returned to the desk in the orderly room, sitting down behind the *Life* magazines and the reports about Japanese infiltrators.

A few seconds later the door opened and Colonel Stockton walked out of his office, carrying briefcase and with his helmet on his head.

"Good night, Lieutenant," he said.

"Good night, sir."

Colonel Stockton left the office and closed the door behind him. Lieutenant Breckenridge took out a fresh cigarette and lit it up, thinking he ought to cut down on his smoking. He recalled Colonel Stockton's offer of a company and a captaincy, and reflected on his answer. Colonel Stockton had taken him by surprise, and he'd answered off the top of his head, but now he was wondering if he'd done the right thing.

Colonel Stockton is right, he thought. *Life would be safer if I was a captain. But if that was true, why did I say I wanted to stay with the recon platoon?* Lieutenant Breckenridge shook his head. *I've been in the jungle too long. I must be losing my mind.*

FOUR . . .

At the crack of dawn, fighter planes and bombers from Guadalcanal swooped down on the Japanese airstrip at Munda Point. They came in low and steady over the trees, strafing and dropping bombs. The Japanese soldiers ran to their posts, manning artillery and machine guns as bombs fell around them and bullets stitched across the runway.

At the edge of the jungle Colonel Stockton lay on his stomach and watched the action through his binoculars. He saw the initial bombs fall, and then the airfield became wreathed with smoke. The bombs continued to fall and the bombers screeched through the sky and dived down on the airstrip. Red flashed of explosions glowed within the smoke and then caused more smoke to billow and churn. Colonel Stockton lowered his binoculars and turned to Major Cobb, who was lying next to him. "Just when we need some wind, we don't get it."

Major Cobb peered through his binoculars, trying to catch a glimpse of Kokengolo Hill. "I don't think they hit that fort, sir."

"Of course they didn't hit it. It's like dropping a can of C rations down a cat's throat at twenty feet. The men will have to take that fort with hot lead and cold steel." He looked at his

41

watch. "It won't be long now. We'd better get back to the CP."

They crawled back into the jungle until it was safe to stand up. Then they got to their feet, brushed themselves off, and headed toward the CP.

Not far away the recon platoon and Able Company were poised at the edge of the jungle, waiting for the order to attack. They watched the planes wreak devastation on the airfield, but all the old veterans knew that the bombing wasn't bothering the Japs too much, because the Japanese tunnel system was dug deep underground, beyond the range of the explosions.

Nearby the tanks rumbled their engines and belched oily black smoke into the air. The tank commanders stood in the hatches, wearing their funny hats, looking at the airfield through binoculars. All the hatches on the tanks were open, and the crew members smoked in the fresh air, their movements nervous and erratic, because tanks are awfully big targets and nobody wants to get blown to bits.

After a while the Japanese fighter planes arrived from Rabaul, and dogfights took place throughout the sky. A few of the Japanese planes broke through the American defensive cover and dropped bombs on the jungle but did little real damage.

The attack was supposed to begin at 0630 hours, and the minutes were ticking away. Everyone looked nervously at his watch, the men apprehensive about putting their heads on the chopping block again, and the officers hoping their elaborate plans would prove successful.

Lieutenant Breckenridge climbed up on the tank that his platoon would follow into battle. "Hi there," he said to the commander. "I'm Lieutenant Breckenridge and my men will be traveling with you."

The commander was smoking a thick black cigar, and he held out his hand. "I'm Sergeant Schuman. How're you doing?"

"Okay."

"Tell your men to stay close behind us, because this tank'll be the only protection you'll get."

"They know."

Lieutenant Breckenridge jumped down from the tank and returned to the recon platoon, dropping to his knees beside Butsko and looking at his watch. "Ten more minutes," he said.

Butsko nodded, puffing a cigarette. He was jumpy and tense,

42

because he was afraid of getting killed. He'd been in so many attacks already, he couldn't add them up, but he'd never been able to overcome the fear completely.

Lieutenant Breckenridge was scared too. Not so scared that he couldn't function, but scared enough to make his hands tremble slightly. Not far away, Bannon lay with his cheek on his forearm and his eyes closed, trying to calm himself down. He'd been feeling demoralized ever since Frankie La Barbara got his stomach cut up. He and Frankie had been together since basic training, and he'd always thought Frankie was his lucky charm. He thought he'd be okay as long as Frankie was okay, but now Frankie was back in the field hospital, and nobody could say for sure whether he was alive or dead.

"All right," Lieutenant Breckenridge said. "Let's get ready."

The men stood up and looked around, trying to draw courage and strength from each other. Butsko led them toward the tank and they formed up behind it. On the airstrip American airplanes were still bombing and fighting off Japanese planes from Rabaul. All around the airfield other companies and battalions were getting into position, and farther back in the jungle General Hawkins was choreographing it all through his field telephones and backpack radios.

Everybody kept glancing at his watch as the final moments ticked away. The men tried not to think of the hell they'd be stepping into as soon as the big hand on their watches reached the six. In the turret of the tank Sergeant Schuman chewed his cigar stub and looked at his watch. Over the airstrip the American bombers were making their final run.

Sergeant Schuman raised his right hand straight up in the air and then moved it forward. "Roll it out!" he yelled.

Something clanked deep within the bowels of the tank and it lurched forward, spewing out fumes at the GIs behind it. The GIs turned around and coughed, waiting for the tank to get several yards away. Sergeant Schuman climbed down into the tank and closed the hatch.

"Okay," shouted Lieutenant Breckenridge, "move it out."

The men from the recon platoon hunched over behind the tank and followed it out of the jungle. The American bombers climbed high in the sky, heading back to Guadalcanal, while the fighter planes stayed behind to keep the Japanese Zeros off the GIs.

The tank rumbled out of the jungle, and so did the other

43

tanks from the Ninth Marine Defense Battalion, each followed by a group of GIs. Gradually the smoke from the bombs lifted and the tank cannons opened fire at targets at the trench system on the edge of the airstrip. Inside the trench system the Japanese soldiers had set up their machine guns and antitank guns. The soldiers with rifles opened fire on the tanks bearing down on them.

The air filled with bullets and flying shells. Japanese mortar rounds dropped down among the Americans, and bullets ricocheted off the tanks. The men from the recon platoon kept their heads low and huddled behind the protection of the tank. They stumbled over the shell holes and moved closer to the edge of the airstrip, numbed by the terrific explosions taking place all around them.

A Japanese antitank shell hit a tank to the right of the recon platoon, and it disappeared in a huge ball of smoke. The smoke cleared and the tank became visible, crushed and twisted.

Bannon shuddered. No one could have survived that explosion. He imagined what it would be like to be in a tank and take a direct hit from a Japanese antitank gun. *Probably wouldn't feel a thing. One moment you're here and the next moment the war is over for you.*

The tanks approached the first Japanese trench network. Sergeant Schuman's machine guns strafed the trench from side to side, and his cannon blew a section of it into the air. The front of the tank reached the trench, nosed down, and crushed the three Japanese soldiers in its path. The tank driver shifted down and gave it some gas, and the tank climbed up the other side of the trench.

The tank rolled over the trench and kept going toward Kokengolo Hill. Lieutenant Breckenridge looked straight ahead and saw that the trench was filled with Japs, and the longer it took his men to get inside it, the more time the Japs would have to get ready.

"Follow me!" he shouted, breaking into a run. *"Take that trench!"*

The men from the recon platoon spread out into a skirmish line as they charged the trench. Inside it the Japanese leaned against the dirt walls and worked the bolt actions of their rifles, opening fire. Private Murdock from the Third Squad caught a bullet in the kneecap and tripped to the ground, hollering in

44

excruciating pain, and Pfc. Barnard was shot through the heart and was dead before he hit the ground.

Lieutenant Breckenridge jumped into the trench, and both of his size eleven combat boots landed on the face of the Japanese soldier in front of him. The Japanese soldier fell onto his back, and Lieutenant Breckenridge kicked his face in to make sure he'd be out of the war for a while, then turned around and saw a Japanese officer running toward him, waving a samurai sword in the air.

"Banzai!" shouted the Japanese officer.

"Banzai your ass!" Lieutenant Breckenridge replied, pointing his rifle and bayonet toward the Japanese officer and planting his feet solidly on the ground.

The Japanese officer swung down with his samurai sword, and Lieutenant Breckenridge raised his rifle, stopping the blade with his rifle stock. Sparks flew into the air, and Breckenridge tried to knee the Japanese officer in the balls, but his aim was off and he hit the officer on the leg. The officer raised his sword for another blow, and Lieutenant Breckenridge punched him in the face with his rifle butt. The officer was stunned and his eyes crossed. Lieutenant Breckenridge drew his rifle butt back and whacked him again. The Japanese officer's head spun around nearly 180 degrees and he fell to the ground like a tree felled by lumberjacks.

A Japanese soldier with rifle and bayonet jumped in front of Lieutenant Breckenridge, screamed, and lunged forward. Lieutenant Breckenridge parried the thrust and the Japanese soldier continued his forward motion, losing his balance and falling onto his stomach. When he landed, Lieutenant Breckenridge was over him and harpooned him through the back. The Japanese soldier screamed, and Lieutenant Breckenridge was about to harpoon him again, when he heard footsteps coming up fast behind him.

He spun around and saw two Japanese soldiers charging him. Lieutenant Breckenridge pulled the trigger of his M 1, the shot rang out, and a red dot appeared on the filthy pale-green shirt that the Japanese soldier on the left was wearing. The Japanese soldier stumbled and dropped as the other Japanese soldier fired point-blank at Lieutenant Breckenridge, who felt the impact of the bullet and thought he was a goner.

But he still was standing, his hands stinging. The bullet had hit the triggerguard of his M 1, shattering it and saving his life. The Japanese soldier pushed his rifle and bayonet forward, trying to impale Lieutenant Breckenridge, who dodged to the side, and the Japanese bayonet tore across Lieutenant Breckenridge's biceps.

Lieutenant Breckenridge was so keyed up that he barely felt the pain. He regained his balance and so did the the Japanese soldier. Both men faced each other, getting ready to kill each other again, when a shot rang out and the Japanese soldier's legs gave way beneath him. Lieutenant Breckenridge looked around and saw a Japanese officer aiming a Nambu pistol at him. In a flash Lieutenant Breckenridge realized that the Japanese officer must have shot one of his own men by mistake, but it didn't look as if he'd make the same mistake again. Lieutenant Breckenridge couldn't run and hide. He thought the party was over.

Then, before his astonished eyes, the Japanese officer's head was split apart by a samurai sword. The force of the blow sent the Japanese officer crashing to the ground, and behind him stood Butsko, the bloody samurai sword in his hand.

"Yaaaahhhhh!" screamed Butsko, spinning around and whacking the samurai sword sideways into the ribs of the Japanese soldier. *"Yaaahhhhh!"* He swung down diagonally, catching another Japanese soldier on the neck and hacking halfway through his rib cage. A third Japanese soldier lunged at him with his rifle and bayonet, and Butsko danced lightly to the side, swinging down, chopping off one of the Japanese soldier's arms. The Japanese soldier dropped his rifle and stared in horror at the stump of his arm gushing blood, and Butsko swung again, lopping off the Jap's head.

Butsko looked around and saw two Japanese soldiers crowding Corporal Gomez against a wall of the trench. Butsko charged, raising the samurai sword in the air. He brought it down, hitting one Japanese soldier on top of his head and splitting it apart like a honeydew melon. Gomez parried the bayonet thrust of the other soldier, and Butsko swung the samurai sword from the side, slicing the Jap's liver in half, then severing his spine. The Jap cracked in half and sank to the ground.

Butsko turned around and *clang,* the samurai sword was knocked out of his hands. His jaw fell open as he saw a Japanese officer in front of him, carrying a samurai sword. The officer raised the sword to split Butsko's head open, when the bloody red tip of a bayonet appeared in the middle of the Japanese officer's chest. The Japanese officer bellowed like a stuck pig, and the bayonet disappeared. The Japanese officer collapsed, revealing Corporal Bannon standing behind him, his bayonet dripping blood, his face and arms flecked with gore.

They heard the snarl of an airplane engine above them, and the chatter of machine guns. Looking up, they saw a lone Zero diving toward the trench, the machine guns in its wings blazing. Behind the Zero was a Grumman Hellcat, its machine guns firing too. The Zero poured lead into the trench, and the GIs and Japanese soldiers dropped down. Butsko covered his helmet with his hands and the ground trembled as machine gun bullets stitched past him. He heard a huge explosion overhead and glanced up. The Zero was gone, and in its place was a twisted wreckage careening toward the ground. It crashed and burst into flame, and the Grumman Hellcat soared past victoriously.

Butsko got to his feet. He couldn't understand why the Japanese Zero had strafed a trench containing Japanese soldiers, but then he noticed that Japanese resistance in the trench had nearly been overcome. No live Japs were near him and only a few struggles still were going on. The Japanese pilot must have thought that the Americans had taken the trench.

Lieutenant Breckenridge climbed the far side of the trench. "Let's go! Keep moving!"

The GIs followed him and continued toward their objective, the old mission station on Kokengolo Hill. As soon as they were in the open the Japanese guns inside the mission fortress opened fire on them. GIs were stopped dead in their tracks, collapsing onto the ground, and the rest tried to get behind the tank commanded by Sergeant Schuman. The tank had stopped and was shelling the fortress while waiting for the GIs to catch up.

The men from the recon platoon clustered behind the tank like a flock of ducklings behind their mother. They held their heads down, their mouths open, gulping air, and their eyes glazed by the horror of the hand-to-hand fighting in the trench. The tank moved forward and Butsko looked around to see American soldiers lying dead all over the ground.

He heard a powerful explosion to his right and saw a tank

47

engulfed by smoke and flames. A ton of earth nearby was blown into the air by another explosion. The Japs inside the fortress were turning loose their artillery, and the battlefield was rocked by the violence of the explosions. Butsko looked around the tank in front of him and saw just ahead the outer runways of the airfield. In the center of the complex of runways was Kokengolo Hill and the old fortified mission on top of it.

The Japanese fire became more intense, and Japanese shells exploded all across the airstrip. Butsko thought the attack couldn't possibly succeed. Japanese resistance was too great. His courage turned to cold, stark fear, and he wished one of those officers in the rear areas would decide to break off the attack. Japanese bullets ricocheted off the Tarmac runway and kicked up clouds of dirt on the open ground around it. The air thundered with explosions. Butsko looked at the faces of his men, and they were all as scared as he was.

Sergeant Schuman's tank was blasted to hell in one incredible thunderclap. It happened so suddenly that Butsko was stunned. The tank had been his platoon's moving wall of protection, but now it was a smoking pile of charred metal. Half the men in the platoon dropped to the ground and flattened out, while the rest looked around at him and Lieutenant Breckenridge to find out what they should do.

Butsko looked at Lieutenant Breckenridge, too, because the young officer was boss in the platoon. Lieutenant Breckenridge was as scared as any of them, but he knew he had to take charge. His last orders were to attack, and that's what he had to do.

He raised his rifle high in his right hand to attract attention to himself. *"Let's go!"* he shouted. *"Follow me!"*

Lieutenant Breckenridge gritted his teeth and ran around the burning tank. Up ahead he saw the runways and the fortress on Kokengolo Hill through the smoke and confusion of the battlefield. His shoulders hunched and his head turtled into his collar. He felt naked before the incredible firepower of the Japanese defenders as bullets whizzed past his ears and kicked up dirt at his feet. He realized that if he continued to lead his men forward, they'd be wiped out.

"Get back!" he yelled, turning around and heading for the shelter of the ruined tank.

He was amazed to see that no one had followed him. All

the others huddled behind the tank, watching him through eyes glowing with fear and excitement. Miraculously he made it back through the hail of bullets and dropped to one knee behind the tank.

Butsko was a few feet away, a cigarette dangling from the corner of his mouth. "Looks like you got carried away there, sir."

Lieutenant Breckenridge's face was flushed with exertion and embarrassment. "Where's Delane?"

"Here, sir!" said Delane, lying on the ground with his walkie-talkie.

"Get over here!"

"Yes, sir."

Delane crawled toward Lieutenant Breckenridge and held out the walkie-talkie. Lieutenant Breckenridge took it and called Captain Ilecki. It took several agonizing minutes for him to get through, and meanwhile the Japanese fire remained hotter than hell. Lieutenant Breckenridge looked around, fearful that the Japs would counterattack, and saw another American tank blown to bits two hundred yards away. Finally Captain Ilecki's voice came through the earpiece.

"Sir," said Lieutenant Breckenridge, "the tank in front of us has been knocked out and we can't go on. We tried, but it's just too hot out there."

"Stay where you are. It's pretty bad where I am too. I'm waiting for new orders, and as soon as they come down I'll pass them on. Over and out."

"What did he say?" Butsko asked.

"He's waiting for orders."

"Why don't we go back to that trench?"

"Nobody told us to."

"Well, sir, maybe you should take it on yourself to move us back there."

Lieutenant Breckenridge nibbled his lower lip. He thought Butsko was right and wasn't embarrassed about it. If the Japs counterattacked, his men would be out in the open where they were.

"Back to the trench!" he yelled. *"Keep your heads down!"*

Bending low to the ground, he waddled back toward the trench, trying to keep the smoking tank between him and Kokengolo Hill. Several times he looked back to make sure and saw his men following him, their faces twisted by tension and fear. The trench wasn't too far away, and Lieutenant Breckenridge jumped in, landing next to a dead Japanese soldier lying on his back, a cloud of flies buzzing around the gaping hole in his chest.

The men from the recon platoon landed in the trench all around Lieutenant Breckenridge. They turned around and rested their rifles on the parapet, in case the Japs attacked.

Butsko walked through the trench like a duck, his head below the parapet. He moved next to Lieutenant Breckenridge and spit out the butt of his cigarette.

"Sir," he said, "sometimes you take this war shit a little too seriously."

FIVE . . .

Colonel Stockton looked down at the map table, his forehead creased with thought. His staff officers looked at him, waiting for his decision. Reports from the front indicated that the attack had been stopped cold, and the Twenty-third had been ripped up badly. Colonel Stockton didn't know if the front-line commanders were exaggerating the ferocity of the Japanese resistance, making excuses for their own inability to take the fortress on Kokengolo Hill. Perhaps a good dose of strong determined leadership could send the men forward to victory. War was a psychological game, after all. The side that thought they were winners usually won.

But on the other hand history furnished many examples of officers ordering foolhardy attacks, like Gallipoli and the famous Charge of the Light Brigade, and Colonel Stockton didn't want to take any chances. His front-line commanders were good men, and they couldn't all be wrong.

He pointed to the map. "Tell the men to retreat to the line of Japanese foxholes and trenches at the edge of the airfield here. Tell them to prepare for a Japanese counterattack."

The officers nodded. They were relieved that Colonel Stockton had finally made his decision, because more soldiers died every minute they were out in the open. Major Cobb picked up the radio headset to transmit the orders to the front.

"Captain Ilecki calling you, sir."

Lieutenant Breckenridge took the walkie-talkie from the hands of Craig Delane and identified himself.

"Pull your men back to the trench we just took," Captain Ilecki said.

"Yes, sir," Lieutenant Breckenridge said.

"Call me as soon as you get there and give me a casualty report."

"Yes, sir."

"Over and out."

Butsko was puffing a new cigarette. "What did he say?"

"He said to retreat to back here and give him a casualty report."

Butsko looked at his watch. "I guess it should take us about ten minutes to get back here, wouldn't you say so, sir?"

Lieutenant Breckenridge frowned and glanced at his own watch. "About that." He looked out at the battlefield and saw devastated tanks and American soldiers dead and wounded, lying on the ground. In the distance, on both his flanks, GIs retreated toward the safety of the trench. The attack had failed. The Japs still owned their airfield, although they couldn't use it.

"Look!" said Craig Delane, pointing straight ahead.

Lieutenant Breckenridge turned his head and saw two figures crawling toward him. They wore American khaki, but that didn't mean they weren't Japs. He raised his binoculars to take a look.

"My God," he said, "it's Gundy, and he's dragging somebody back here."

"I'll go help him," said Butsko.

Lieutenant Breckenridge placed his hand on Butsko's shirt. "Stay here. I don't want you taking any chances."

The Japanese fire was directed toward the retreating GI units; evidently the Japs didn't notice the young medic and his patient. The men from the recon platoon watched with fascination as Gundy drew closer, and then they saw who was with him: Corporal Gomez, unconscious.

Butsko grunted. "Another squad leader down the hatch."

Gundy reached the edge of the trench, and hands reached out to drag him and Gomez in. They landed in the bottom of the trench and Gomez lay still, while Gundy leaned over him, feeling his pulse. Lieutenant Breckenridge crept toward Gundy and Gomez to determine how much damage had been done.

"He's still alive," Gundy said. "It's a chest wound, though. Real bad."

Gomez was bandaged and sedated. Lieutenant Breckenridge was amazed that Gundy had done all that work during the retreat. "Good work, Gundy."

Gundy grimaced as he examined the bandage. "This damned war," he said.

Lieutenant Breckenridge and Butsko moved back to where they were before. "I'm afraid that medic of ours isn't going to be around much longer," Lieutenant Breckenridge said.

"I'm afraid *I* won't be around much longer," Butsko replied.

Lieutenant Breckenridge looked at his watch. It was almost time to call Captain Ilecki.

"Japs!" somebody screamed.

His hair nearly standing on end, Lieutenant Breckenridge looked over the battlefield. In the distance he could see Japs streaming like ants down the side of Kokengolo Hill.

"They're coming!" Lieutenant Breckenridge said. *"Get ready!"* He turned to Craig Delane. "Tell Captain Ilecki that the Japs are counterattacking!"

Delane pressed the button of his walkie-talkie as shells swooshed over their heads. The shells were heading toward the Japs, and Lieutenant Breckenridge realized that the counterattack had already been spotted and reported. He raised his binoculars and watched as the ground became covered with a carpet of smoke and flames, but then, through the tumult, Japanese soldiers appeared, shaking their rifles and bayonets and shrieking *"Banzai!"*

Butsko moved down the trench, positioning the men, making sure machine guns and BARs were ready to fire. Many machine-gun crewmen had been killed since morning, and he had to recruit riflemen to help out with the machine guns. He kicked, pushed, and swore his way along, because there was no time to spare.

Lieutenant Breckenridge cupped his hands around his mouth. "Don't fire until I give the order! Make every shot count!"

The American artillery adjusted their sights and inflicted a creeping barrage on the Japs, but the attack had begun too suddenly, and not all the artillery was zeroed in. The Japanese soldiers sped across the runway, urged onward by their sergeants and officers waving swords in the air. They swarmed past the disabled tanks, and some paused to jab bayonets into wounded American soldiers.

"Get ready!" Lieutenant Breckenridge ordered. *"Fire!"*

The machine guns chattered viciously, and Japs fell to the ground. Their comrades jumped over their fallen bodies and continued the charge into the hail of American bullets. Lieutenant Breckenridge watched through his binoculars, nearly deafened by the rifle and machine-gun fire on either side of him. He saw Japs falling, but the attack continued, the first wave of the Japs closing with the trenches.

Bannon sat behind a machine gun, swinging it from side to side on its transverse mechanism, mowing the Japs down. He was supposed to let go of the trigger after every burst of six rounds, to let the barrel cool, but there was no time for that now. Private Shaw, the flamethrower on his back, fed the cartridge belt into the machine gun, which ate it up and spat out hot lead. Bannon tried to remain calm, to sit where he was and not flee as he wanted to, because the Japs kept coming, hordes of them with slaughter and mayhem in their eyes.

Butsko leaned against the parapet, firing his rifle as fast as he could pull the trigger. He barely aimed because the Japs were so thick. All he had to do was keep the M 1 level and the Japs fell down.

But not enough of them fell, and at different points in the Twenty-third's line they caught up with GIs who hadn't made it back to shelter. The GIs were shot and bayoneted in the back as the Japanese soldiers swarmed forward.

Lieutenant Breckenridge fired his carbine on automatic as he saw his life flash before his eyes. A boy fishing in the streams of Virginia, a student at the university, the lover of debutantes and townie girls, he was going to die in a ditch on a filthy bug-infested island—for what? He saw the Japanese soldiers pass Sergeant Schuman's ruined tank. They were so close now that he could see the whites of their eyes.

"Hold fast!" he screamed. *"Don't let them pass!"*

As soon as the words were out of his mouth, he felt stupid.

He was playing army officer at a moment when the rules of war were irrelevant. From now on it would be blood and guts until everybody was dead.

"I need some help on this gun!"

It was Bannon's voice. Butsko swung his head around and saw Shaw lying on his side, covered with blood. Bannon was trying to unjam the belt of cartridges from the chamber of the machine gun. Butsko ran across the trench, keeping his head down. He dropped to his knees beside the machine gun and pushed Shaw out of the way.

"Pull back the lever!" Butsko said.

Bannon pulled it back and Butsko yanked hard. The cartridge belt pulled free and Butsko laid it in the chamber. Bannon pulled the trigger and the gun barked angrily. Butsko fed the cartridge belt in and looked over the top of the ditch. The Japs were only fifty yards away, huge gaps in their line, but they still were charging, screaming for American blood.

Private Gundy dropped to one knee beside Shaw, unfastened the flamethrower from his back, and saw the big bloody wound on the side of Shaw's face. It looked as though a big chunk of his cheek and jaw were gone, and all Gundy could do was pour on the sulfa powder and apply the biggest bandage he had.

The machine gun danced as Bannon swung the barrel from side to side. Butsko held the cartridge belt in his sausage fingers, watching the Japanese soldiers close the distance between them and the recon platoon.

"Just keep firing," Butsko said grimly. "The only thing we can do is take as many of them as we can before they get us."

At regimental headquarters the harrowing news was coming in. The Japs had counterattacked and the line was cracking. Lieutenant Stockton puffed his pipe calmly and looked down at the map, figuring out how to handle the situation. He'd had the roof cave in on him many times in his military career, and the only thing to do was treat it like a chess game and move his strongest forces to the spots of greatest trouble.

"All right," he said to Major Cobb. "We'll take the Third Battalion out of reserve. Move Company I in here, Company J over here, and hold King Company right here." He pointed to the spots on the map. "Understand?"

"Yes, sir."

Colonel Stockton turned to Private Levinson. "Get me General Hawkins!"

"Yes, sir!"

Farther back in the jungle, in a tent underneath camouflage netting, General Hawkins was assaying the situation. Removed from the battle, its sounds only a faint rumble in the distance, he could be even more dispassionate than Colonel Stockton.

He looked at his map and repeatedly pinched his chin with his fingers. The events at the front were crystal clear to him, for he could see the big picture.

The attack by the Fifteenth, from the northeast, was bogged down at the edge of the airstrip. It had not even taken the first line of Japanese trenches and bunkers, but it was minus one whole battalion, a third of its striking force, which had set up a roadblock between the airfield and Bairoko Harbor.

The Twenty-third had crashed through, and the Japanese responded by directing at it all its strength on Kokengolo Hill. The Japanese had stopped the Twenty-third and rocked it back on its heels. Now the Japanese were counterattacking, and since the Twenty-third was weak and tired, the Japanese might break through.

General Hawkins wasn't overly concerned, because his ass was safe. He had the Thirty-Eighth Regiment between him and the Japs, and all he had to do was move them in behind the Twenty-third and counterattack the counterattack. Colonel Brill, the CO of the Thirty-eighth, was a tough, resolute commander. He'd turn the tide. The Japs couldn't have that many soldiers out there.

He looked at Brigadier General Searles, his executive officer. "Tell Colonel Brill to bring his regiment up on the line here," he said, pointing to the map.

The Japs were only twenty yards away, and the GIs kept firing their rifles and machine guns, poised to jump up and fight hand-to-hand. Bannon held the trigger of the machine gun pulled up all the way, and the bullets chopped down the charging screaming Japs, but there were so many of them—too many of them. They shouted as they fell to the ground, and the ones on their feet shouted as they charged forward, eager to recapture the trench for the glory of the Emperor.

They were so close that Butsko couldn't hold still anymore. His eyes fell on the flamethrower lying on the ground beside Private Shaw, and he got an inspiration. In quick, decisive moves he picked up the flamethrower, hoisted one of its straps onto his right shoulder, and aimed the nozzle at the Japanese soldiers, who now were only a few yards from the rim of the trench, led by an officer waving his samurai sword in the air. The other GIs were standing up, pointing their rifles and fixed bayonets at the Japs, hoping to impale them on the way down.

Butsko flicked the switch on the nozzle, and flaming, gelatinous petroleum shot out. Lumps of the hideous burning stuff fell on the first wave of Japs and set them afire. The officer with the samurai sword became a sheet of flame jumping up and down, shrieking horribly. The jelly burned his flesh and melted his bones, and he sizzled as he fell to the ground. Butsko angled the nozzle upward, and the flaming jelly fell on the Japs like rain, burning through their uniforms and flesh and kept burning no matter how they tried to snuff it out.

Butsko stood upright, swinging the nozzle from side to side, and the flame-thrower accomplished what bullets couldn't: The Japanese attack faltered right on the edge of the trench. No one, not even a fanatical Japanese soldier, can move when he's on fire, and the thought of burning up alive was enough to dishearten even those soldiers who hadn't yet been touched by fire.

The GIs got down and resumed firing their rifles as Butsko sprayed the Japs with flames. The horrible stench of burning flesh filled the air, and a black cloud of smoke rose to the sky. The Japs couldn't advance and didn't want to retreat, and the GIs pumped lead into them, slaughtering them in bunches. The bodies piled up, many still burning, and then even the bravest and wildest Japanese soldiers couldn't take it anymore. Nobody gave an order, but they broke and ran. Those still able to reason concluded that they'd be more valuable to the Emperor alive than dead, and the rest just ran for their lives. They turned tail and hotfoooted it toward Kokengolo Hill, while the GIs kept firing. Bannon's machine-gun bolt flew forward, made a clunk sound, and stayed there. He looked and saw that the belt had run out. He had no more ammunition. The attack had been turned back in the nick of time.

Butsko turned off the nozzle of the flamethrower. He unhooked the harness from his arm and let the apparatus fall to the ground. Picking up his rifle, he put the butt to his shoulder and wearily sighted down the barrel so that he could kill a few more of the Japs before they reached the safety of Kokengolo Hill. But it was difficult for him to fire from the level of the trench, because so many dead Japs were piled up in front of the parapets, still burning, giving off a horrendous odor. He heard a sound like a herd of horses behind him and turned around.

It was I Company moving up on the line. Captain Hastings, the company commander, landed in the trench beside Butsko and looked around as his men jumped amid the exhausted, hollowed-eyed men from the recon platoon.

"Where's all the Japs?" Captain Hastings demanded excitedly.

"Gone," replied Butsko. "You're too late."

"Who's in charge here?"

"Lieutenant Breckenridge. He's down thataway."

Captain Hastings, who had the face and build of a bulldog, charged down the trench, looking for Lieutenant Breckenridge. He saw him with Private Gundy, bending over the prostrate body of Private Stevenson, who had a stomach wound and was screaming and twisting around.

"I've got no more morphine, sir," Private Gundy said.

"Lieutenant Breckenridge?" asked Captain Hastings, kneeling down.

"That's me," replied Breckenridge. "You got a medic with you?"

"Sure do."

"Get him over here, will you?"

"Kaloudis!" shouted Captain Hastings.

"Yes, sir!"

"Get over here!"

"Yes, sir!"

A short, stout, swarthy soldier, huffing and puffing, a red cross on his arm, waddled toward them, carrying his medicine back.

"Help this man out!" Captain Hastings said.

"Yes, sir."

Lieutenant Breckenridge stood, took off his helmet, and

wiped his forehead with the back of his arm.

"I heard you were being overrun by Japs," Captain Hastings said. "Where the hell are they?"

"They retreated," Lieutenant Breckenridge said. "They didn't overrun us. We pushed them back."

"Well, I suppose I should report that."

"You do that," Lieutenant Breckenridge replied. "And while you're at it, ask for medicine and ammunition, because my platoon is out out of the first and almost out of the second."

"Sure thing, Lieutenant," Captain Hastings said, gazing at the mounds of charred Japanese soldiers. "What the hell happened here, anyway?"

"I'll tell you after you make the call."

SIX . . .

The big walled tent was set up in a thick part of the jungle, and the jeep screeched to a halt beneath the camouflage netting. Colonel Stockton jumped out, his pipe sticking out of his mouth, and carried his briefcase into the tent, making his way to General Hawkins's desk, saluting, and reporting.

"Come back here and tell me what happened," General Hawkins said.

Colonel Stockton walked behind the desk, looked at the map spread out in front of General Hawkins, and described the attack, counterattack, and subsequent events.

"Some of my units held and some didn't," he said. "My reserves moved into position in the nick of time, and when the Thirty-eighth arrived, the line really solidified."

"Yes, good," General Hawkins said, although from his point of view it was immaterial whether or not Colonel Stockton's regiment held, because the Thirty-eighth Regiment would have stopped the Japs anyway. "Where did you say you were?"

"From about here to about here," Colonel Stockton said, pointing to the map.

General Hawkins made marks on the map. "Your approximate casualties?"

"I'd say my regiment is less than half strength."

"That bad?"

"Yes, sir."

"I'll have to give you less of the line to cover. We don't want to spread you too thin, do we?"

"No, sir."

"Swing to your right and occupy a length of line from here to here, understand?"

Colonel Stockton took his map out of his briefcase and marked the spots. "I'm having an ammunition shortage in some units," he said, "and I need medical supplies desperately."

"All front-line units will be resupplied today and tonight," General Hawkins said with irritation, because Colonel Stockton was introducing a new subject when the old one wasn't finished yet. The man always was a damned hothead, in a hurry to go nowhere. "You'll link up with the Thirty-eighth Regiment on your right, with the ocean here on your left. Don't let any of the Japs get around your flanks on the ocean side, understand?"

"Yes, sir."

"Tomorrow we intend to harass the Japs and make them think we're attacking, but we won't. The next day we'll attack, bright and early, with reinforcements from Corps and plenty of artillery preparation. The Japs on Kokengolo Hill won't be able to do the damage they did today."

"It'll be hard to get them in there," Colonel Stockton pointed out. "They're dug in deep."

"All we want to do is keep them out of action until the men are knocking on their doors. Then we'll break down the doors and get them on the inside, like rats in their holes."

"That won't be easy, sir."

"I never said it would be easy, but I said we're going to do it, Colonel."

"Yes, sir," replied Colonel Stockton.

Throughout the rest of the day the GIs rearranged their line. The Twenty-third Infantry Regiment swung left, occupying approximately two-thirds of the line that it had held in the morning. The recon platoon was on the far left flank, in the jungle next to the beach.

The men ate C rations for dinner and watched the sun sink on the horizon. They didn't look forward to nightfall, because

62

they expected Jap infiltrators to bother them and maybe even launch a full-scale night attack intended to roll up the flank.

Butsko sat down next to Bannon and dug his spoon into his can of franks and beans. "You did a good job with that machine gun today. 'Course, I expect you to do a good job all the time, but just thought I'd mention it."

Bannon was eating sausage patties, chewy and greasy, the worst kind of food to eat in the tropics. "Thanks, Sarge."

Butsko chewed on a length of frankfurter. Flies buzzed around his can, and he wiped them away with a wave of his hand, but then they came back and he resigned himself. One probably would get into the can and die and he'd probably eat it, but he'd eaten bugs before. All you had to do was open your mouth and one would fly down your throat.

Butsko glanced at Bannon. "You've been acting strange today, kid. Anything wrong?"

Bannon looked at Butsko guiltily. "How've I been acting?"

"I dunno, kid. You don't have your usual moxie."

Bannon sighed and his shoulders drooped. "I don't feel so good, Sarge."

"You sick?"

"No, I'm not sick."

Butsko waited for Bannon to explain, but Bannon gloomily continued eating.

"What's bothering you, kid?" Butsko asked.

Bannon shrugged. "It's a hard thing to talk about, Sarge."

"You get bad news from home or something?"

"We ain't had any mail since we got here."

Butsko didn't feel like asking any more questions. If Bannon didn't want to say what was bothering him, to hell with it. He relaxed and finished eating his franks and beans, tossed the empty can over his shoulder, and opened the can of fruit salad, his favorite portion of the C ration package, except for the cigarettes.

Bannon lit a cigarette and blew smoke toward the afternoon sky. "Sarge, do you ever think about dying?"

"All the time."

"You ever had a strong feeling that you might get killed."

"Sure."

Bannon sucked smoke out of his cigarette, held it in, and inhaled while saying, "I think I'm gonna get it tomorrow."

"Why tomorrow?"

"Because that's what I think."

"How come?"

Bannon smiled sheepishly. "This is gonna sound fucked-up."

"It won't be different from anything else you ever said."

"I think I'm gonna get it because of Frankie. He and I've been together since Fort Ord, and I always figured I'd stay alive as long as he was okay, but now he's dead for all I know, and I think I'm going too."

Butsko leaned back his head, held the empty can of fruit salad in the air, and let the last drops fall into his open mouth. Bannon watched, amazed, because he'd expected Butsko to take his revelation more seriously than that.

"Goddamn, I love that stuff," Butsko said. "If I ever get out of this war, I'm gonna eat fruit salad until it comes out of my fucking ears." He tossed the can over his shoulder and lit up a cigarette. "Well, kid, lemme tell you something." He tucked his pack of cigarettes back into his shirt pocket. "Every soldier, sooner or later, thinks he's gonna die the next day. We see other guys get it and we can't help thinking it's gonna happen to us, especially when one of our buddies gets it. But one thing doesn't have anything to do with the other. I've been through a lot more of this war than you, and I'm still here. If you use your head, you've got a better chance than the guys who are walking around with their heads up their asses, like Frankie La Barbara. So don't worry so much, although it won't do any good for me to just tell it to you like that. And as for Frankie La Barbara, you don't know that he's dead. He's too much of a stupid asshole to die. Only the good die young, and he's no fucking good, he never has been any fucking good, and he never will be any fucking good. And you're no good, either."

"Gee, thanks, Sarge," Bannon said sarcastically. "I really feel a lot better now."

"Glad to help you out, kid." Butsko puffed his cigarette and looked at his watch. "It's gonna be dark soon. Come on with me and I'll tell you where I want you to put your people tonight."

They arose and brushed the mud and dirt off their uniforms. Slinging their rifles, they trudged toward the beach, two dirty nondescript GIs with helmets askew on their heads and helmet

64

straps hanging loose, smoking cigarettes, their eyes glazed over with war-weariness. Butsko glanced up at the treetops, because there always were rumors about Jap snipers in the trees, and Bannon gazed at the ground, certain he'd be killed as soon as the fighting started again.

American intelligence was right about Kokengolo Hill: It covered a labyrinth of hidden tunnels and rooms dug deep into the ground. Two companies of Japanese soldiers lived like moles in the cool, dank maze, augmented by two platoons of artillery, and they gathered that late afternoon in one of the larger underground rooms to hear an address from their commander, Captain Kazuyoshi Hisahiro.

The room was damp, and the only light came from a solitary kerosene lamp. At one end of the room were crates of ammunition, rice, canned goods, and other supplies, and at the other end Captain Hisahiro stood with his back to the dirt wall, the flickering lamp making shadows dance on his thin, sallow face. Before him, packed tightly together, were all the men in his command except those on guard duty on the upper floors of the mission fortress.

"Men," said Captain Hisahiro, "the Americans will attack tomorrow morning, and we can expect their attack to be more severe than the one today, which we stopped. Americans are poor fighters individually, and they can defeat us only if they outnumber us hugely in men and material. They are bringing up reinforcements, and I imagine we can expect a thorough artillery bombardment in the morning, followed by their attack.

"It has been my experience," Captain Hisahiro continued, "that Americans can be stopped by determined, spirited fighting. Japanese spirit always can overcome American material, for even in death we are victorious, because our cause is just. I am speaking with you now because I want you to be prepared for tomorrow. I expect you to fight with desperate intensity, with the full knowledge that your ancestors are watching you and judging you carefully to determine whether or not you will be worthy to join them in heaven. So do your best tomorrow. Fight hard. Remember that Colonel Hirata has ordered each of us to kill ten Americans, but I say to you that you must kill ten Americans *every day* if you want to call yourselves good Japanese soldiers.

"Our time is drawing near. The Americans will attack in

twelve hours or so. I have nothing more to say to you at this time, except that I would like to wish you good luck. When we meet again in the land of our ancestors, we shall smile and embrace, for we shall always be comrades throughout all eternity. You may return to your posts now."

"Atten-*hut!*" shouted Sergeant Akai.

The soldiers bumped into each other as they scrambled to their feet. Captain Hisahiro marched out of the room, and his footsteps echoed back through the earthen corridor outside. Then the men filed out of the room, those closest to the door leaving first, putting on their helmets, carrying their long bolt-action Arisaka rifles.

Toward the rear of the room, standing in the darkest shadows, was Private Takashi Nanamegi, barely over five feet tall, with a scrawny frame; the others called him Mosquito. He was from Tokyo and had been a pimp and pornographer before being drafted into the Imperial Army. He'd tried to buy his way out and had paid a lot of money, but he'd been cheated by crooks in high places who'd been more clever than he.

He watched the other soldiers leave the room and hated them all. Nearly all of them were farmers from prefectures far from Tokyo, and they were ignorant and naive, just the kind of fools who'd be moved by Captain Hisahiro's sentimental little speech. They'd actually fight like maniacs, thinking of their ancestors in heaven. The Mosquito wanted to spit disgustedly on the floor, but he didn't dare do that. Sergeant Suzuki would punch him in the mouth if he tried it.

The room emptied out slowly, and finally the Mosquito could leave. He followed the others into the corridor and made his way through the dark passageways to the room where he lived cheek by jowl with the other twenty-two soldiers left from his platoon, which originally numbered fifty men.

The Mosquito found a vacant spot in a corner and lay down on his side, resting his head on his hand. Some soldiers prayed silently nearby, sitting in the lotus position, and others muttered in little groups. Sergeant Suzuki sat with his back against a wall, staring blankly into space. The Mosquito wanted to smoke a cigarette, but smoking was permitted only in the upper floors of the fortress, where there was fresh air, and the Mosquito didn't like to go up there unless he had to, because you never knew when a bomb would fall on you.

66

The Mosquito wanted desperately to survive the war. He knew that the odds were against it, but he had to try. Never had he felt so alone in his life, because he could discuss his inner thoughts with no one. All the others wanted to die for the Emperor. The Mosquito wasn't a religious man, and he didn't believe in the divinity of the Emperor, who was just another man as far as he concerned, while the royal family was just a family business. He didn't want to die for the Emperor or anyone else. He wanted to live somehow.

He didn't know how he could do it. When the Americans attacked next time, they'd turn Kokengolo Hill into a huge crater filled with corpses, and his corpse would probably be among them.

But maybe not. Perhaps there'd be a way out. If there was, he'd find it. And if not, he'd just die like the lowlife everybody believed he was. He rolled onto his back and rested his head on his hands. *Better get as much sleep as I can,* he thought. *I'll need every bit of strength I have when the Americans attack tomorrow.*

Frankie La Barbara opened his eyes and didn't know whether he was dreaming or not. A woman in an Army uniform stood in front of him, pointing a camera.

Click!

Frankie flinched. "Where the fuck am I?" he asked.

The woman turned away, fingering a knob on the camera. Her armband said: PRESS.

A man materialized out of the fog, and he wore a similar armband. He carried a note pad and pencil in his hand.

"What's your name, soldier?" he asked, steel-rimmed glasses over his eyes.

"What's going on here?" Frankie asked, dazed. He was shot full of morphine but could feel the ache in his stomach. He recalled being bayoneted by a Jap in the jungle southeast of the Jap airfield.

"We're war correspondents," the man said with a smile. "We'll get your picture in your hometown paper, maybe. What's your name?"

"Frankie La Barbara."

"Your rank?"

"Buck private."

67

"Where you from?"

"New York City."

The correspondent wrote it all down. "Good luck, soldier," he said, moving away.

"Where the hell am I?"

The man disappeared. Frankie felt numb all over. Even his brain felt numb. He focused on the OD-green canvas wall of a tent. *I'm in a tent,* he thought. *I wonder if I'm gonna die.* Somebody groaned nearby. Through the numbness Frankie could feel the throbbing ache in his stomach. *I hope it's not too bad. Just bad enough to get me shipped the fuck out of here.*

He blinked his eyes. A young woman wearing an Army uniform stood in front of him, black hair curling out underneath a fatigue cap crooked on her head.

"Are you real or am I dreaming you?" Frankie asked.

She smiled. "I'm real." Taking his wrist, she looked at her watch.

"Where am I?" he asked.

"Your field medical unit."

"This is still New Georgia?"

"Yes, but you'll probably go to Guadalcanal tomorrow or the next day."

"Am I hurt bad?"

"Not that bad."

"Will they ship me back home?" Frankie asked eagerly.

She could hear the desperate desire in his voice. "I don't think so."

"Shit," Frankie said.

"I know how you feel."

Frankie looked at her, and she had the features and coloring of an Italian like himself. "You a guinea too?" he asked.

"Yeah."

"Where you from?"

"Boston."

"I'm from New York What's your name?"

"Mary Falvo."

"I'm Frankie La Barbara."

"I know." She let his wrist go.

"Am I okay?"

"Yes. Close your eyes and get some sleep."

"Why don't you get in here with me and we'll sleep together?"

"You couldn't get it up if your life depended on it, so go to sleep."

"Frankie La Barbara can *always* get it up."

"I said go to sleep."

She retreated into the shadows and was gone, but her presence and her touch made Frankie feel better. She was the first woman he'd seen since leaving Guadalcanal. He closed his eyes and drifted off into the warm black ocean, a smile on his face.

Colonel Stockton lay on the cot in his office, reading a dog-eared copy of Ulysses S. Grant's memoirs. It was night and he'd go to sleep soon. All his work was done, hours of poring over maps and issuing orders, and now he was relaxing before undressing.

The cot was positioned along a wall in his big headquarters tent, and he read by the light of a kerosene lamp. His favorite books were by or about the great military leaders of history; Alexander, Julius Caesar, Napoleon, von Clausewitz, General Pershing—under whom he'd served in World War One—and now General Grant, one of the best—and maybe the very best—field commander the United States had ever produced.

Colonel Stockton was convinced that General Grant was a better strategist and commander than General Lee, although conventional wisdom said otherwise. Most people believed that the Southerners lost the Civil War only because they were outnumbered by the Northerners, but if you examined the numbers, as Colonel Stockton had, and took into consideration the fact that the South had many part-time militia and guerilla fighters that were never counted in their rosters, while the North used many of its soldiers to guard and maintain its long supply lines into the depths of the Confederacy, it became clear that both sides had similar numbers opposing each other in the field.

Colonel Stockton's military reading took his mind away from his immediate concerns while maintaining his military point of view. He continued to read about the battle of Vicksburg, admiring Grant's straightforward writing style and the clarity of his ideas.

"Sir?" said a voice on the other side of the tent flap.

"Yes?" replied Colonel Stockton, looking up from the book.

"I have to speak with you, sir."

"Come in."

The tent flap was pushed aside, and Lieutenant Wooster, the OD, entered and saluted. Colonel Stockton swung his feet around to the floor and sat up.

"Sir," said Lieutenant Wooster, "there are two war correspondents outside, and they want to see you. One of them's that famous photographer Lydia Kent-Taylor."

"Shit," Colonel Stockton said. "Just what I need."

"They've got passes from General Griswold that say they can go anywhere. They want to talk to you about moving up to the front here."

Colonel Stockton groaned as he stood up. He stretched and hobbled to his desk. "Send them in in five minutes, will you?"

"Yes, sir."

Lieutenant Wooster left the office, and Colonel Stockton sat heavily behind his desk. He opened a drawer, took out a comb and a steel mirror, and combed his silvery hair. He needed a shave but he supposed front-line officers weren't supposed to look like they were on parade. Favorable publicity might help get his star, but reporters twisted everything and could make a fool out of you, even ruin a career. Colonel Stockton didn't feel like dealing with a famous lady photographer, especially after 71 men were killed and 123 wounded that day.

"May I come in?" asked a female voice.

Colonel Stockton stood behind his desk. "Please do," he said in his most charming voice.

The flap was swept aside and the famous Lydia Kent-Taylor entered the office, followed by a man in glasses, a bookworm type, whom Colonel Stockton didn't recognize.

"Hello," said the woman, "I'm Lydia Kent-Taylor, and this is Leo Stern. We're both from the Universal News Syndicate out of New York."

"I've heard of you Miss Kent-Taylor," Colonel Stockton said, shaking her hand. "Please have a seat. I apologize for the lack of comfort here, but I'm sure you understand." He shook Leo Stern's hand, then everyone sat down.

Calmly, without any self-consciousness, Lydia raised her Leica camera and snapped a shot of Colonel Stockton, who didn't know whether to smile or frown and wound up looking into the lens with a stolid expression on his face.

Lydia wore Army fatigues and a battered old safari hat. She carried a canvas haversack containing camera equipment and

Kodak film, and wore the Leica around her neck. Colonel Stockton judged her age at around thirty-five, and she had light-brown hair, short, fine, and wavy. The features of her face were Anglo-Saxon, just like his.

She reached into her haversack. "I have a letter here from General Griswold," she said. "It authorizes me to go anywhere and requests local commanders to assist me however possible."

She handed over the letter and Colonel Stockton read it. The signature looked authentic, and she surely was Lydia Kent-Taylor because he'd seen her picture in magazines. He recalled from his reading in *Stars and Stripes* that she was in the Pacific Theater.

"What can I do for you?" he asked, handing the letter back.

She folded it carefully and placed it in a pocket in her haversack. "I understand there's going to be a big attack here the day after tomorrow. I want to go up to the front and photograph it before, during, and after."

Colonel Stockton straightened his spine, because she was fingering her camera and he thought she might take another picture. "Ever been to the front before?" he asked.

"Many times," she replied.

"When there was hard fighting going on?"

"Yes."

Colonel Stockton paused to think, because her concept of heavy fighting might be vastly different from his. "My regiment suffered very heavy casualties today. The Japs don't discriminate between my soldiers and photographers from the States. If you'd been at my front today, you might become a casualty too."

"I know all about your casualties," she said. "I just came from your field hospital and I saw them. I want to go where the fighting is the hottest, and I'll take my chances. So will Leo."

Leo Stern nodded as he wrote in his notebook. *What the hell is he writing?* Colonel Stockton thought. *I'd better get these two out of my office before they get me in trouble.* Then he had an idea, and it made him smile. He'd send them to the recon platoon and let Butsko handle them. Butsko would cut this high-falutin lady photographer down to size. He'd show her what the war was all about at its rawest, most brutal level.

"Well," Colonel Stockton said, "if you want to go where

71

the fighting is the hottest, I guess you ought to go where my recon platoon is. They always get the toughest missions and they're usually in the thickest fighting. Does that sound all right to you?"

"I just want to be with regular American front-line soldiers," Lydia said.

"That's what they are," Colonel Stockton replied. "They're from all over America, from all walks of life. Some enlisted, some were drafted, and a couple of them are career soldiers. I don't think you'd want to invite many of them into your home, Miss Kent-Taylor, but they're regular front-line American soldiers."

An expression of hostility passed over her face, and Colonel Stockton was sorry about his remark as soon as the words were out of his mouth. He looked nervously at Leo Stern, who was writing away, and Lydia raised her camera to take another picture. Colonel Stockton tried to smile.

Click!

She lowered the camera. "You'd be surprised who I'd invite into my home for dinner," she said sweetly. "Why, I might even invite *you* into my home for dinner, Colonel."

"That'd be my great pleasure, ma'am," he replied, trying to be charming again.

"Can you explain how I can get to this platoon?" she asked. "What did you call it . . . the *recon platoon*?"

"Yes, it's my reconnaissance platoon. It does all my dirty work. I'll have somebody take you to them. And I think both of you had better wear steel pots, because, as I said, that's where the war is."

"I heard you," she answered, "and back here is where you are."

Their eyes locked into each other. *I hate this bitch,* Colonel Stockton thought. *I hope she gets a bullet up her ass.*

"Lieutenant Wooster!" Colonel Stockton shouted.

Lieutenant Wooster burst through the tent flap so quickly that Colonel Stockton realized he'd been waiting out there.

"Tell Lieutenant Harper to escort Miss Kent-Taylor and Mr. Stern to the recon platoon, Lieutenant."

"The recon platoon, sir? But they've reported enemy activity in the jungle in front of them."

Colonel Stockton looked at Lydia. "Still want to go?"

"More than ever."

Colonel Stockton turned to Lieutenant Wooster. "I just gave you an order."

"Yes, sir!"

Lieutenant Wooster led Lydia and Leo Stern out of the office.

"And get them some steel pots!" Colonel Stockton shouted after them.

"Yes, sir!"

They left the office and Colonel Stockton sat behind his desk, shaken up. "They should keep these fucking civilians away from me," he muttered. He drummed his fingers on his desk, thought about smoking his pipe, but decided on a cigarette instead. Opening his desk drawer, he took one out and lit it up. *Goddamn fucking reporters*. He puffed his cigarette and thought he'd better send a message to the recon platoon to warn them.

Goddamn, he thought as he stood behind the desk. *Why'd they have to come to my regiment, of all the regiments at the front?*

SEVEN . . .

"Amelican, you die!" yelled the Jap in the jungle.

Bannon and Longtree crouched in a foxhole, peering over the edge. The night was pitch-black; clouds blocked the light of the moon. Insects buzzed around them and lizards crawled over the ground.

"Amelican, I kill you!" said the Jap.

Bannon thought of Frankie La Barbara. Frankie liked to shout back at the Japs at night, calling them cocksuckers and motherfuckers. Bannon wondered how Frankie was. *I'm gonna die tomorrow,* Bannon said to himself. *The Japs are gonna get me.*

"Amelican, you die."

"I wish the son of the bitch would shut up," Bannon said.

"We can shut him up," Longtree replied. "He's right over there." He pointed.

"Yeah?" Bannon asked.

"Yeah. Not more than twenty thirty yards."

"We shouldn't leave our post," Bannon said.

Butsko's growling voice came to them out of the bush. "You're goddamn right you'd better not leave your post."

Butsko's head appeared out of the bush, followed by his big, burly body. He dropped into the foxhole with the both of

75

them; he had his souvenir samurai sword strapped to his waist.

"If I ever catch anybody away from his post without permission, I'll fucking kill him," Butsko said.

Bannon and Longtree didn't reply. They knew he meant it.

"You really think you know where he is, Chief?" Butsko asked.

Longtree pointed with his chin. "Right over there."

"Let's go get him. Bannon, you stay here."

"Alone?"

"Yeah, or should I call the chaplain for you."

"Fuck you," Bannon muttered.

"What was that?"

"I said I'll stay here alone."

"Good for you. Let's go Longtree. Show me where the cocksucker is."

Longtree crawled out of the foxhole, and Butsko drew the samurai sword out of its sheath. Holding it in his right fist, he followed Longtree into the thick jungle. Bannon watched the night swallow them up and held his rifle tightly. He didn't like to be alone in the jungle, because two guns are always better than one. He'd just have to be alert, that was all. Hear them before they got too close.

"Amelican, I fuck you mother!" the Jap shrieked, and then laughed maniacally. Bannon felt the gall rise in his throat. He hated the Japs because they'd ruined his life. They tortured prisoners and mistreated the natives. He hoped Butsko and Longtree would get that noisy Jap out there.

Longtree and Butsko crawled slowly and silently over the ground as the jungle around them buzzed and chattered with the sound of bugs. The bugs landed on their shirts and sucked their blood. Both had crotch itch from not bathing, and both had mild cases of trenchfoot. Pain was constant to them, including the pain of fatigue, but they carried on anyway, now as at any other time, because pain had become their constant companion and they were used to it.

Longtree stopped and touched his finger to his mouth. Butsko crawled beside him and stopped too, raising his face to indicate *Why?*

"He's moving," Longtree whispered. He moved his finger to indicate the path the Japanese soldier was taking, then motioned for Butsko to follow.

76

They moved out again, Butsko watching Longtree's legs and ass in front of him. Longtree traveled over the ground like a snake, every movement flowing into the next one, making no sound at all, whereas Butsko was tense and straining to keep himself under control, and he knew he made little sounds once in a while, sounds that an Indian like Longtree could hear, but he hoped the Japs weren't that sharp. They hadn't been yet.

"Amelican, you die!" yelled the Jap from his new position.

He sounded close by, not more than ten yards away. Longtree and Butsko could rush him, but the Jap might shoot one of them. They had to get closer.

They'd done this many times on Guadalcanal.

Longtree slowed down, and so did Butsko. This permitted them to be extra careful, and even Butsko was silent now. Raise the hand and place it down very gently. Raise the leg, move it forward, and lower it as if it were a feather falling to earth.

"Amelican, I kill you!"

Longtree stopped and pointed. Butsko looked and made out a big bush. No Jap was in front of it, so evidently he was right behind it. There was no way to get under the bush, because it was too thick. It seemed to be very wide. All Butsko could do was charge through the bush or jump over it. Butsko pointed his thumb at his chest, and Longtree nodded. Slowly drawing himself into a crouch, Butsko gripped the samurai sword tightly.

"Amelican, fuck you!"

Butsko leaped like a lion, tore through the bush, and swung the samurai sword. The Jap was kneeling on the ground, his hands cupped around his mouth. The Jap turned to Butsko, rising a few inches, his face just beginning to show horror.

Butsko swung the samurai sword, and its razor edge caught the Jap on the throat. The blade passed through the Jap's neck with an ugly *thunk* sound, and the Jap's head went flying into the air like a grapefruit hit by a baseball bat. It didn't travel far, and Butsko saw approximately where it landed. He looked down at the decapitated Jap lying at his feet, arms and legs splayed out.

"Gotcha," Butsko said with a grin.

Everyone in the recon platoon heard the jeep coming through the jungle, but they gave it no special attention because military vehicles were always traveling around behind the lines. They heard the jeep engine grow louder, and after a while they realized it was coming their way.

Lieutenant Breckenridge was in his foxhole, sleeping soundly, when the jeep's rumble woke him up. It was close, and he figured it probably carried an officer, because the troops usually traveled around on foot. "Uh-oh," he muttered. "I hope it's not coming here."

"I think it is," replied Craig Delane.

Lieutenant Breckenridge listened with sinking heart as the jeep was driven unmistakably toward the recon platoon. Its driver shifted gears, gunned the engine, let up on the gas.

"I bet it's the colonel," Craig Delane said.

Lieutenant Breckenridge took a swig of water from his canteen, then rubbed some over his face, hoping it would wake him up. He felt the stubble on his chin; he hadn't shaved for three days. Taking off his helmet, he ran his fingers through his hair, being careful not to touch the cut on his scalp. He lit a cigarette as the jeep stopped close by.

"Look sharp," Lieutenant Breckenridge said to Craig Delane, "just in case."

"Yo."

Lieutenant Breckenridge heard voices and thought one of them belonged to a woman. No, it couldn't be. There weren't any women out there. Footsteps headed toward him, and Lieutenant Harper, Colonel Stockton's aide, emerged from the jungle, accompanied by two figures, one of medium height and one short. The short one looked awfully frail. *No, it's impossible,* Lieutenant Breckenridge thought.

Lieutenant Harper approached, looking neat and clean as always. Lieutenant Breckenridge believed Harper had never fired a shot in anger in his life; Harper was a decent guy, a graduate of the University of Michigan, and he'd wanted to become a lawyer before the draft got him. The two others were a few paces behind him, and Lieutenant Breckenridge examined the frail one. *It can't be.*

But as they drew closer, Lieutenant Breckenridge realized with mounting anxiety that it was indeed a woman, not bad-looking but no spring chicken, either.

"Hello, Dale," Lieutenant Harper said.

"'Lo, Bob."

"I'd like to introduce Lydia Kent-Taylor and Leo Stern of the Universal News Syndicate."

Lieutenant Breckenridge shook hands with both of them; he'd heard of Lydia before. "A pleasure to meet you, ma'am," he said in his southern accent.

"Nice meeting you, Lieutenant," she replied.

"They're going to be spending some time with you," Lieutenant Harper said.

"They are?"

"Yes. Colonel Stockton's orders."

"Here?"

Lydia took the letter from General Griswold out of her haversack. "I have full authorization." She handed over the letter.

Lieutenant Breckenridge held the letter up but couldn't read it clearly in the darkness.

"It's authentic," Lieutenant Harper said. "Colonel Stockton wants you to cooperate to the extent that you can."

"Gee, I don't know," Lieutenant Breckenridge said. "I'm not set up for this kind of thing."

"Don't worry about it, Lieutenant," she replied. "We have our own transportation, tents, and supplies."

"But, ma'am," Lieutenant Breckenridge said, "there are Japs around here. Anything can happen in a place like this."

"That's why I'm here," she replied. She turned to Lieutenant Harper. "Thank you very much for bringing us here. We'll be all right now."

Lieutenant Harper walked off, leaving Lieutenant Breckenridge with Lydia and Leo Stern. Craig Delane crawled out of the foxhole and stared at Lydia as if she were a geek.

"I suppose," Lieutenant Harper said unhappily, "that you should pitch your tent somewhere near my hole here."

"Don't you have a tent, Lieutenant?" she asked.

"We don't have time for tents. We've got to be ready to move out at a moment's notice."

Leo Stern wrote that down. Lydia turned and saw a lone soldier approaching.

"Hey, Lieutenant!" shouted Butsko. "Catch!"

Lieutenant Breckenridge turned around and raised his hands, catching the head of the Japanese soldier Butsko had ambushed in the jungle.

79

"Good grief!" said Lieutenant Breckenridge, gazing down at the closed eyes and open mouth of the Jap.

"I caught the cocksucker back there," Butsko said, pointing behind him with his thumb.

Lydia Kent-Taylor stared at the object in Lieutenant Breckenridge's hands. "I do believe that's a human head!"

"It is," Lieutenant Breckenridge replied, tossing it back to Butsko.

Butsko realized he'd just heard a woman's voice. Squinting his eyes, he approached her, carrying the head under his arm like a basketball.

"Miss Kent-Taylor, may I present my platoon sergeant, Master Sergeant John Butsko."

"Is that a woman?" Butsko asked incredulously.

"Yes, she's a photographer. And that's Leo Stern, a war correspondent."

Butsko stared at Lydia Kent-Taylor. "Well, I'll be a son of a bitch."

She wrinkled her nose in disgust as she looked at the head under his arm. "Where did you get that?"

Butsko held it in the air. "This? I got it off the Jap who owned it." Snorting viciously, he lobbed it toward Lydia Kent-Taylor.

She screamed and hopped out of the way. The head landed in the muck, and she stared at it.

Lieutenant Breckenridge was getting angry at Butsko, but he didn't want the two civilians to see him chew Butsko out. "Sergeant, Miss Kent-Taylor and Mr. Stern will be in our area for a few days."

Butsko blinked. "What for?"

"To take pictures and write stuff."

"Yeah?"

"Yes, and Colonel Stockton wants us to be as helpful as we can."

"Oh, shit!"

Lieutenant Breckenridge tried to grin, as if it all were a big joke, but it wasn't.

"Why here?" Butsko asked. "What did we do to deserve this?"

Lydia Kent-Taylor cleared her throat. "You have an objection to us being here, Sergeant Butsko?"

He looked her in the eye. "Yeah."

"What's the nature of your objection?"

"You'll probably get somebody around here killed."

"And how will I do that?"

"By getting in the fucking way."

"I won't get in anybody's way."

"You already are."

Lieutenant Breckenridge looked sternly at Butsko. "Don't you have something to do, Sergeant?"

"I always got something to do." He took one step backward, saluted, and walked away.

"He forgot his head," Lydia Kent-Taylor said dryly.

"Delane!" Lieutenant Breckenridge said. "Bury that head right now."

"Maybe Butsko wants it for something."

"I said bury that head!"

"Yes, sir."

Delane scooped up the head and carried it off into the night. Lieutenant Breckenridge smiled.

"Well," he said, "I guess the front isn't a tea party, and some of the men get a little rough. I apologize for the behavior of Sergeant Butsko, but he's been in the war since the very beginning. He was on the Bataan Death March, you see. Escaped from a Jap POW camp on Luzon. He's not exactly what you would call a boy scout."

"Neither am I," Lydia Kent-Taylor said. "We'll pitch our tents right here, and if we need you for anything, we'll ask. By the way, there's only one item I'll require: I'd like to have one of your men dig me my own latrine."

"I'll have Private Delane take care of it as soon as he comes back."

"Very good, Lieutenant. I look forward to seeing you in the morning."

"We get up pretty early around here."

"So do I."

"Do you have a weapon?" Lieutenant Breckenridge asked.

"What kind of weapon?"

"A knife or a gun."

"What would I need that for?"

"Jap infiltrators."

"Here?"

"Sometimes in the morning we find men whose throats have been slit by the Japs during the night."

"My goodness!"

"I take it you don't have a gun."

"Well, no."

"I'll post a guard at your tent, ma'am."

She remembered what Butsko had said about her being in the way. "That won't be necessary, Lieutenant. I'm sure we'll be all right."

"I'm not so sure, and I'm the one in command here. I'll post a guard." He raised his rigid right hand to his temple and saluted her. "Good night, ma'am."

Butsko dropped into the foxhole with Longtree and Bannon. "You'll never believe what just happened."

"What was it?" Bannon asked.

"There's a cunt in the platoon area."

Longtree's ears perked up. "A cunt?"

"Yeah, a lady photographer, a real la-di-da bitch."

"What's she doing here?" Bannon asked.

"I guess she's gonna take pictures of us."

"She pretty?"

"She's not bad for an old broad."

"Nice ass?" asked Longtree, who was an ass-and-legs man.

"I couldn't see."

"Any tits?" asked Bannon, who was a tit man.

"I just told you I couldn't see."

"Where's the head?" asked Longtree.

"Oh, fuck, I got so pissed off at that broad, I forgot it."

"Somebody's coming," Bannon said.

Lieutenant Breckenridge emerged from the jungle and knelt at the edge of the foxhole, looking directly into Butsko's eyes.

"You son of a bitch!"

"What I do?" Butsko asked.

Lieutenant Breckenridge pointed at Butsko's nose. "From now on you're going to be nice to that lady."

"She ain't no lady—she's a war correspondent."

"I don't care what she is—you're going to be nice to her!"

"Aw, come on, Lieutenant."

"If she complains about us to General Griswold, all our asses will be in a sling."

Butsko snorted. "What's he gonna do to us, put us all before a firing squad? Fuck him too."

"There are a lot of things he can do to us, and you know it. So be nice to her. Maybe she'll take a few pictures tomorrow and leave."

"Let's hope so. We don't need any broads wandering around here. We're having enough problems as it is. Hey, by the way, where's my fucking head?"

"It's still on your shoulders, from what I can see."

"I mean the Jap head."

"I told Delane to bury it."

"What you tell him that for?"

"What did you expect me to do with it?"

"I wanted to put it on a pole out there in the jungle to scare the fucking Japs."

"See Delane about it." He pointed at Butsko again. "You're going to be nice to Miss Kent-Taylor, aren't you?"

Bannon widened his eyes. "Lydia Kent-Taylor, the famous photographer?"

"That's her."

Butsko frowned. "I'll be nice to her, sir. If I get close to her, I'll stick my finger up her ass. If she behaves herself, maybe I'll let her take a picture of my cock."

Lieutenant Breckenridge looked at his watch. "I think it's time I hit the hay. You-all might as well turn in too. I don't know what we're gonna do tomorrow, but I think we'll start shelling the Japs pretty early. Just remember Butsko, if you mess with that woman, she'll make you regret it. She's got friends in high places. She even knows General MacArthur, according to something I read a few months back."

"Fuck him too," Butsko snarled.

"Jesus Christ," Lieutenant Breckenridge said, standing. Shaking his head in despair, he walked away.

EIGHT . . .

The artillery bombardment began at the first glimmer of dawn, around four-thirty in the morning. The loud rumbling didn't wake up Lydia Kent-Taylor, because she hadn't slept much all night. She'd lain with a bayonet at her side, and every time she heard a sound, she thought it was a Japanese soldier creeping up on her to slit her throat. She cursed Lieutenant Breckenridge for planting the fear in her mind. She had an artist's personality and tended to get obsessed by things.

She'd slept with her clothes on, and now all she had to do was lace up her boots, put on her hat, and get her ass in gear, but first she had to go to the toilet. She crawled out of her tent, saw that Leo wasn't up yet, and looked around at the recon platoon area in the first light of dawn. Nearby, Lieutenant Breckenridge sat in his foxhole, eating something out of a can.

"Good morning, Lieutenant," she said cheerfully, although she didn't feel so hot.

He looked up from his map. "Morning. Sleep okay?"

"Yes, thank you. Yourself?"

"Okay."

"Did you have my latrine dug?"

"Yes, ma'am."

"Where is it?"

"Over there."

"Thank you very much."

She walked in the direction he'd indicated and found a fresh path leading to the latrine, which surrounded by an OD tarpaulin to ensure her privacy. Smiling, she went inside and saw the hole with the pole suspended over it so that she could sit and hang out her bottom.

She unbuttoned her fatigue pants, pulled them and her underwear down, and moved toward the hole. Something was inside it, and she squinted her eyes to make it out. Her jaw fell open when she saw what it was: the head of the Japanese soldier, face up.

She wanted to scream, but managed to suppress the sound coming up from her throat. Then she became angry. Somebody had done this deliberately to upset her, and she had a good idea of who it was.

Pulling up her pants and buckling her belt, she stormed out of the latrine and marched toward Lieutenant Breckenridge, who was still looking at his map.

"Lieutenant Breckenridge!" she said.

"Ma'am?" he replied, glancing up.

She placed her hands on her hips. "Somebody is trying to make a fool of me! The head of the Japanese soldier is in my latrine!"

Lieutenant Breckenridge closed his eyes and groaned. "Are you sure?"

"Of course I'm sure!"

"It's probably a little dark in there. You might have been seeing things."

"I wasn't seeing things!" She realized she was screaming and brought her voice under control. "Would you care to see for yourself?"

"Okay." Lieutenant Breckenridge folded his map and put it in his map case. He left the case in the hole with his other belongings, slung his carbine, and walked with her into the woods.

"I think it's a disgusting, vindictive thing to do!" she said. "And I bet I know who did it!"

"Who?"

"That sergeant you introduced me to last night."

"Butsko?"

"That one."

Lieutenant Breckenridge moved into the jungle with long strides. He knew that if anybody had placed the head in her latrine, it probably was Butsko. *That maniac is driving me nuts,* Lieutenant Breckenridge thought.

They came to the latrine, and Lieutenant Breckenridge let Lydia go in first. She looked down into the hole. "It's gone!"

Lieutenant Breckenridge stood beside her. "You sure you saw it in the first place?"

"Yes!"

Lieutenant Breckenridge shrugged. "Well, I don't know. It sure as hell isn't here now."

She turned to him angrily. "Do you think I'm lying to you?"

"No, ma'am, but maybe your eyes were playing tricks on you before. You do look a little peaked."

"Peaked!"

"Yes, ma'am."

"I am not peaked!"

A faint smile broke out on her face, and she knew she'd lost. One woman all alone among an army of men had to take a lot of shit, and that's all there was to it. If a man had been alone among an army of woman, it would have been the same thing.

"Well," she said, calming down, speaking coldly and with a faint tinge of derision, "I know what I saw, but it's not here now and I can't prove anything. Hereafter I'll handle these matters myself. Would you kindly advise me as to where I can find Master Sergeant John Butsko?"

"I imagine he's with the First Squad over there." Breckenridge pointed.

"Are you very busy right now, or do you think you could take me to him?"

"I'm busy, ma'am, but I'll have Private Delane take you."

"That would be most kind of you."

"I want to be as helpful as I can, ma'am."

They walked away from the latrine and passed through the jungle, returning to the foxhole, where Craig Delane lay, listening to the walkie-talkie.

"Delane, take Miss Kent-Taylor to Sergeant Butsko."

"Yes, sir."

Delane jumped up and approached Lydia. "This way, please."

She walked beside him toward the jungle. A big bug landed on her forehead and she slapped it, splattering all over her forehead. "Damn," she said, reaching into her pocket, taking out her handkerchief, and wiping it off. "Is Sergeant Butsko far from here?"

"No."

"By the way, what was your name again?"

"Craig Delane, and I believe we've met before."

Lydia stared at the filthy, unshaven soldier next to her; he smelled to high heaven. "We have?"

"Yes, in New York City. A charity ball at Delmonico's, given by Henry Rutherford, I believe. We were introduced by my uncle, Lemuel Decatur."

Her eyes bugged out of her head. "Why, yes, I believe I remember! I'm an old friend of your uncle's! My God! What are you doing here?"

"I enlisted in the Army after Pearl Harbor."

"Why didn't you get a commission at least?"

"Patriotic foolishness. I thought I should serve with the ordinary soldiers—you know, the real men."

"Well," she said, "I'm not so sure that was a good idea."

"It wasn't, but it's too late to do anything about it now."

"Can't anybody get you out of this—someone in your family? Your Uncle Lemuel has very good contacts in Washington, you know."

"Nobody's been able to do anything, or at least that's what they tell me. I think they're letting me stew in my own juice, to teach me a lesson or something."

"Let me tell you what happened to *me,* this morning."

Ahead of them was a clearing, and Lydia spotted Butsko standing with a bunch of other soldiers. She'd calmed down considerably while talking with Craig Delane, but now the fury returned like someone slowly turning on a faucet full blast. Butsko was a stupid pig who'd tried to frighten and humiliate her, and she was from the old East Coast Yankee aristocracy. Nobody was going to pull that shit with her and get away with it.

"Wait for me here one moment, would you, Mr. Delane?" she asked sweetly.

"Certainly, Miss Kent-Taylor."

Setting her jaw, she balled up her fists and stomped across the clearing toward Butsko.

"Don't look now," said Longtree, "but here she comes. I'd say she's in a pretty bad mood."

Butsko couldn't help chuckling. "I'd give anything to have seen the look on her face when she saw the Jap's head."

Bannon tossed his cigarette at the ground and glanced at her. "She really looks fit to be tied."

Butsko chuckled again, because he was having fun. "Just relax and let me handle everything. Women, even when they're pissed off, are nothing to handle if you just know what you're doing."

He heard her approach, combat boots mashing into the mud, and pretended he didn't hear anything, as casual and loose as an old soldier could be. The angrier she got, the calmer he'd get: He knew from experience that that was a good way to handle women. If they wanted to fight and you didn't, it really drove them nuts, because it made them think you didn't care about them enough to get mad.

Pow!

Lydia Kent-Taylor punched Butsko directly in the mouth with all her strength, and it astonished him more than it hurt. She kicked him in the shins and he screamed in pain, holding one leg in his hands and hopping around on the other. Pulling back her arm, she lambasted him in the face, knocking him on his ass.

If she had been a man, Butsko would have got up and killed her; but she was a woman and he couldn't strike a woman. He rolled away, trying to escape, but she jumped forward and kicked him in the ass. The men from the recon platoon watched in horror as she kicked him in the stomach, and when he doubled up she kicked him in the ass again. She was beating up the man they thought was the toughest in the world.

"Halp!" Butsko screamed.

He tried to get up but she tripped him and he fell down again. She kicked him in the thigh and he howled in pain. None of the men dared touched her, because she was woman and they couldn't cold-conk a woman.

Suddenly she stopped. She looked down contemptuously at

Butsko quivering and whimpering on the ground, then turned and walked resolutely back to Craig Delane, her head held high.

Bannon bent over to help Butsko to his feet. "You really showed us how to handle her, Sarge," he said.

Captain Ilecki had black hair, a thin face, and a ratty, furtive manner. His CP was a hole in the ground in back of a boulder ten feet high, because he tended to feel insecure. He sat in the hole, looking at his map, a Pittsburgh stogie held between his yellow teeth. Lieutenant Breckenridge approached and knelt down.

"You wanted to see me, Joe?"

"Yes. How're you doing, by the way?"

"We're okay, except that we've got Lydia Kent-Taylor traveling with us."

"Really?"

"Yes."

"You lucky bastard! She'll probably make you famous! You could go home and run for Congress if you wanted to, I'll bet."

"Who in the fuck wants to run for Congress, and what makes you think I'll live that long?"

Captain Ilecki had always been interested in politics, and his father was an alderman in Chicago. After the war Captain Ilecki wanted to run for Congress. But he too had to survive first, and that brought him back to his map.

"We've got orders from Battalion," he said. "They want us to occupy this jungle all the way to the airfield."

"When?"

"Sometime today. They're gonna shell it first and they'll let us know."

"What makes them think there are Japs in there?"

"I don't know."

"Didn't you tell them there are no Japs in there?"

"I don't know that there are no Japs in there. Do you *know* there are no Japs in there?"

"I couldn't say for sure, but I don't think there are. Some were in there last night, but they're gone now."

"How do you know?"

"It's common sense, Joe. If there were Japs in there, we'd know about it."

"What makes you think so?"

"We would've heard them."

Captain Ilecki smirked. "C'mon, you know better than that. You don't have to hear them for them to be there."

Lieutenant Breckenridge was getting tired of the argument. "Okay, we'll do it your way."

"It ain't my way, it's Battalion's way."

"Okay, okay. When do we jump off?"

"I'll let you know as soon as I find out. Any other questions?"

"No."

"You can go back to your zoo now, the one they call the recon platoon. And by the way, you can tell Lydia Kent-Taylor that if she really wants to take a picture of a handsome officer, she can take a picture of me."

"I'll tell her that," Lieutenant Breckenridge said, standing up. "I'm sure she's just dying to meet you."

Craig Delane was lying in his hole, smoking a cigarette and listening to the walkie-talkie. The airwaves buzzed with messages, and a red spider crawled along the rim of the foxhole. Birds chirped in the trees and a monkey leaped from branch to branch.

Lydia Kent-Taylor came into his line of vision, held up her camera, and took a picture of him. Leo Stern was two steps behind her, a shit-eating grin on his face.

Lydia took another picture of Craig Delane, then jumped into the foxhole with him. "I've been thinking about you," she said, "and I got a great idea for a story: *Society Playboy in a Foxhole*. About how you wanted to be an enlisted man instead of an officer, so you could be with the men. I'll take the pictures and Leo here will write it up. What do you think?"

"Sounds awfully corny to me."

"It is corny, but it's the kind of thing that sells newspapers."

Leo joined them in the foxhole and asked Craig Delane questions as Lydia snapped pictures. Lieutenant Breckenridge returned, his carbine slung over his shoulder and his helmet straps hanging loose. He looked at all of them together and scratched his jaw.

"Delane, get Butsko for me."

"Yes, sir."

Craig Delane rose quickly and climbed out of the foxhole, ending the interview. Lydia and Leo Stern would have liked to continue, but they knew better than to interfere with the war. Lieutenant Breckenridge dropped into the foxhole, sat down, and took out his map.

"I've got work to do," he said. "Hope you don't mind."

Lydia snapped his picture. "Do what you have to. Don't pay any attention to us."

Lieutenant Breckenridge looked at his map, wondering how he could ignore a woman taking pictures of him. Lydia changed position, taking profile shots, overhead shots, and after changing lenses, low-down wide-angle shots. Presently Craig Delane returned with Butsko, who was black and blue, with a split lip and his left eye half closed.

Lieutenant Breckenridge took one look and nearly shit a brick. "What in the hell happened to you!"

"I fell down," Butsko replied in an apologetic tone.

"You fell down! You didn't fall down! You've been fighting again! If I told you once, I told you a thousand times that I don't want any more of that goddamned idiotic fighting in this platoon! I told you to save it for the Japs! Get it?"

"Yes, sir."

Butsko glanced at Lydia Kent-Taylor, who eyed him haughtily. She raised her camera and pointed it at Butsko. "This will make a very good picture," she said. "A real battle-scarred combat veteran."

Butsko scowled as she took his picture.

Lieutenant Breckenridge cleared his throat. "I wonder if I can speak with my platoon sergeant alone for a few moments."

Lydia Kent-Taylor blew dust off her fifty-millimeter f2 Summitar lens. "Sure thing, Lieutenant. Is anything going to happen here this afternoon?"

"Yes, but I'll tell you about it after I discuss it with my platoon sergeant."

"I understand, Lieutenant. We'll talk with you later."

Lydia and Leo Stern walked back to their tents, leaving Lieutenant Breckenridge with Butsko and Craig Delane.

"I don't know how much more of those two I can handle," he said.

"I know what you mean," Butsko replied.

Craig Delane thought it was time to let his platoon leader

and platoon sergeant know he was no ordinary dogfaced GI like all the others.

"Miss Kent-Taylor and I knew each other quite well in New York," he said, exaggerating somewhat because he was an asshole despite his upper-class background, or maybe because of it.

Butsko and Lieutenant Breckenridge stared at him.

"Yes," Craig Delane continued, "her family and my family are quite close."

Butsko and Lieutenant Breckenridge looked at each other.

"It was such a strange coincidence seeing her here."

Butsko took one step toward Craig Delane and grabbed his shirt in his fist. "Well, you'd better make sure she puts in a good word for us higher up, because if she doesn't, it's gonna be your ass."

"Yes, Sergeant!"

Butsko let him go and pushed him away. "Take a fucking walk."

"Yes, Sergeant!"

Craig Delane scurried away, and Butsko turned to Lieutenant Breckenridge. "We've got to get rid of that bitch," he said.

"We've got to be nice to her. I don't want any more funny business from you. Don't think I don't know that you had something to do with that head being in her latrine."

Butsko looked him in the eye. "Who, me?"

"Yes, you. Cut that shit out."

"But, sir—"

"Don't *but* me," Lieutenant Breckenridge interrupted. "Just do as I say, and I don't want to hear anything more about it. Come over to my foxhole and I'll tell you what we're going to do this afternoon. And by the way, I don't know who kicked the shit out of you, but he did a great job."

Craig Delane joined Lydia Kent-Taylor and Leo Stern, who were sitting cross-legged in the shade of a huge, lush canopy of leaves. Leo wrote in his notebook, and Lydia cleaned out the interior of her Leica camera with the camelhair brush.

"Any news?" she asked, as Craig Delane sat down.

"Yes, but I don't know what it is. Lieutenant Breckenridge is telling it to Sergeant Butsko right now."

Lydia shuddered. "What a stupid brute he is!"

"Sergeant Butsko?" Craig Delane asked. "Well, he may be a brute, but he's not stupid. He knows more about small-unit tactics than most officers, and he's absolutely without fear. The men in this platoon would follow him anywhere."

"Really? Would you?"

"I have. With all his shortcomings Butsko is a helluva soldier. If you want to do a story about someone, you should do one about him. He's probably the most decorated soldier in the regiment."

"But he's such an animal!"

"Well," Craig Delane said thoughtfully, "he's certainly an animal. You wouldn't want to go to the ballet with him, but in a war there's nobody I'd rather be with than Butsko. I could tell you stories about him that you wouldn't believe, but I believe them because I was there and I saw them happen with my own eyes. In fact, when this war is over and if I'm still alive, Butsko can visit me anytime and he can stay as long as he likes. I'd be honored to have him with me. I think he's a great man."

Lydia was confused by what Craig Delane was saying, because she couldn't imagine how Butsko could be a great man, but she knew from her previous interview with Delane that he'd been in a lot of combat with Butsko. Delane would be in a position to know, and he was no fool, although he certainly was an asshole at times.

"Leo," she said, "maybe we ought to do something on Butsko, and Lieutenant Breckenridge seems kind of interesting too; we haven't done that much with officers." She looked at Delane. "What do you think of Lieutenant Breckenridge?"

"Well," Delane said, "let me put it this way: Lieutenant Breckenridge is the only officer I've seen who can handle Butsko."

"Why's that?"

"Because Lieutenant Breckenridge is a big, tough son of a bitch," he said, "and Butsko respects him."

NINE . . .

At eleven o'clock the artillery barrage began, plastering the jungle in front of Company A and the recon platoon. Birds shrieked and flew away, but the other creatures couldn't escape. Trees containing families of monkeys crashed to the ground, and lizards, which thought they were safe in their burrows, were blown into the air. Huge chunks of shrapnel whizzed in all directions, slashing apart trees and decapitating animals. Fires broke out and huge clouds of smoke rose into the sky.

Lydia photographed it standing on the hood of her jeep, using her 135-millimeter telephoto lens. "Beautiful," she mumbled, twirling dials and aiming. "Like the end of the world."

Nearby the recon platoon lay in a skirmish line, ready to move out. It would be on the extreme left flank, with a portion of the jungle and the beach in front of it, and Company A linked up on its right. The men smoked cigarettes and talked with each other. Some reread letters from home or Bibles that they'd been carrying around with them since the war began. A few watched the bombardment listlessly, because they'd seen so many others just like it.

Lydia jumped down from the jeep and advanced toward the skirmish line. She got in front of the men, dropped to one knee, screwed the 35-millimeter lens into the Leica, and took a picture. *The recon platoon prepares to move into action* would be the caption. She duck-walked toward Lieutenant Breckenridge, and snapped one of him. *The platoon leader studies his map prior to the battle.* She moved the camera to her left and Butsko filled the frame, gazing malevolently at her. *Master Sergeant Butsko waiting for the order to move out.*

The shelling lasted until noon, augmenting the sound of the bombardment of the mission fortress on Kokengolo Hill. In the rear areas artillerymen stripped to their waists fed shell after shell into their big guns, while other artillerymen pulled the cords that fired them off. Nearly all of them suffered hearing impairments from the terrific ear-shattering sounds of artillery in action. Many of them had busted eardrums even before they'd left their training camps in the States.

The shelling stopped on time, and everybody's ears rang, whistled, or buzzed. The forest was filled with smoke, and Lydia thought the atmosphere would be marvelous for pictures of war as it really was.

Lieutenant Breckenridge stood up. "All right," he said, "let's move it out! Stay dressed right and covered down! Let's go, and keep your eyes open!"

The men stood, lined up, and advanced cautiously toward the jungle, with Lydia and Leo Stern following even more cautiously. The GIs passed through a nightmare landscape of broken trees and smoking shell craters. Pfc. Hart heard something in front of him and fired off a round, making everyone drop down, but a patrol investigated and found nothing there. The platoon moved out again, combing the jungle and watching the beach. They met no resistance after one hundred yards, and it became obvious that no Japs were in the jungle. Lydia ran ahead with her camera, got low in the bushes, and photographed the men coming toward her. *The recon platoon advances cautiously through a Jap-held jungle somewhere in the South Pacific.*

At three o'clock in the afternoon they reached the edge of the jungle. In front of them was the open ground of the airfield, and in the distance were airstrips and the fortress on Kokengolo Hill. They deployed across the edge of the jungle closest to Kokengolo Hill, because they'd attack from that direction during the big push scheduled for the following morning.

Lieutenant Breckenridge told them to dig in and they took

out their entrenching tools, looking for spots where the earth wasn't so rocky or interlaced with roots. Lieutenant Breckenridge walked toward Lydia Kent-Taylor, who was now photographing the men digging their foxholes. *The recon platoon digs in, expecting a Jap counterattack.* Leo Stern sat on a fallen log nearby, scribbling furiously.

"Are you going to stay, ma'am?" Lieutenant Breckenridge asked.

"Of course."

"I'll have Private Delane dig you a foxhole."

"Do you think we'll need one?"

"You never can tell," Lieutenant Breckenridge replied.

Private Nanamegi, known as the Mosquito, was on guard duty in the fortress and gazed out at the landscape around him through binoculars. There was a lull in the shelling, and he had to see if an American attack was being launched. Scanning the jungle at the edge of the airstrip, he could see nothing suspicious.

He aimed his binoculars south and saw something glint in the sun. His heart beat faster as he focused on that spot: It looked as though American soldiers were there, digging in.

"Sergeant Suzuki!" he cried.

"What is it!" demanded Sergeant Suzuki.

"I see Americans over there!"

"Where?"

The Mosquito pointed, and Sergeant Suzuki trained his binoculars in that direction. "I see them! Good work, Private Nanamegi!"

Sergeant Suzuki picked up the phone and reported the sighting to Captain Hisahiro, in his office deep in the fortress. Captain Hisahiro looked at his map and realized that the Americans were occupying new ground in that jungle, evidently preparing for an attack. He had to be economical with his shells, saving them for the American attack, but it wouldn't hurt to lay a barrage on those Americans over there, because they weren't dug in yet and he could inflict casualties, maybe even make the Americans pull back.

He picked up the phone on his desk and called his artillery officer to arrange for the barrage.

• • •

97

The first shell landed while the GIs were digging in, and they all dived into their holes. Lydia Kent-Taylor whipped out her camera, because it was just another picture situation to her. *GIs hit the dirt during artillery bombardment.* The next shell landed close by, startling her. She realized that she would have been killed by that shell if she'd been standing closer, and a wave of fear swept over her.

Something enormous and heavy hit her from behind, sending her flying into the muck. She thought she'd been hit by a bomb, but then she felt someone crawl off her and looked around to see Butsko.

He pushed her face into the muck. "Keep your head down, stupid!"

"Now just a moment . . . !"

Another shell landed in their vicinity, and she jerked as if somebody had plugged her into a wall socket. She could feel its concussion in her stomach and easily could imagine being blown apart. Terrified, she hugged the ground and trembled, feeling naked and vulnerable.

"C'mon with me, nitwit," Butsko said, grabbing her collar.

She was paralyzed with fear, so he dragged her behind him, heading toward a shell crater. He crawled in and pulled her in after him. She toppled to the bottom beside him and looked up fearfully.

Butsko took out a cigarette. "You'll be safe in here," he said. "And besides, they say you never hear the one that lands on you." Flicking the wheel of his Zippo, he took a drag on his cigarette.

She looked at him in disbelief. He was leaning casually against the wall of the crater, smoking a cigarette as if nothing were happening. Shells slammed into the ground all around them, and tiny clods of earth rained down on them. A small rock landed on Lydia's cloth fatigue hat, stunning her.

"You ought to wear a helmet," he said, "but I guess it's hard to focus your camera when your're wearing a helmet."

She stood on her hands and knees in the bottom of the crater, trembling all over and flinching hard whenever a shell landed. She wished she'd worn the helmet Lieutenant Harper had given her, but it had been too heavy, had clanged against her camera whenever she raised it to her eyes, and had not been very flattering. Her heart beat like a tom-tom; she was scared to death. A shell landed close to the crater, caving in one of the walls, and she screamed, leaping onto Butsko and hugging him tightly.

Butsko patted her ass and chuckled. "Take it easy. The Japs can't keep this up for long, and it could be worse. They have only three artillery pieces out there, and they have to watch their ammunition. Can you imagine what it'd be like if they had as much artillery as we do?"

She held him tightly, smelling his masculine odor, his stubbled cheek against her smooth one, and his big hands on her nice round ass. Dirt covered her left leg, the sky was full of thunder, the earth shuddered, and she felt herself getting turned on.

She pushed away from him, pressed her back to the opposite side of the crater, and tried to pull herself together.

Butsko puffed his cigarette and looked at her through narrowed eyes, one of them blackened by her earlier in the day.

"Lady," he said, "If you keep hanging around this platoon, I'm probably going to fuck you, you know that?"

Her eyes widened, and she became so angry and confused that she didn't know what to say. Her hands trembling, she checked her cameras and equipment to make sure everything was all right.

He watched her and chuckled. "Relax," he said. "Your problem is that you're too tense all the time. Nobody ever gets out of this world alive, so what in the hell are you worried about?"

In the late afternoon, as the sun dropped toward the horizon, a meeting was held in General Hawkins's CP tent. All staff officers, regimental commanders, and battalion commanders were there, standing around the map table as General Hawkins stood with his swagger stick, holding an end in each fist, the swagger stick horizontal at thigh level.

"All right, gentlemen," he said, "the battle for this miserable little island has gone on long enough, and tomorrow we're going to bring it to an end. I will tolerate no excuses, and there will be no room for failure. Any commander who fails to attain his assigned objective will be relieved of command. Is that clear?"

The room was silent, and the officers gazed at General

Hawkins, who clearly was in an ass-kicking mood. Colonel Stockton, his waist abutting the table, looked down at the map, which showed Kokengolo Hill at its center, three inches higher than the flat terrain around it. All terrain features were represented on the map: the jungles were green plaster molds and the flatland was sand. The runways of the airstrip were plaster strips painted black.

"All right," General Hawkins continued, "let's move on. Here we are"—he pointed his swagger stick at the map and waved it back and forth—"and here's Corps. We're bringing all our power to bear on the airfield, and it will be in our hands by nightfall. Our objective is Kokengolo Hill and all ground to the south of it. Kokengolo Hill is the key to the entire campaign, not just in our sector but on the whole front. It is the strongest fortification that the Japanese have have left on New Georgia. It will not be easy to assault, but assault it we will, from all sides, with unrelenting violence, until it is ours." He pointed to the maps. "All of you can see your regiments, indicated by colors on the map. The Twenty-third is here, the Fifteenth here, and the Thirty-eighth here. Your orders are quite simple. When the bombing and artillery barrage ends tomorrow morning, you attack from where you are right now and you continue attacking until the airfield is ours. That means sweeping all the way up to Kula Gulf and the Solomon Sea. Instruct your men to kill every Jap they see unless they're surrendering, but tell them to make sure they're surrendering. If they have any questions, tell them to shoot first and ask questions afterwards. General MacArthur thinks we've been on New Georgia too long and he's getting impatient. He wants this campaign to end, and that's precisely what we're going to do tomorrow. Any questions?"

It was night on New Georgia. In the area held by the recon platoon and Company A, guards were posted and the troops were asleep. Ammunition for the attack in the morning was stacked up in special foxholes dug into the ground. All the men had been issued C rations for the day. Before dawn they'd wake up and move into position for the attack.

A short distance behind the recon platoon line, not far from her tent, Lydia Kent-Taylor paced back and forth in a small jungle clearing, chain-smoking cigarettes, crossing and uncrossing her arms. She thought she was losing her mind, and she couldn't remember any time in her life, except for when her mother died, that she felt so distraught.

"Is that you, Lydia?" asked Leo Stern in the darkness.

She spun around. "Yes, it's me, Leo."

He walked toward her and appeared in the dim light of the half-moon. "I thought I heard somebody out here. Are you all right?"

"I can't sleep," she said.

"What's wrong?"

He stood in front of her, about a foot taller than she, gawky and goggle-eyed in his glasses; he'd always reminded her of a buzzard, but he had a heart of gold.

"I want to leave here," she said.

He paused for a few moments. "You can't be serious."

"I am very serious."

"What's wrong?"

She looked away from him. "I'm afraid."

He placed his hands on her shoulders and squeezed reassuringly. "That bombardment was hell today, and it scared me, too, but it sounded worse than it was, and it's over now anyway. We're safe here, and tomorrow you'll get some great pictures and I'll get a great story."

"It's not the bombardment," she said. "It's something else." She looked into his eyes. "I'm afraid something terrible is going to happen to me here, Leo."

"Do you mean you think you'll be killed?"

"No, worse than that, I'm afraid."

"What could be worse about being killed?"

"Being humiliated."

"By what?"

She leaned against him, and he wrapped her arms around her. She took a few moments to organize her thoughts.

"I don't know if I can explain it, and I don't know if you can understand," she said.

"Try."

"Well, I feel like I'm losing control of myself, as if I'm not myself anymore."

He laughed softly. "I've never known you to lose control of yourself in all the time I've known you. I think that bombardment shook you up a little too much today, but it's over

101

now. You've got to understand that it's over now, and you were never in any real danger."

"I told you, it wasn't the bombardment, Leo."

"Then what is it?"

"You promise you won't laugh?"

"I promise."

"And you must never never tell anybody."

"I promise that too. Tell me already, because the suspense is killing me."

She pushed away from him, fidgeted with her feet, and finally threw up her hands in exasperation. "It's that goddamned Butsko!"

"What'd he do this time?"

"He hasn't done anything." She drew back her foot and kicked a rock twenty feet. "Remember that you promised not to laugh."

"I remember my promise."

"Well . . . I . . . *shit!* I don't know how to say it, so I guess I'll just say it. I'm falling in love, or in lust, with the big, smelly son of a bitch!"

Leo's jaw dropped open and the features on his face went slack. "No!"

"Yes."

"But he's just a brute! You said so yourself!"

"That's what's so arousing about him—that's it!" She balled up her fists. "He *is* a brute. Cant you see it? He's a male *in extremis*, all power and energy and sexuality, and what is that if not a brute? For God's sake, Leo, he literally *reeks* masculinity. When I'm near him I feel faint. I'm afraid I'll just throw myself at his feet! But if he were just a brute, I think I could deal with him. I could dismiss him if he were a brute, do you know what I mean? But he's not stupid, and all the men here worship him. Even Craig Delane, who's even more of a snob than I am—and *that's* saying something—even he worships him. Butsko is a decent man, maybe a hero, underneath the scars and lumps all over him. This war has torn his body apart, and he probably doesn't even believe in it to the extent that many Americans do, but he fights anyway out of professionalism and a sense of honor. He's a man of honor, Leo. He could have taken advantage of me today—I would have been putty in his hands—but instead he saved my life

102

and let me be. That scares me. A man like that could own me. I'd be his slave. If I was ever alone with him, I think I'd lose my mind, and I can't afford that, Leo; I've got too much to lose; my career, my family, everything. That's why I want to get the hell out of here right now, tonight, and go to another part of this front. I know it sounds crazy, but that's how I feel." She looked up at him and held his skinny biceps. "Let's get out of here, Leo. Come with me. If I stay with this damned recon platoon, I think it'll be the end of me!"

He took her arms off his biceps and stared intently at her for a full thirty seconds while she examined his face, alarmed, because she'd never seen such intensity and concentration in Leo's face.

"This is not the Lydia Kent-Taylor I know," he said in a soft deep voice. "This is not the famous photographer who's been everywhere, photographed everything, and subordinated everything else to her career in journalism, a career that has made her famous, practically a household world. This is not the Lydia Kent-Taylor who's pulled strings and buttonholed generals for three months so she could go to the front—not the front behind the front where the other photographers and journalists hang around, but the real front, where the real GIs are doing the real fighting, to show America and the world for all time what this war is like in its fiercest, hottest place. The Lydia Kent-Taylor I know would be itching to start tomorrow. She'd be up cleaning her camera and polishing her lenses, writing down information, planning what kind of story she wanted to do. You're not the Lydia Kent-Taylor I know. You're a high school girl with a crush on the football coach, and I'm not going anywhere with you, because this is my big moment too. My ambitions are no less than those of Lydia Kent-Taylor. I want to write about this war in such a way that it'll be read not just by the folks on the home front but by historians and students who'll want to know what this war was like for centuries to come!"

She stood frozen for a few moments, thinking about what he said. Taking out a cigarette, she lit it with her Zippo, turned away, and paced back and forth. It was true, tomorrow would present a fabulous opportunity for her, an opportunity she'd been moving toward for a long time, and how could she throw it away?

"C'mon," Leo said gently. "Pull yourself together. If Butsko bothers you that much, don't ever let yourself be alone near him. I'll stick to you like glue if you want. You know that nothing will happen to you if I'm around."

She realized he was right. If she felt herself losing control, a few well-chosen words from Leo would snap her back to reality. She couldn't let her passion for Butsko, which seemed a little melodramatic and silly to her now, get in the way of her career. If she could become a war photographer, an enormously difficult career for a woman, she could handle Butsko, especially if Leo was with her to help out. The bombardment today must have unhinged her a little—that and lack of sleep.

"Thank you, Leo," she said. "I do think you've brought me back to my senses."

"It's been a hard day. I feel a little strange myself."

"Will you really stay with me all the time, as you said?"

"Sure. We're in this together, you know. This war is going to make us, and we've got to help each other, because when you get right down to it, we have only each other out here."

She lurched toward him and clasped him in her arms, resting her face on his flat, bony chest. "Oh, Leo, thank you so much!" she said.

A half hour later, alone in her tent, Lydia lay on her low canvas cot and smoked her last cigarette of the day. She still felt nervous and jumpy, but Leo had calmed her down a lot. She'd get through tomorrow somehow. She'd just concentrate on the images of war and not think about Butsko.

Although he scared her, she let herself think of him now, because she knew enough about psychology to understand that the harder she tried to push him out of her mind, the more energy he'd have in her unconscious mind, and that energy would mess her up. She recalled how he'd looked during the bombardment, husky and brave in his tattered uniform, scars all over his face and arms, an atmosphere of calm strength about him. "I'm probably going to fuck you," he'd said. God, what a discourteous way to talk to a woman; yet, when those words had struck her brain, she'd thought she'd jump out of her pants.

He was uncouth, there was no doubt about that. He was also arrogant, brutal, and utterly ruthless. If he had a kind side, she'd never seen it, although she could sense that it was there. At least she hoped he had some kindness in him. Without kindness he'd be terrifying.

All her life she'd wanted to fall in love with someone like Leo: a decent man who was courteous and intelligent, shared her interests, and treated her with respect. Unfortunately men like that didn't excite her. She could take them or leave them. But the big, burly, hairy-chested ones like Butsko, who were impolite, far beneath her intellectual level, and didn't understand her at all—they were the ones who excited her. Men like Leo had natures too similar to hers; there was no mystery to them. She could never go to bed with someone like Leo, whereas Butsko was provocative and different, like landing on another planet where everything was turned upside-down.

Lydia had very little sexual experience. A few clumsy young men when she was a student, a few men like Leo, and one rough, tough carpenter in an unfinished attic once—that was the extent of her love life. She'd never had a really good fuck in her life, and sometimes she thought she was frigid. Unsure of herself sexually, she couldn't cope with someone who affected her like Butsko.

Well, she thought, *in a few days I'll be gone from here, and this'll all be a memory. Besides, people really don't need sex as much as they think they do. It's all a big delusion.*

She tossed and turned for most of the night, trying to believe that.

TEN . . .

Lydia finally fell asleep but was awakened a few hours later by explosions in the distance and the roar of airplane engines overhead. She shook her head and looked at her watch: It was a quarter to five in the morning, just light enough to see the hands on her watch's dial.

Crawling toward the front of her tent, she pulled aside the flap and looked out. Directly in front of her, about thirty yards away, Lieutenant Breckenridge was talking with a few of his men, one of them Butsko. Vapor rose from the jungle floor as if small fires were burning, and in the dim light the soldiers with their rifles and helmets were phantasmagorical. *There's enough light there for a picture,* she thought, reaching for her camera bag. She pulled out her Leica and screwed in the ninety-millimeter F4 Elmar lens, because it would distort perspective and add to the eeriness of the scene. She raised the camera to her eye and turned the lens barrel until the lines converged and the soldiers came into focus.

"The artillery barrage will continue until we're approximately here," Lieutenant Breckenridge was saying, pointing to the map. "Then it'll stop and we'll charge the mission station. We'll have to get inside before they start shooting back."

Butsko frowned. "They'll rebound real fast. Those last few yards are gonna be awful hard. We'll be at point-blank range."

"That's why you'll have to run like hell. Tell the men that they've got to really move it out when the order comes down."

"Nobody can move faster than a bullet," Butsko said.

"There'll always be casualties," Lieutenant Breckenridge replied, looking at his watch. "Okay, go talk to the men. We should be moving out in about an hour."

The meeting broke up. Butsko turned and headed back to the First Squad. Lydia's tent passed into his line of vision. She was lying inside the tent with the flap open, pointing her camera at him. He felt like throwing her a French salute, because he enjoyed needling her, but decided against it. Colonel Stockton might see the picture and really get mad at him. Instead he held up his two fingers in the *V* for Victory sign and grinned at her long enough for a picture to be taken, then turned toward the First Squad and resumed his walk.

Lydia lowered her camera and retreated back into her tent, closing the flap behind her. The meeting was over and she had no more good picture possibilities, but Butsko's gesture disturbed her. Was his *V* for Victory an expression of his confidence about the outcome of the attack that morning, or was it a signal to her that he was going to do what he said: fuck her.

The mere thought of him doing that made her shiver. She couldn't let a man like that conquer her, but yet she knew she craved him. The collision of opposing thoughts in her mind made her feel a little light-headed, and she reached for her first cigarette of the day.

As long as Leo stays with me, I'll be all right, she thought.

Drugged and in pain, Frankie La Barbara opened his eyes and looked at the morning light glowing through the OD of the hospital tent. He could hear the bombardment in the distance and couldn't tell who was on the receiving end, the Japs or the GIs.

He thought of Butsko and Bannon and all the others out there in foxholes, probably having breakfast now—or trying to have breakfast. Frankie had been with them for over a year, and now he was with other men crowded into a hospital tent, far from the action. He felt a little homesick for the good old recon platoon.

Nurse Falvo entered the tent, followed by an orderly carrying a tray with pills, thermometers, hypodermic needles, and other medical paraphernalia.

"Hey, what's going on out there?" Frankie asked.

"There's a big attack this morning," Mary Falvo said. "Open your mouth."

Frankie opened his mouth and Nurse Falvo dropped in a thermometer, looking at her watch and holding his wrist.

The thermometer felt uncomfortable underneath his tongue, so he moved it to a better spot, but Mary Falvo noticed and pushed it back where it was.

"Leave it alone," she said. "And keep your mouth shut."

Frankie looked up at her long eyelashes and big brown eyes. She had a faint mustache and the suggestion of sideburns, and her features weren't particularly delicate, but she wasn't bad-looking otherwise. She had large, upstanding breasts, just the kind he'd like to rest his head upon.

Explosions rumbled in the distance, and Nurse Falvo pulled the thermometer out of his mouth, reading it.

"How am I?" he asked.

"You don't have a temperature," she said, moving on to the next man, whose legs had been blown off the day before and who hadn't come to consciousness yet. He'd also been wounded in his chest and stomach and didn't have long to live.

Frankie La Barbara listened to the peals of thunder in the distance. *Boy, I'm glad I don't have to go on this one,* he thought.

Colonel Stockton stood beside his desk and strapped on his Colt .45 service pistol. He pulled it out of its holster, checked the clip, and worked the bolt. The Colt .45 was accurate only at short range, but if you hit somebody with one of its fat bullets, you'd blow him apart.

He put on his helmet and positioned it low over his eyes. Grim-faced, intending to lead his regiment's attack personally, he walked to the tent flap and whacked it aside.

In the next tent section Lieutenant Harper, Major Cobb, Sergeant Major Ramsay, and Private Levinson were waiting for him.

"Let's go," he said.

They followed him outside. Private Nick Bombasino was

standing beside the jeep and snapped to attention. Colonel Stockton marched resolutely toward the jeep and Private Bombasino snapped to and saluted. Colonel Stockton returned the salute and climbed into the front passenger seat.

"To the front," Colonel Stockton said.

The Japanese soldier known as the Mosquito sat in a tunnel near the top of the fortress, his back pressed against a dirt wall, trying not to shiver or show fear as American bombs and artillery shells slammed into the ground and building just above him. The shelling had been going on for over an hour, and the Mosquito was apprehensive about the attack that he knew would come soon.

On both his sides and on the other side of the tunnel, other Japanese soldiers sat like he did, knees in the air and rifles pointed upward. Sergeant Suzuki had his eyes closed and was probably asleep. How could anyone sleep at a time like this? Yet, Sergeant Suzuki's rifle was straight up in the air. Even in sleep he was a soldier.

Footsteps could be heard approaching in the tunnel. Sergeant Suzuki leaped to his feet and shouted, *"Attention!"*

Captain Hisahiro came into view, followed by staff officers. He stopped in the midst of the men and posed, fingers resting on the handle of his samurai sword.

"Stand easy," he said.

The soldiers went slack. The Mosquito gazed with hatred at the face of Captain Hisahiro. *Officers like that get men like me killed,* he thought. *Officers like that have started this damned war.* He wanted to raise his rifle and shoot Captain Hisahiro but was too much of a trained infantry soldier to do that.

"The American attack will come soon," Captain Hisahiro said. "Be ready to fight. Your orders are to kill ten American soldiers each, and I expect you to do it. Aim straight and be thoughtful. Obey your officers and remember your training. Think of your ancestors in heaven who are watching you. Carry on."

Captain Hisahiro thrust out his left foot and continued his march throughout the labyrinth, issuing brief pep talks to his men. He'd positioned them all near the top of the fortress so that they could rush to the parapets as soon as the shelling stopped. He knew there would be several minutes during which

110

he could inflict heavy casualties on the Americans attacking over open ground, and he intended to make the best use of them.

The Mosquito turned toward the wall and bit his lower lip in an effort to hold back the tears. He wasn't a sentimental man, and he'd seldom cried in his adult life, but he knew that he probably wouldn't live to see another dawn.

The Twenty-third Regiment was lined up in foxholes at the edge of the jungle, ready to advance across the airstrip toward the mission fortress on Kokengolo Hill. In the distance planes dropped bombs on the fortress, and artillery shells hammered it constantly. All they could see was a huge cloud of smoke flashing yellow and orange as the bombs and shells detonated.

Longtree watched the cloud, trying to see what effect the bombardment was having, and Bannon sat in the foxhole, smoking a cigarette and staring into space. He felt certain that he'd be killed in the attack.

He knew that he and the others would soon be charging across open ground and that there would be a few minutes when the Japanese could rip them apart. Usually he was philosphical during times like this, but Frankie La Barbara wouldn't be with him today, and so he didn't feel very philosophical.

He'd seen many men die during the year he'd been in combat, and some of them had shrieked with pain for a long time before the medics reached them. The pain must have been excruciating for them to shriek so loudly, and some had been brave men—not crybabies. If such men could be reduced to tears and babbling, how would he hold up?

He'd seen other wounded men just go slack, their eyes glazing over, but still they were alive, with faint pulses. It must be terrible to feel your life dripping away through a stomach wound or a hole in your chest. How awful to lose control that way as Death dragged you off. The pain and horror must be almost beyond human endurance, and yet men went through it every day. Bannon wished he could be Frankie La Barbara, safe in a hospital far behind the lines. *Oh, God, I never should have joined the Army,* he thought. *I should've got on my horse and rode to Mexico and hid for the duration, maybe shacked up with one of those almond-eyed Mexican honeys*. He lit a fresh cigarette with the butt of his old one.

111

"You okay?" asked Longtree.

Bannon looked to the side and saw Longtree's concerned face. "I'm gonna die today," he replied in a disembodied voice that sounded strange to both of them.

"You really think that?" Longtree asked.

"I really think that."

Longtree was as superstitious as a human being could get, and he believed in premonitions, omens and portents. "Well," he said, "then all you can do is die like a warrior, fighting hard. I will fight beside you. It is a good day to die."

"What's so good about it?" Bannon snapped back.

Longtree looked up at the red ball rising in the cloudless sky. "At least it isn't raining."

"If you're dead, what does it matter whether or not it's raining? Who gives a fuck?"

"I suppose any day is a good day to die," Longtree admitted. "There is nothing we can do except die with honor, like true warriors."

"I shoulda never enlisted in this motherfucker," Bannon said weakly.

"It's a little too late for that," Longtree told him.

The jeep stopped among tall thick-trunked trees bedecked with huge leaves shaped like elephants' ears. Colonel Stockton swung his feet around and climbed out, glanced at the soldiers in foxholes nearby, then trudged through the jungle, heading for the open ground.

Private Bombasino stayed with the jeep, while Major Cobb, Lieutenant Harper, and Private Levinson, carrying the backpack radio, followed him. Men in the foxholes nearby looked at Colonel Stockton as he passed. They weren't surprised to see him, because often he chose to lead major attacks personally to show them all that he wouldn't ask them to do anything he wouldn't do himself.

Colonel Stockton passed through the jungle and walked into the open area. Ahead of him were the outer runways of the airstrip and in the distance the throbbing cloud that enveloped Kokengolo Hill. Enough wind was blowing to provide an occasional glimpse of the mission station, but then it would disappear in explosions again. Standing with one leg ramrod stiff and the other bent in front of him, Colonel Stockton raised his

112

binoculars to his eyes and studied the mission fortress.

He couldn't see much of strategic significance, but that wasn't why he was there. The main thing was to show himself to his men and give them confidence. It was possible that a stray chunk of shrapnel would tear a hole in him, but that was unlikely, and besides, the colonel had overcome most of the fear inside him long ago when he'd been a young lieutenant in the Second Division, under Major General Lejeune. Colonel Stockton was a professional soldier, and he'd realized then that a professional soldier had to overcome fear, and he'd done it through the exertion of his will. His father had been a general, and so had his grandfather. They had molded him to be the kind of man he was.

Major Cobb, Lieutenant Harper, and Private Levinson lagged behind him in the woods, because they didn't want to expose themselves. Colonel Stockton calmly swung his binoculars from side to side, then raised them and looked at planes streaking across the blue sky, shooting at each other, dropping bombs. It was hard to see which were friendly and which weren't. Lowering the binoculars, he studied the mission fortress again, and all the soldiers nearby gazed at him in awe, because none of them would stand out there if they didn't have to.

In the sky above Kokengolo Hill a Japanese fighter pilot in a Mitsubishi A6M Zero-sen happened to spot the lone figure down there at the edge of the jungle. Bullets whizzed all around the pilot and his Zero was full of holes. His engine sputtered and his communications system was knocked out.

It looked as if the Americans were about to attack from out of those woods down there, and he leaned his wheel to the side, banking in that direction. He couldn't notify his squadron leader of what he'd seen, and indeed doubted whether his squadron leader was still alive, because so many Zeros had been shot down already, but he would fly down himself and indicate what he saw.

His engines screamed as he rolled to the side, and then he dived down toward the figure standing in the open, positioning his thumb over the button that would fire his machine guns.

"Look out!" shouted Major Cobb.
"Get down!" yelled Lieutenant Harper.
Colonel Stockton looked up and saw the Zero swooping

113

toward him. Lightning spurted from its wings and he realized it was firing at him. He could turn and run away, but he couldn't let his men see him to that. Besides, it would be awfully difficult for a single plane to shoot a solitary man at the speed the plane was traveling.

He stood solidly where he was and aimed his binoculars at Kokengolo Hill, as the Zero dived toward him. At the edge of the jungle, antiaircraft batteries shot at the plane, but it was coming too fast to be a good, reliable target.

Colonel Stockton heard the plane's engines become louder, but he didn't react. His men stared at him in disbelief.

"Watch out!" screamed Major Cobb.

Antiaircraft shells burst all around the Zero, making it rock and roll as it continued its dive. The Japanese pilot hung on to his stick and pressed the button, bullets firing out of the machine guns in the wings. An American machine-gun bullet zipped through his cockpit, leaving holes on either side, but the Japanese pilot accelerated and kept his aim on the American soldier in front of him. Why didn't the fool run for cover?

Colonel Stockton heard the plane approaching and its machine guns rattling, but he was confident that the bullets would miss him. They stitched two lines toward him, and still he studied Kokengolo Hill through his binoculars, cool as a cucumber. The twin paths of bullets kicked up dirt toward him and shot past him on both sides, so close that some of the dirt spattered his leg. He flinched slightly when he felt it, and thought for a split second that he'd been hit, but he didn't look down; he just stood his ground as if nothing were happening. The Zero passed overhead and started to climb, but an antiaircraft gunner on the ground got lucky and blew off the Zero's left wing. The Zero bellied over and wobbled in the air. It skimmed the tops of the trees, lost altitude, and crashed into the jungle, sending a blossom of orange flame rising into the sky.

Lydia Kent-Taylor had captured Colonel Stockton's performance with her camera, and she was glad she hadn't run out of film in the middle of the action. She'd seen Colonel Stockton appear on the battlefield, moved closer to take a

114

picture, and had been in a good position behind him and to the left when the Zero opened fire.

She'd held him in her sights as the Zero fired at him and the bullets kicked up dirt. It had been a beautiful shot in the viewing lens, as good as anything Robert Capa or Edward Steichen ever did, and she hoped the picture would come out all right after it was developed.

She walked toward Colonel Stockton after the Zero had been shot down. Leo Stern was behind her, his notebook ready. She angled to the side and took a profile shot of Colonel Stockton as he peered ahead through his binoculars. *Colonel Stockton studies the field of battle before the attack.* He lowered his binoculars as she moved into his line of vision and took a frontal shot.

"I think you'd better take cover, Miss Kent-Taylor," he said.

Bombs were bursting on Kokengolo Hill in the distance, but she felt safe where she was, and besides, this was a fabulous sequence of pictures. *I'm going to make you famous,* she thought. *I'll bet we can sell these pictures to* Life.

Leo Stern approached Colonel Stockton, his notebook and pen ready. "That was some feat, Colonel."

Colonel Stockton scowled as he looked at Kokengolo Hill through his binoculars again. "I think you're too far forward. You'd better go back where it's safe."

"Why didn't you take cover when that Zero strafed you."

"I knew he couldn't hit me. I was a small target and he was coming too quickly to aim straight."

"But he came awfully close." Leo Stern looked at the marks the Japanese machine-gun bullets had made in the ground.

"Close doesn't mean anything. You've got to land on target if you want to shoot a man. Otherwise you've just wasted ammunition." He watched Leo Stern writing. "Is this on the record?"

"Everything you say to me is on the record, sir. How do you think the attack'll go this morning."

"We'll take Kokengolo Hill before sundown or my name isn't Bill Stockton."

"Why are you so far up front, sir? Isn't it an unnecessary risk?"

Colonel Stockton looked at him sternly, and Lydia snapped the picture. "I'm up front here because I'm leading the attack."

"You mean in person?"

"Yes."

"Why are you doing that?"

"It's my job."

"Other regimental commanders don't lead attacks in person."

"I guess some of them see their jobs a little differently from the way I see mine." Colonel Stockton glanced at his watch. "The barrage will be ending soon and I have things to do. I hope you'll excuse me."

"Of course," said Leo Stern.

His hands clasped behind him and his Colt .45 slapping his side, Colonel Stockton walked back to the jungle, where Major Cobb and the others were. "Direct all commanders to move their men up on the line!"

Lydia Kent-Taylor snapped the picture. *The colonel issues his final orders.*

American soldiers would attack Kokengolo Hill from three sides, and they all came out of their foxholes, moving into position at the edge of the woods. First they would be ordered to move out, to advance across the airstrip under the cover of the bombardment, drawing their noose around Kokengolo Hill. Then the bombardment would end and the attack would begin.

Lydia Kent-Taylor took photographs of the recon platoon lining up as Leo Stern approached her. "Listen," he said, "do you think you can take a picture of Butsko for me?"

"Why?"

"Because I'm building a story around him and I'd like some pictures."

Lydia was still thrilled by the great pictures she'd got of Colonel Stockton standing up to a Zero. "Sure," she said.

Leo Stern walked toward Butsko, who was shouting orders to the recon platoon and pointing to where he wanted the men to stand.

"Hello, Sergeant," Leo Stern said.

Butsko spun around and gazed at Stern malevolently.

"What are your thoughts before going into battle, Sergeant?"

"I don't have time to think. *Cameron, move your men twenty paces to your left!*"

"Yo!"

116

Leo Stern wrote on his pad. "Are you afraid?"

Butsko ignored him. *"Fix bayonets! Longtree, who told you to go over there! Get back where in the fuck you belong!"*

"How do you think the battle will turn out?"

"How should I know?"

Click!

Butsko turned and saw Lydia Kent-Taylor pointing her camera at him. He stared at it in disbelief. *Are these people crazy?* he wondered.

Click!

Butsko wanted to scream a horrible obscenity at her, because he thought she was a total idiot, but instead he unslung his M 1 and affixed his bayonet to the end.

She took his picture again. *The platoon sergeant adjusts his bayonet in the moments before the attack.* Then she lowered her camera and looked at him, her head angled to one side. He was all business and absolutely fierce, and she'd put him on film forever. He turned away from her, and she looked at his broad shoulders and big, meaty ass. She wondered what it would be like to grab a handful of it.

Leo Stern grabbed her epaulette and pulled her away. "C'mon," he said, "you've been around the great warrior long enough."

Colonel Stockton looked at his watch. It was nearly time to start moving forward. "All right," he said to Major Cobb, Lieutenant Harper, and the others, "you all know what you have to do. Good luck."

He turned and walked out of the jungle to the edge of the airstrip. Looking around, he saw soldiers standing to his left and right, holding their rifles and bayonets ready, waiting for the order to advance on Kokengolo Hill. Colonel Stockton looked at his watch. It was only a few minutes until six o'clock, when the attack would begin. He drew his Colt .45 from his holster, checked the bolt, ejected the clip, and rapped it back in. Behind him Major Cobb, Lieutenant Harper, and Private Levinson got ready.

Colonel Stockton raised the pistol high in the air, then waved it forward in the direction of Kokengolo Hill.

"Move it out!" he yelled.

He stepped out toward Kokengolo Hill, aiming his pistol at

it from the waist, and Lydia Kent-Taylor took the picture. *Colonel Stockton leads his regiment in the attack.* She looked from left to right, excited to be part of such a huge military effort, and here she was in the middle of it, right up front with the real soldiers.

The Japs in Kokengolo Hill hadn't fired a shot yet, because bombs and artillery shells rained down upon them and made it impossible to man the parapets. The Zeros had been either shot down or chased back to Rabaul. There was no enemy resistance yet.

Lydia wondered whether to stay with the colonel and perhaps take a picture if he was wounded. Robert Capa had taken a famous picture of a soldier getting shot in the Spanish Civil War, and if she could take a picture of Colonel Stockton stopping a bullet, it'd really be spectacular.

She realized it was unlikely that the colonel would get shot while the bombardment was going on, so she moved down the line to take pictures of the men. Her steel helmet on the back of her head, she dashed about lithely, taking pictures of the serious young soldiers walking along with their eyes focused on Kokengolo Hill.

The light was perfect and the long, curving skirmish line picturesque. She forgot who and where she was as she became lost in aiming, focusing, and clicking off the pictures. She screwed in the 135-millimeter lens so she could get some good head-and-shoulder shots. Focusing on Sam Longtree, she could see the concentration in his face as he narrowed his eyes and moved toward Kokengolo Hill. Gundy, the medic, had downcast eyes, and she thought he looked sad. She moved the camera to the right and flinched when Butsko filled the frame, his lips moving, talking to his men. She clicked off the picture and then looked at him, admiring his strong, decisive manner.

Lieutenant Breckenridge walked toward her. "Nice day to take pictures, huh?"

He sounded hostile, and she wasn't sure what he was getting at. "Yes, the light is very nice."

"You know what you are?" Lieutenant Breckenridge asked. "You're a war profiteer, just like the ones who own the factories that make the bombs."

"No I'm not," she replied. "I'm just trying to show the people at home what it's really like."

"Yeah, but do you *know* what it's really like?"

"The camera doesn't lie," she said.

"Bullshit."

He walked by her, heading toward Kokengolo Hill, and she looked at his back. She was surprised by the vehemence of his remarks, because he was only a young first lieutenant and she could get him into a lot of trouble.

But then she moved her head to the side and looked at Kokengolo Hill. The Japs weren't firing back yet, but when they did, the battlefield would become hazardous for young lieutenants. Facing that danger, how could he be worried about what a woman photographer might do to him?

Leo approached her. "We'd better lag back a little bit. The Japs will start firing soon."

"When they do, I'll get down," she said, "but first I want to get as many pictures as I can."

The American regiments advanced toward Kokengolo Hill. American airplanes dive-bombed the mission fortress, and artillery shells howled as they fell through the air toward it. The noise was painful to the GIs' ears, and the ground shook beneath their feet. Lydia Kent-Taylor dashed about, her helmet tipping from side to side on her head, snapping pictures, feeling the mounting excitement. Leo Stern was several yards behind the recon platoon line, scribbling in his notebook as he walked along, recording his impressions and feelings and trying to imagine what the GIs were thinking about.

Gradually the ring tightened around Kokengolo Hill. The huge pulsating cloud of smoke and flame drew closer. Colonel Stockton checked his watch and noted that the shelling would stop soon. His ears ached from the sound of the bombardment, and his mouth was dry with anticipation. It wouldn't be long now. The last act in the battle for New Georgia was about to begin.

ELEVEN . . .

In the hospital tent Frankie La Barbara lay on his cot and listened to the bombardment in the distance. He knew that the big attack was under way—he'd heard it on the grapevine—and he knew that the recon platoon was out there someplace: Butsko, Lieutenant Breckenridge, Bannon and all the rest, their bayonets fixed and their M 1s locked and loaded, waiting for the order to charge.

Frankie had been on many big attacks with the the recon platoon, and all the feelings came back, the fear and anxiety, the rage and determination to win and survive somehow against the odds and the possibility that a stray Jap bullet or chunk of shrapnel could end a GI's life.

His stomach ached, and never in his life had he experienced such a deep, horrible, never-ending pain. Whenever he moved, it hurt more, and he was afraid to cough, because he'd done that once and it had been nearly as painful as the initial wound.

He'd been in the hospital on New Caledonia with malaria once, but that hadn't been painful. This was much worse; he felt weak and helpless. He couldn't even get up to piss: He had to do it in a bottle. He'd watched while the nurse had changed his bandage the morning before, and the sight of the gash in his stomach, all stitched up, almost made him faint.

Suddenly in the distance the bombardment stopped. Frankie perked up his ears and his eyes darted around wildly. He knew that the attack was beginning just then. All his buddies were rushing forward toward the barrels of the Japanese guns, and it would be hell. Every GI would think he'd be cut down in a minute or two, and he'd be able to see other GIs getting shot. And somehow you just kept going, because there was nothing else to do. You had to charge and lay your head on the chopping block, because that's what everybody else was doing.

Frankie gripped the sides of his cot and stared at the top of the tent. He thought about his buddies in the recon platoon galloping toward Kokengolo Hill.

"On your feet!" shouted Sergeant Suzuki. *"Hurry!"*

In the dark, narrow corridor the Japanese jumped up and ran in two single files toward the incline that led to the top of the fortress. They held their rifles at port arms and their faces were grim, because they knew they were hugely outnumbered. The battle for which they were waiting had begun. Now it would be vicious and bloody until the bitter end.

The soldiers ran toward the uppermost section of the mission fortress. The Mosquito saw smoking rubble everywhere. Artillery soldiers hauled their cannons to the parapets, and machine-gun crews set up their weapons. The top of the fortress had been devastated, but the piles of debris would provide all the cover that the defenders needed.

The Mosquito choked on the smoke and strong odor of cordite. Visibility was poor, the sun making a gray haze in the smoke.

"Move quickly!" Sergeant Suzuki shouted. *"Open fire!"*

The Mosquito dropped down behind a pile of boulders that had once been a wall of the mission. He pulled his rifle butt to his shoulder and lined up the sights. The wind was blowing away the smoke, and he could see the long green line of American infantrymen running toward the base of Kokengolo Hill. A cannon fired nearby, and for a moment the Mosquito thought his head had collapsed from the shock waves. The shell exploded at the base of the hill, blowing GIs into the air. Rifle fire crackled around the Mosquito, and then another artillery shell was fired.

The Mosquito aimed at a GI, held his breath, and pulled the trigger of his bolt-action Arisaka rifle. Its butt kicked into his shoulder and the barrel rose several inches into the air. The Mosquito worked the bolt, ejecting the spent shell, and pushed a fresh one into the firing chamber while looking down at his target.

The GI had fallen and his comrades jumped over him or swarmed around him as they charged Kokengolo Hill. The Mosquito took aim at one of them and squeezed his trigger again. When the smoke cleared he saw that he'd shot that soldier too. It was hard to miss at that range.

The bullet hit Longtree in the center of his chest and he blacked out while still on the run. His legs lost coordination and he fell to the ground, rolling over and flattening out on his back.

"Medic!" shouted Bannon, who had been beside Longtree. *"Medic!"*

Bannon knelt beside Longtree and saw the big bloody chest wound. *Oh, my God, he's dead,* Bannon thought. Longtree's chest was covered with blood, and he lay so slack on the ground Bannon thought there couldn't possibly be any life in him.

"Medic!" he yelled again, looking around, but he couldn't see Gundy. *Maybe he's been shot too.*

Ka-pow—a Japanese artillery shell landed fifty yards away, shaking the ground and sending clods of earth flying through the air. Bannon wanted to feel Longtree's pulse, but there wasn't time. He had to get up there with his squad again. He turned to see where they were and found himself looking into the camera of Lydia Kent-Taylor.

Click!

She took the picture. *A GI weeps over his fallen buddy.* As she wound the film, Bannon jumped up and ran past her to join his squad. She looked around for another good shot; they were everywhere: She had to make up her mind which was best. Her thirty-five-millimeter wide-angle lens was screwed into the camera so she wouldn't have to worry about focusing, and the light was constant. All she had to do was wind, aim, and shoot.

She snapped the shutter, then sped forward to keep up with the main line of attack. Her fear of being shot or blown up

123

was overwhelmed by all the great pictures she saw. She shot one of Lieutenant Breckenridge running forward, holding his carbine in his right hand over his head, leading the recon platoon toward Kokengolo Hill. She filled the frame with a long rank of GIs running toward the hill, and just as her finger came down on the shutter button, one of them was stopped by a bullet.

Click!

She caught him as he was halfway down. *What a picture!* she thought, feverishly winding the knob. Getting to her feet, she ran toward the fallen GI and saw him squirming on the ground, his face wrenched with pain.

Click!

Gundy, the medic, dropped to his knees beside the fallen soldier, who was Pfc. Solomon Mayer from Atlanta, Georgia. Mayer had a bullet through his left shoulder, and Gundy cut away his shirt with his razor-sharp Ka-bar knife.

Click!

The GIs raced up the sides of Kokengolo Hill as the Japanese fired everything they had at them. GIs were raked with machine-gun and rifle fire and blown to bits by Japanese artillery. But still they attacked, their officers and noncoms urging them on.

"Move it out!" yelled Colonel Stockton.

He ran up the hill, holding his Colt .45 in his right hand, firing wildly at the mission station.

"Keep going!"

He saw soldiers falling all around him, and he expected to be shot at any moment, but he wasn't afraid. He wanted to get inside that fort, where the artillery would no longer be a problem and where the GIs would be able to kill Japs face-to-face.

"We're almost there! Charge!"

Bannon's heart chugged in his chest as he ran up the side of the hill. Private Bollings dropped to the ground beside him, a bullet in his head, but Bannon didn't stop to take a look at him. Close to the Japs now, he was a big target and didn't dare let himself become stationary. Nearby he heard the voices of Lieutenant Breckenridge and Sergeant Butsko shouting orders. He thought of Frankie La Barbara in the field hospital and Longtree lying motionless on the ground. Bannon pumped his legs and raced up the side of the hill. They had only about fifty yards to go and then they'd be inside the fortress.

Barrrooooommmmmm!

Bannon felt himself being lifted into the air, tumbling, spinning, twisting. He blacked out, saw flashes of light, came to, and went out again. A Japanese artillery shell had blown him twenty feet in the air, and he had landed on his left shoulder, rolling over and coming to a stop on his stomach.

He wasn't unconscious but he wasn't fully awake, either. His head ached fiercely, and he couldn't figure out what had happened. He was just a tiny glimmer of consciousness without any moorings, floating in a black sea.

"Holy shit!" said Butsko.

Bannon opened his eyes and saw Butsko's face spinning above him. Bannon was aware that his face was wet, and his vision was tinged with red.

"You okay?" Butsko asked above the din of battle.

Bannon opened his mouth to speak, but no words came out. He was dizzy and felt weird. His head felt as if somebody had buried the head of an ax in it. "Ooooohhhh," he said.

"Medic!" screamed Butsko.

Lydia Kent-Taylor heard Butsko's voice and turned toward it, thinking he'd been hit. She saw him on his knees beside a soldier with a terrible head wound. She raised her camera and pressed the button.

Click!

The composition and lighting were perfect. The wounded soldier's blood soaked into the ground, and Butsko's face was contorted with concern.

"Medic!"

Lydia moved closer for a tighter shot and then recognized the man on the ground, Corporal Charles Bannon from somewhere in Texas. Lydia recalled speaking with Bannon once, and he'd made a nice impression on her.

Then she realized that this wasn't just another picture for a magazine back home: It was a man with a bleeding head wound, and Butsko leaned over him, worry on his face. Butsko pulled out Bannon's first-aid pack, ripped off the wrapping, and applied it to the wound on Bannon's head. The gauze quickly became soaked with blood.

"Medic!"

Lydia moved her camera to the side and dropped down

125

beside Bannon, whose eyes were wide open and staring.

"You'll be okay, kid," Butsko said. "Just take it easy."

"I can't see anything, Sarge," Bannon said through quivering lips. "I'm scared."

"Medic!"

"Am I gonna die, Sarge?"

"They say if a head wound doesn't kill you right away, it's probably not too bad."

"Butsko, where are you!" shouted Lieutenant Breckenridge.

"Over here!"

"Get the fuck up here!"

Butsko looked at Lydia. "Can you stay with him till the medic gets here?"

"All right."

Butsko took one last look at Bannon, then turned around and jumped to his feet, running up the hill. Lydia looked down at Bannon, who was moaning softly, his eyes closed. She felt his pulse. It was beating, but she didn't know whether it was strong or weak; she was no nurse.

"Just take it easy, soldier," she said. "You'll be all right."

Bannon shuddered and Lydia thought he was going to die. She gazed at his face and saw the pain and confusion. A tear rolled out the corner of his eye.

"I'm gonna die," he whispered.

"You're not going to die."

She felt weird saying that, because she didn't know for sure that he wouldn't die. Gazing at his face, the reality of war came through to her. She'd seen Bannon roaming around the bivouac for two days, full of life, strong and healthy, and now he was dying on the ground. Bullets whizzed over her head and one kicked up dirt nearby. She was no longer a photographer snapping shots of the war: She was in it and a bullet could hit her too.

She dropped lower, looking up the hill. The GIs were close to the fortress, too close for the Japanese artillery to fire. They were just about ready to go inside.

"I can't see," Bannon muttered, as if in a dream.

She held his limp hand and squeezed it. *He's so young and he's probably going to die,* she thought. She felt sick inside, because she didn't want to watch him die. She didn't think she could handle it, but she couldn't leave him alone, either.

126

"Hold on," she said. "You're not hurt that badly."

Private Gundy dropped down beside her and grabbed Bannon's wrist, looking at his watch. Then he let go of Bannon's wrist and took away the bandage Butsko had put on. Blood welled up from a hole the size of a half-dollar. He sprinkled on the coagulant powder to stop the bleeding, then reached into his haversack for an ampule of morphine.

Lydia realized she could leave then. No more shells were falling, and few bullets were being fired over her head. The battle was somewhere else; the GIs were ready to storm the fortress.

She stepped back and looked on as Gundy jabbed the ampule into Bannon's ass. It was a great picture, but she didn't feel like lifting her camera. Looking around, she saw the side of the hill littered with bodies of American soldiers and pockmarked with shell craters. Blood was everywhere, and her eyes fell on a leg severed from a body.

"My God," she thought, feeling nauseous, and dropped onto her ass. She felt vertiginous and weak. *So many men have been killed and wounded—for what? A hill on an island nobody has ever heard of? What the hell's going on up here?*

Leo Stern appeared next to her, his face smudged with dirt. "You okay?" he asked.

"I feel sick."

"My God, what a battle! Why aren't you taking any pictures?"

"I don't feel so good, Leo," she said, covering her face with her hands.

"C'mon, don't be such a woman. Let's show the folks at home what it's like out here."

"You go on without me. I'll catch up."

Leo gripped his pen and pad and ran up the hill. Lydia, still shaky, took out a cigarette and lit it, trying to put her thoughts in order. She recalled what Lieutenant Breckenridge had said about whether she could show the war as it really was.

All her pictures made the war appear interesting. The attack on Kokengolo Hill had looked through the lens of her camera like a wild, thrilling charge, and indeed it actually had seemed that way to her while the attack was going on. The GIs who'd been shot had appeared heroic as they dropped to the ground, like brave warriors on their way to Valhalla, but now, sur-

127

rounded by blood and gore, she saw the war in a new way. It may have been thrilling and heroic for a while, but now it was all horror and misery.

The folks back home should see this part too, she thought, raising her camera to her eyes. Looking through the viewfinder, she saw the American bodies lying on the side of the hill, some doubled up in pain, others motionless forever.

Click!

She moved closer to one soldier, whose eyes were shut, his mouth trickling blood and his rib cage blown apart. The peaceful expression on his face somehow didn't fit with his bones glistening in the sun. Lydia's teeth were on edge as she carefully composed the picture.

Click!

She heard running footsteps and turned around. Two medics were carrying Bannon away on a stretcher, and his lifeless hand hung over the side, bouncing up and down.

Click!

She lowered the camera. "Is he going to be all right?" she called out after the medics.

They paid no attention to her as they ran with Bannon toward the surgical tents set up in the jungle. The sun rose in the morning sky behind them, silhouetting them against the blue sky, while dead soldiers lay everywhere amid shell craters and pieces of equipment that had been thrown away.

Click!

Troops from the Thirty-eighth US Regiment breached the northeast wall of the fortress, hollering and screaming, bayoneting Japanese soldiers.

"Hold fast!" shouted Sergeant Suzuki.

The Mosquito turned to see hand-to-hand fighting at the other end of the fortress. He couldn't see how it was going, but he was scared to death. From all sides, Americans were converging on the shattered walls, and he knew he'd be fighting hand-to-hand with one of them soon if he didn't do something first.

Sergeant Suzuki spotted him. *"Turn around and fight!"* he screamed.

The Mosquito hated Sergeant Suzuki. He wanted to raise his rifle and shoot him down, but he didn't have the guts.

Facing straight ahead again, he saw American soldiers only a few yards away!

"*Over the top!*" yelled Lieutenant Breckenridge, leaping into the air.

He sailed over the Mosquito, who became so frightened that he fainted dead away. He collapsed on the ground and Lieutenant Breckenridge landed behind him, followed by Butsko and the rest of the recon platoon.

Lieutenant Breckenridge found himself a few paces in front of Sergeant Suzuki, who aimed his pistol at him.

Blam!

The pistol fired, and Lieutenant Breckenridge heard the bullet whistle past his ear. He leveled his carbine and fired a shot from the waist, but Sergeant Suzuki didn't fall down. Sergeant Suzuki steadied himself and took aim at Lieutenant Breckenridge, pulling the trigger, but before his Nambu pistol fired, a group of GIs got in the way.

Blam!

One of them dropped to the ground, and the rest turned toward Sergeant Suzuki, opening fire. Two of them missed but three didn't, and their bullets lifted Sergeant Suzuki into the air. His pistol dropped from his hand and he fell onto his back, where he lay still, never to issue a command again.

Lieutenant Breckenridge saw the Japanese soldiers retreating toward the doors and passageways that led to the bowels of the fortress. American soldiers pursued them, shooting them in their backs, while other Japanese soldiers couldn't run away because they were engaged in hand-to-hand fighting with American soldiers.

Butsko faced one of them, a steely-eyed Japanese corporal with a Fu Manchu mustache. The Japanese soldier bent his knees and lunged at Butsko, thrusting his rifle and bayonet forward, and Butsko parried it easily, slamming the Jap in the mouth with his rifle butt, kicking him in the balls, and bashing him again with his rifle butt. The Japanese soldier fell to the ground and Butsko rammed his bayonet through his heart, the blood gushing out red and shiny in the light of the morning sun.

"*Stay after them!*" shouted Lieutenant Breckenridge. "*Follow me!*"

He headed toward one of the passageways, which was pitch-black inside. He couldn't see anything, so he fired a few rounds from the waist as he ran forward, to make sure no Japs were standing there.

Suddenly a Japanese hand grenade came flying out of the black hole and landed at Lieutenant Breckenridge's feet. He bent down, picked it up, bobbled it, got a grip on it, and threw it toward the passageway. The grenade flew about ten yards and exploded in the air, driving chunks of shrapnel into Lieutenant Breckenridge's chest, stomach, and pelvis. He felt as if his body were being torn apart, and he bellowed in pain as he staggered from side to side, dropping his rifle, pressing his hands against the bleeding holes.

I'm hit! he thought. He didn't know what to do. A terrible chaos came over his mind, and he felt his legs give out underneath him. He tried to catch his footing but didn't have the strength, and he fell onto his face.

He wanted to get away. Pulling together all his energy, he pressed his hands against the ground and tried to raise himself. He managed to push himself up a few inches, then everything went black and he fell onto his face again.

Butsko ran toward him. *"Medic!"*

"Yo!" replied Private Gundy, working on a wounded soldier from another outfit.

"Lieutenant Breckenridge is hit!"

"Be right there!"

Butsko looked down at Lieutenant Breckenridge and saw all the holes. *He's a goner,* Butsko thought. But Lieutenant Breckenridge's chest rose and fell with his breathing. He was a big strong man and he was still alive. Butsko thought about Bannon, Frankie La Barbara, Gomez, Shaw, and all the others who'd been wounded. *There ain't gonna be no recon platoon left after today.*

Colonel Stockton appeared in that section of the fortress, followed by Major Cobb, Lieutenant Harper, and Private Levinson, who carried a backpack radio. The fighting on the top of the fortress was over, and bodies of soldiers, most of them Japanese, were everywhere. The sounds of shouting and shooting could be heard from the passageways and trapdoors, because the fighting now had moved to the labyrinth below.

Colonel Stockton's eyes fell on Butsko. *"What the hell are you doing, Sergeant?"*

Butsko looked up, a dazed expression on his face. *"It's Lieutenant Breckenridge, sir!"*

"You're not a medic! Get back to your damned platoon!"

"Yes, sir!"

Butsko jumped up, adjusted his helmet on his head, took one last look at Lieutenant Breckenridge, and turned away, running toward the passageway from which the grenade had been thrown. Colonel Stockton looked at Lieutenant Breckenridge and thought he must be dead. He moved to find out if that was so, when Private Levinson called out to him.

"Major Berman wants you, sir!"

Colonel Stockton reached for the headset and pressed it against his face. "Colonel Stockton here!"

"This is Major Berman, sir. Colonel Hunt has been killed in action, and I'm taking command of the Third Battalion, with your permission, sir!"

"Continue your attack!" Colonel Stockton replied.

Private Gundy ran toward Lieutenant Breckenridge and knelt beside him, dropping his haversack onto the ground. He unbuttoned Lieutenant Breckenridge's shirt and looked at the holes. None of them bubbled, which meant neither lung had been punctured. He could see that Lieutenant Breckenridge still was breathing, so he took out the blood coagulant powder and sprinkled it over the wounds.

Colonel Stockton and his entourage walked away, leaving Private Gundy alone with Lieutenant Breckenridge and a carpet of motionless American and Japanese soldiers. Gundy unwrapped bandages and taped them to Lieutenant Breckenridge's chest and stomach. Then he bent over and pressed his ear against Lieutenant Breckenridge's heart.

It beat strongly and steadily. *This guy's as strong as a horse,* Gundy thought, becoming erect again. Something moved in his line of vision and he turned to it. His eyes bulged as he saw a Japanese soldier raising his head and shoulders from the ground, aiming a Nambu pistol directly at him!

Gundy couldn't believe his eyes. The Jap's arm shook as he tried to aim, and Gundy could see him gritting his teeth. He was lying in a pool of blood.

Blam!

The bullet whizzed past Gundy and brought him back to the real world. He knew he had to do something, and he had no desire to become a casualty. He picked up Lieutenant Breck-enridge's carbine.

Blam!

The Japanese soldier fired and missed again. Coughing blood, he drew a bead on Gundy, who lined up the sights of the carbine on the Jap's face, holding steady and pulling the trigger.

Blam!

His aim was off; the bullet hit the ground in front of the Jap and ricocheted upward, hitting the Jap on the throat, sev-ering his windpipe. Blood spurted out of the Jap's mouth and his head dropped down to the ground.

Gundy stared at him, his jaw hanging open. *I've killed a man!* He blinked his eyes, wishing that the dead Jap and the whole battlefield would go away and that he was back at Saint Joseph's Abbey in Massachusetts, safe with all the other Trapp-ist monks. But when he opened his eyes the dead Jap still was there, lying in an ever-widening pool of blood. *I've killed him!*

Gundy closed his eyes and all his strength drained away. He toppled to the side and fell onto the ground, where he lay still beside Lieutenant Breckenridge, trying to think.

He'd left the abbey because he felt he had to help stop the evil being spread through the world by the Nazis and the Japs. He'd become a medic because he didn't want to kill anybody, but now he'd killed somebody just to save his own skin.

I should have let him kill me, Gundy thought. *I should have turned the other cheek as Christ said I should. Then I would've been killed, but I would've had eternal life with Christ. Now I don't know what will happen to me.*

He recalled that he hadn't hesitated a moment before shoot-ing the Jap. He'd had no tug of conscience, no second thoughts. He'd just killed the poor son of a gun. His prayer life, his three years at the abbey—nothing had mattered when he'd seen the Jap. He was just like everybody else: trying to save his skin instead of trying to save his soul. *I'm a fraud,* he thought. *I don't really believe what I say I believe. Oh, God, I'm sorry.*

"Hey, looks like they got one of our medics."

Gundy opened his eyes and saw legs and feet nearby. He pushed himself upright, and a medic he'd never seen before ran toward him.

"Hey, you all right, buddy?"

Gundy nodded. "Yes, I'm all right."

The medic cocked his head to the side as he examined Gundy's face. "What happened to you?

"I must've passed out." Gundy pointed at Lieutenant Breckenridge. "He needs to be evacuated right away."

The medic turned and cupped his hands around his mouth. "Stretcher-bearers!"

Two medics with a stretcher ran toward them and lay their poles on the ground, moving the canvas under Lieutenant Breckenridge and lifting him.

"Gee, he's heavy," one of them said as they carried him away.

Gundy picked up his haversack and adjusted it on his shoulder. He walked toward the dead Jap and gazed down at him. *God forgive me,* he thought.

Nearby, a wounded GI moaned. Gundy turned toward him and put one foot in front of the other, moving jerkily, like a robot. *I've got to keep going,* Gundy told himself. *Later, when things settle down, I'll think about all this.*

TWELVE . . .

Butsko ran through the dark tunnel and caught up with the remnants of the recon platoon. They pressed their backs to a wall of the tunnel, and Private Morehouse tried to peer around the corner to see if any Japs were there.

Beeooowwwwww went a Japanese bullet, ricocheting past his nose.

"We got a flamethrower here?" Butsko asked.

"Nope," replied Sergeant Cameron, his face streaked with sweat and filth.

"Morehouse, get outta the way."

Morehouse moved away from the wall and Butsko took his place. Butsko tore a hand grenade from his lapel, yanked the pin, and held the lever down.

"When this grenade blows, follow me," he said.

The men poised themselves. Butsko bent his knees and chucked the grenade around the corner as hard as he could. Three Japanese bullets whizzed past in the moments his hand was out. He heard the iron grenade fall with a thud on the dirt floor of the tunnel, and the Japs jabbered frantically. Butsko held his M 1 rifle up like a baseball bat, because he knew what would happen next.

Sure enough, the grenade came flying back, having been thrown by one of the Japs. Butsko swung his rifle as if he were Joe DiMaggio trying to hit the center field bleachers at Yankee Stadium. His rifle butt connected with the grenade and batted it back.

The grenade exploded with a deafening roar that echoed around and through the tunnel system. Clods of earth fell from the walls and ceiling, and Butsko jumped around the corner, aiming his M 1 from the waist.

"Follow me!"

He saw Japanese soldiers everywhere in the dimness. Some lay on the floor, some were huddled on their knees, and others ran away. He shot into the Japs crouching before him, and then came a fusillade of fire from the recon platoon. The bullets cut up the Japs still alive in that section of the tunnel system, and Butsko waded through them, kicking and kneeing, stabbing with his bayonet. In the distance he could hear the footsteps of the Japs running away.

Butsko advanced cautiously, and the light became dimmer as he moved into the tunnel system. He noticed a torch standing in a holder mounted on the wall of the tunnel. Taking down the torch, he flicked the wheel of his Zippo and set it afire. The tunnel glowed and trembled in the light of the torch.

"Delane?" Butsko said.

"Hup, Sarge."

"Hold this."

Butsko passed the torch to Delane, then motioned with his hand. He moved deeper into the tunnel system, and Delane walked beside him, holding up the torch to light the way.

The tunnel slanted downward, and the air became cool and damp. Sections of the tunnel were shored up by log posts and beams. Butsko heard muffled explosions and gunshots coming from other sections of the tunnel system. He knew that only a small percentage of the Japs had been killed in the initial assault on the fortress, and most of them had retreated into the tunnel system, where they were now fighting GIs in a last ditch hara-kiri defense. Butsko wished he had a flamethrower, but he had to get along as best he could with what he had. The battle for New Georgia was almost over and he was hoping for a nice long rest before the next campaign. That kept him anxious to kill all the Japs and get the battle over with.

They came to another curve in the tunnel. Butsko motioned with his hand, indicating that they should get close to the wall. "Gimme the torch," he whispered to Delane.

Delane handed it over, and Butsko held it in his big fist. He drew back his arm and threw the torch around the corner, hearing it land on the floor of the tunnel. A split second later the tunnel filled with the sound of rifle shots as Japanese soldiers opened fire. It sounded as if at least ten of them were ahead.

Butsko gritted his teeth in frustration, because this kind of fighting was worse than anything that happened aboveground. It was difficult to see, and all the Japs had to do was wait for them to move out into the open.

Butsko peeked around the corner to see where the Japs were, and a Japanese bullet hit a rock a few inches from his nose, sending flakes of the rock into Butsko's face. He pulled back quickly, and little dots of blood appeared where the bits of rock had embedded themselves.

"See anything?" asked Sergeant Cameron.

"Not a goddamned thing." Butsko wiped the blood away with the back of his hand. "We're not gonna make much headway here without a flamethrower." He looked at Craig Delane. "Go topside and get us a flamethrower."

"From whom?"

"That's up to you to figure out. Get your ass in gear."

"Hup, Sarge."

Delane handed the walkie-talkie to Butsko, turned, and walked up the incline toward the opening to the outside. Butsko looked around and gave the walkie-talkie to Private Briscoe.

"Hang on to this."

Briscoe nodded. Butsko took out his pack of Camels.

"Smoke break," he said, dropping down to a sitting position at the bottom of the cave. "Have your weapons ready in case the Japs counterattack."

Topside, in the rubble of the former mission station, the Mosquito lay amid dead Japanese and American soldiers, breathing as shallowly as he could so that he wouldn't show any movement. Blood from the others had flowed over him, making it appear that he'd been shot, too, and the hot sun baked his back. Swarms of flies buzzed around him, landing on his face and eyelids, tickling him and driving him nuts, but he stayed still and tried not to be too aware of the physical sensations.

He heard American soldiers walking back and forth all around him. Sometimes he opened his eyelids a tiny bit and saw the Americans soldiers carrying away their wounded or bringing supplies into the passageways that led below. He also saw American officers and their staffs looking at maps and issuing orders. Soldiers with radios spoke earnestly into their mouthpieces.

The Mosquito thought that if he was a good loyal Japanese soldier he'd jump up and kill one of those high-ranking American officers. It would be suicidal, but Japanese soldiers weren't supposed to worry about death, and indeed had been taught to look forward to it.

The Mosquito didn't look forward to dying, and he didn't want to do anything that might get himself killed. He was even afraid to get up and surrender to the Americans because they might shoot him on the spot. He'd heard rumors that sometimes Americans shot their prisoners, just as the Japanese sometimes shot theirs, and he didn't want to take any chances. He'd surrender if he had to, but if he didn't, he'd wait until nightfall and try to sneak away, hiding in the jungle and living on coconuts until the war was over and it was safe to come out.

Flies buzzed around his eyelids as he opened them to slits and saw a young American soldier emerge from the entrance to a tunnel, puffing a cigarette. He took off his helmet, wiped the perspiration off his brow with the back of his arm, and walked away.

The Mosquito closed his eyes and wondered how many hours it would be until night. He guessed it wasn't even noon yet, so he had a long way to go. Somehow he had to make it, so that one day he could return to his whores in the Shimbashi district of Tokyo, and he could be a pimp again, rolling in money, wearing the finest suits and eating the best food.

I'll do it, the Mosquito thought. *Somehow I'll survive even this.*

The soldier who'd emerged from the tunnel was Craig Delane, and he'd spotted Colonel Stockton and his staff not far away. Lieutenant Harper was there, and Delane was fairly friendly with him, although Harper was an officer and Delane an enlisted man. Both had graduated from prestigious colleges and had a certain commonality.

Delane saluted Lieutenant Harper as he approached. "Sir," he said, "do you know where I can get a flamethrower?"

Colonel Stockton heard the question and turned toward the voice. He recognized Craig Delane as a member of the recon platoon. "What happened to your platoon's flamethrower, soldier?"

"Private Hansen was carrying it, sir, and somehow we lost him. We think he was killed or wounded during the attack."

"Well, maybe you'd better go look for him if you want a flamethrower. I'd say that would be your best bet."

"Yes, sir."

Delane turned and walked away, looking for the route the recon platoon had taken when it stormed the outer defenses of the mission. He saw soldiers from both armies lying on the ground everywhere, grim testimony of the fierce hand-to-hand struggle. Medics had taken away most of the American wounded, and now the graves registration squads were moving through the area, removing dog tags from the dead and preparing the bodies for burial.

Delane's roving eyes fell on a slim figure with a camera and short light-brown hair: Lydia Kent-Taylor photographing a dead American whose face was covered with blood. She'd lost her helmet and looked unusually pale. Walking toward her, he saw that her uniform was torn and filthy, just like a GI's. He wondered why she was photographing such a grisly corpse.

"Hi," said Craig. "How's it going?"

She lowered her camera and looked at him as though she didn't recognize him. Then she smiled faintly. "Hello, Craig—so you made it."

"So far." He noticed that she looked different, as if the wind had been knocked out of her. "Are you okay?"

"I'm fine."

"Why are you taking a picture of a dead soldier? No paper or magazine back home would print a picture like that."

"I want to show what this damn war is really like," she said, moving toward the next American soldier.

Craig snorted. "The people back home don't care what this war really looks like."

139

"I don't care what they think. I just care about what I think."
She saw a graves registration soldier pulling off the dog tags
of a dead corporal. Raising her camera, she snapped the picture
of the soldier jamming one of the dog tags into the corporal's
mouth, so it wouldn't get lost while he was being transported
to his grave.

Craig thought she looked a little weird. "You sure you're
all right, Lydia?"

"I'm fine."

"I've got to do something for Sergeant Butsko. I'll see you
later."

"He still alive?"

"Yes."

Delane walked away, and Lydia aimed her camera down at
an American soldier who'd been bayoneted through the heart.
Blood was caked on his shirt, and his eyes were wide open
and staring. His lips were drawn back in a snarl, frozen there
forever, and a fly walked across his teeth. Lydia aimed her
camera, pressed the button, and took the picture. Then she
turned the knob, but it stopped halfway. She'd come to the end
of the roll.

Sitting on the ground next to the dead soldier, she rewound
the film and took it out of the camera. The air smelled sweet
with the odor of dead bodies in their first stage of decompo-
sition; soon they'd stink terribly, but that wouldn't be for a
few hours. She put the used roll into her camera bag and took
a fresh roll.

Leo Stern knelt next to her. "Are you all right, Lydia?"

"I'm fine."

"You look distraught."

"I told you, I'm fine."

"Are you still taking pictures of dead soldiers?"

"Yes."

"I think you'd better start taking pictures of live ones—of
the victors."

"What victors?" She sniffed disdainfully. "There are no
victors."

Leo looked at her more closely. "Listen to me, Lydia. You've
got to get hold of yourself. This was a battle that American
soldiers won and Japanese soldiers lost. That means the American soldiers are the victors. The American people have a right

140

to see their soldiers as victors. Show them ordinary GIs as victors. The home front can use some morale-boosting."

"I don't know Leo," she said, shaking her head, "I just don't know anymore."

He wrapped his fingers around her slim female biceps and squeezed. "We've got to be journalists. We've got to give the American people the real story."

"But what the hell's the real story?" she yelled.

Her vehemence startled him and he let her go, moving back a few inches, furrowing his brow. "The real story is that the US Army has won the battle for New Georgia and now is engaged in mopping-up operations. Now, take your camera out and show that."

She indicated with a wave of her arm the heaps of dead soldiers all around her. "What about them?"

"They're dead. They died bravely, for their country."

"Did they really?"

"Lydia, you know they did. The Japs bombed Pearl Harbor, remember? They'd bomb San Francisco, too, if they could get close enough."

She nodded slowly. "That's true."

Leo stood and held out his hand. "Then get to your feet and go to work. We have to do our part to help win this war too."

Lydia reached out and let Leo pull her up. He patted her shoulder and smiled. "I'm going to interview Colonel Stockton. You might want to take some photographs of him and his staff, now that the big battle is over."

"Lead the way."

Leo took his notepad and pencil from his shirt pocket as he walked toward Colonel Stockton and his staff. Lydia followed a few steps behind him, trying to pull herself together, trying to convince herself that there was more to the war than the dead American soldiers lying all around her.

Craig Delane found Private Hansen lying dead on the side of Kokengolo Hill, a dog tag jammed between his teeth. The flamethrower was on his back, the tube and nozzle stretched on the ground like a dead snake. Delane rolled Hansen over onto his stomach. Hansen was stiffening from the initial stages of rigor mortis. Hansen, a big Swede from South Dakota who went beserk whenever he got drunk but was docile the rest of the time, had been fairly new to the recon platoon. *He'll never drink again,* Delane thought as he unstrapped the flamethrower. It weighed over seventy pounds, and he lifted it up with some difficulty, pushing his arms through the straps. He pulled the nozzle to him and twisted the knob, and a jet of flaming jellied gasoline shot out. It was still in good working condition.

He trudged up the hill toward the mission, recalling how he'd gone that way not much more than an hour before and how scared he'd been with all the bullets flying past and the artillery shells exploding everywhere. He'd just stayed close to Butsko and kept working his legs. The only thing he could do was keep moving, and somehow he'd stayed alive.

He passed through an opening in the wall and entered the top of the fortress again, thinking that the battle wasn't over for him and that there'd be a lot of dirty work below; killing fanatical Japs making their last stand in the dark tunnels. *I might wind up like Hansen,* he thought.

Craig Delane made himself numb whenever he got scared. He stopped thinking about whatever was scaring him and focused on narrow immediate concerns, such as carrying the flamethrower to Butsko. More officers were on top of the mission station now, and trucks dragged artillery pieces into position in case the Japs staged a major bombing run from the air. He entered the dark tunnel where Butsko was and made his way through the dark shadows.

"It took you long enough," Butsko said, getting to his feet, his second cigarette dangling from the corner of his mouth.

"I had to look for Hansen. He's dead."

"You think you can handle that flamethrower?"

"It's awfully heavy."

Butsko looked him up and down and figured that Delane wasn't very sturdy or aggressive. He always did only what he had to do, and Butsko needed somebody better than that now.

He looked around and saw that most of his best men weren't with him anymore. Ten men were left out of the original forty, and the best of those, except for himself, was Sergeant Cameron.

"Put on the flamethrower, would you, Larry?"

Sergeant Cameron nodded, pulled the apparatus off Craig Delane's back, and put it on his own. "You check this out before you brung it here?" he asked Delane.

"Yes."

Sergeant Cameron tightened the straps and held the nozzle in his right hand. "I'm ready."

"Spray some around the corner, and when you turn it off, the rest of us'll charge out there and take whatever cover we can."

"Now?" asked Cameron.

"Now," replied Butsko.

Sergeant Cameron pressed his back against the dirt wall and eased toward the bend in the tunnel. He poked the nozzle around the corner and turned the knob. Gelatinous flame leapt out of the nozzle and crackled as it flew through the air. The cave lit up and shadows shook erratically.

Butsko pulled his next to last hand grenade from a lapel. *"That's enough!"* he shouted. *"Let's go!"*

He charged around the corner, saw flaming jelly on the floor and walls of the tunnel, and leaped past, heading down a length of straight tunnel twenty yards long.

Beeaannnggggg—a bullet ricocheted near him and another zipped over his head. He ran three more steps and dived toward the ground, rolling to the side and pulling the pin on the hand grenade. Muzzle blasts of Japanese rifles flashed ahead of him, and he let go of the lever; it popped into the air, arming the hand grenade. Butsko counted to three and hurled the grenade with all his strength. It sailed down the tunnel and hit the wall where the tunnel veered to the right, landing on the ground. A Jap dashed into the open to pick it up and throw it back, but Pfc. Fischer, a survivor of the Third Squad, shot him in the kidney, and the Jap screamed as he went flying toward the same wall that the grenade had hit.

Butsko heard a garbled hysterical Japanese conversation and then the hand grenade blew, rocking the tunnel and filling it with billows of smoke.

"Follow me!" yelled Butsko, jumping to his feet.

He ran toward the bend in the tunnel, pulling the last hand grenade from his shirt. He pulled the pin, released the lever, counted, and dropped to his stomach.

"Hit it!"

His men flopped onto the ground behind him, and Butsko hurled the hand grenade at an angle, so it'd bounce off the far wall and land around the bend. The Japanese conversation

143

became even more hysterical, and one of the Japanese soldiers screamed in horror.

The grenade thundered and roared, and Butsko was on his feet again, charging after the hand grenade.

"Follow me!"

He rounded the bend, held his M 1 steady at his waist, and fired at the figures in the smoke. Visibility was poor, and he didn't know whether he'd hit any or not, but then he tripped over a dead Jap on the floor and fell on his hands and knees while the others from the recon platoon shot the fleeing Japanese soldiers.

Butsko got to his feet. The smoke was lifting and he saw dismembered Japanese soldiers lying on the floor. A few of them were splattered against the walls. He kicked one out of his way and proceeded down the tunnel, holding his M 1 ready to fire.

He saw a door straight ahead to his left. It was closed and framed by logs, and a bulletin board was next to it. Butsko held his hand out behind him, signaling that the others should slow down and be quiet. Butsko tiptoed to the door, pressed his back against the wall beside it, reached out, and knocked three times.

A machine gun opened fire on the other side of the door, filling it with holes.

"Temple," said Butsko, "shoot out the lock!"

Pfc. Temple was from the Second Squad and been a high school football star in Akron, Ohio, before the war. He carried a BAR slung over his right shoulder and held level with the ground, waist-high. Butsko got out of the way and Pfc. Temple took his place, aiming the BAR at the doorlatch. He pulled the trigger and the automatic weapon kicked in his hands, but he held it steady and the lock was blown apart, along with the latch and splinters of wood, while the Japanese soldiers inside the room fired their machine gun through the door, their bullets banging harmlessly into the opposite wall. Letting go the trigger, the latch and part of the door gone, Temple lashed out with his foot and kicked the door open. Butsko pulled a hand grenade from the lapel of Private Morgan Chambers, yanking the pin, releasing the lever.

He counted to three, tossed the hand grenade into the room, and heard the excited voices of Japanese soldiers as they rustled for cover. The grenade blasted, sending a flash of orange-yellow flame into the tunnel. Butsko got out of the way, and Sergeant Cameron moved into position, thrusting the nozzle of the flamethrower into the room.

He turned the nozzle and fire spurted out. Japanese soldiers in the room screamed and moaned. Butsko leaped past Cameron and charged into the room, holding his M 1 ready to fire. The room was full of burning bodies, some still on the floor, others running around or jumping up and down. Butsko raised his M 1 to his shoulder and plugged one of them, while Pfc. Temple fired his BAR from the waist, chopping down two. The other recon platoon members shot the rest of the Japs, putrid fumes swirling everywhere.

Butsko covered his nose with the back of his hand. "Let's get out of here," he muttered.

He led the recon platoon into the hallway. Coming at them from the right was a platoon of American soldiers, a lieutenant in front of them.

"What's going on here?" asked the lieutenant.

"We just cleaned out that room," Butsko said.

The lieutenant poked his head into the room, took a sniff, and pulled back, his nose wrinkled. "What a mess. Okay, you men fall in with us. Let's move it out."

The platoon passed by and the recon platoon tagged along at its rear. Butsko took out a cigarette and lit it up, taking deep breaths, feeling tired. *Let that other platoon do the work for a change,* Butsko thought. The crowd of men proceeded through the tunnel, approaching the next bend, when suddenly a Japanese soldier jumped into the open, holding a machine gun in his hands.

"Banzai!" screamed the Jap, pulling the trigger.

His first burst caught the lieutenant and hit a few men in the front rank. Everybody else hit the dirt, and one soldier from the other platoon managed to get off a shot that came close enough to the Jap to make him flinch. Then Private Verderosa from Butsko's First Squad fired a bullet that hit the Jap in the guts. The Jap keeled over and fell on his face, the machine gun underneath him. The GIs got to their feet stealthily, and Butsko moved forward to see if the lieutenant still was alive, when something shiny and small flashed through the air in front of him.

145

"Hit it!" he bellowed.

It was a Japanese hand grenade, and it landed several feet in front of the GIs, bounced once, and exploded. The sound was deafening and the top of the tunnel collapsed; earth dropped to the floor.

The GIs rushed toward the piles of dirt. Butsko knelt over the dead lieutenant, whose chest was mangled by direct hits from two bullets.

"Who's next in charge of this platoon?" Butsko asked.

"I am," said a soldier whose rolled-up sleeves covered whatever rank he had. "I'm Tech Sergeant Clancy."

"I'm Master Sergeant Butsko, and I guess I'm your boss now."

"Guess you are."

"I need somebody to throw a hand grenade around that corner there. You wanna do it?"

"Naw, do you?"

"Gimme a grenade. When it blows, everybody follow me."

The sergeant took a grenade out of one of the big side pockets of his fatigue pants and threw it to Butsko, who crawled toward the wall.

"Cover me," he said.

The GIs raised their rifles over the pile of dirt, ready to shoot anybody who might aim a rifle at Butsko. Butsko stood up, placed his back against the wall, and slid toward the turn in the tunnel, the grenade in his hands, one forefinger hooked through the ring fastened to the pin, ready to pull it.

Six inches of Arisaka rifle barrel appeared around the bend, and the GIs opened fire at it all at once, forcing it to withdraw. Butsko moved sideways, keeping his back close to the wall, where he'd be a difficult target. He came to the bend, pulled the pin of the hand grenade, and turned the lever loose. Counting to four, he hurled it around the corner and darted backward, dropping to the floor.

Barroooom!—the hand grenade exploded, and Butsko jumped to his feet. *"Follow me!"*

He ran around the corner and fired his rifle before he could take stock of what was there. Through the clouds of smoke he saw Japanese soldiers lying dead on the tunnel floor, and other Japanese soldiers running away.

Behind Butsko the GIs shot Japanese soldiers who looked

like they might still have some life in them.

"Keep going!" Butsko said.

He ran down the tunnel, away from the smoke, and peered into the shadows, looking for doors to rooms where Japs might be hiding. Ahead was a fork in the passageway, and Butsko slowed down. The rest of the GIs caught up with him.

"Clancy, you take your men down the passageway to the left and I'll take mine down here." He indicated the tunnel on the right with his chin. "Give us some hand grenades."

"Hey, we need them for ourselves!"

"You've got a lot more than us. If half your men give each of us one, we'll be okay."

"But we need them!"

Butsko, his eyes ablaze, pointed his M 1 at Sergeant Clancy. "I said gimme some hand grenades, you cheap son of a bitch!"

Clancy looked at the rifle and smiled. "You wouldn't dare pull that trigger."

Butsko raised his M 1 a few inches and pulled the trigger. The firing pin shot forward into the bullet and its cartridge exploded, sending the bullet spinning down the barrel and through the air a few inches from Sergeant Clancy's right ear, making Sergeant Clancy flinch.

The smile was wiped off Sergeant Clancy's face. "You're crazy, you know that?"

"Gimme the hand grenades."

Sergeant Clancy told every other man in his platoon to give Butsko one grenade. The men fearfully stepped forward and laid them at Butsko's feet, retreating quickly.

"Get going!" Butsko said.

Sergeant Clancy scowled at Butsko, then led his men into the tunnel on the left. Butsko knelt down and fastened a grenade to his lapel.

"Help yourselves, boys," he said.

The men scooped up the grenades, fastening them to the lapels of their shirts. Butsko got three and so did some of the others, but most of them ended up with two.

"Okay," Butsko said, standing. "Let's get going. The sooner we clean out the Japs, the sooner we'll get a rest."

Hunched over, carrying his M 1 in both hands, Butsko advanced into the tunnel, looking for Japs. His men followed him. Their path was fairly level for several paces, then it in-

147

clined down sharply. Butsko's head bounced up and down as he descended the incline. In the darkness ahead he saw a door.

"Uh-oh," he said. "Everybody against the wall."

The men moved toward the wall and pressed their shoulders or backs against it, while Butsko prepared one of his grenades, pulling the pin but not turning or letting go of the lever.

"Cover me," he said.

He tiptoed forward, intending to lay the grenade in front of the door to blow it down, when suddenly the door was flung open and a bunch of Japs spilled into the passageway, firing rifles and pistols wildly, led by a lieutenant screaming *"Banzai!"*

The GIs were huddled against the wall, and most of the bullets whizzed by them. Pfc. Ruehlmann from the Fourth Squad was shot in the stomach, and Private Carter from the Second stopped a bullet with his shoulder. They dropped down as the other GIs fired back at the Japs, who were in the middle of the passageway, easy targets. Butsko tossed his grenade at the Japs.

The Japs were so excited, they didn't even see the grenade roll into their midst. Butsko dived to the ground. *"Hit it!"*

The GIs dropped down and the grenade exploded, ripping Japanese arms from Japanese bodies, cracking bones and caving in heads. A Japanese torso landed in front of Butsko, and the air was filled with smoke.

Butsko took another grenade, pulled the pin, and tossed it through the open door. The grenade detonated, blowing the door off its hinges and sending a cloud of smoke billowing over Butsko's head.

"Get that flamethrower in there!"

Sergeant Cameron jumped up and ran toward the door, leaned beside it, stuck the nozzle into the room, and turned on the gas. Fire poured into the room. Then Butsko hurled himself forward, streaking toward the door.

"Follow me!"

Sergeant Cameron turned off the flamethrower and burst through the door, followed by the rest of his men. Butsko charged into the room, waving his M 1 from side to side, looking for Japs to shoot. Blankets burned and stank on the floor, but nobody was there. At the other end of the room was a passageway.

148

"Let's go down there," Butsko said.

They advanced cautiously toward the passageway and entered it, noticing that the air was gradually becoming cooler and damper. Butsko wondered how far beneath the ground they were. *Where does this damned thing end?* he wondered.

The tunnel twisted and turned, and then they came to another closed door. Butsko readied a hand grenade and motioned for Sergeant Cameron to get next to him. Butsko and the others got down on their stomachs, hugging the wall, and Butsko lobbed the grenade toward the door.

The grenade exploded, blowing the door apart. Before the sound ended, Sergeant Cameron charged forward, his flame-thrower spurting lightning into the room.

"Now!" Butsko cried.

He ran toward the door, hearing the footsteps of his men behind him, and jumped into the room, his eyes smarting from the smoke as he searched for Japs, holding his M 1 waist-high, ready to shoot anything that moved.

Through the clouds of smoke he perceived that he was in a large room, perhaps thirty feet by twenty feet, with crates stacked against the walls. He stepped toward the crates nearest him; they were burning, and his hair stood on end because he realized that the boxes had the markings he'd seen in the past on captured Japanese ammunition.

"Get the fuck out of here!" Butsko screamed.

He spun around and plowed into the GIs behind him, heading toward the door. They followed him and bumped into each other, elbowing and clawing, trying to get out of the room. Butsko ran into a long winding corridor, wondered for a split second which way to go, and decided to flee in the direction from which they'd come. He veered to the left and raced up the incline, huffing and puffing, aware that the ammunition would blow at any moment. He stretched his legs out in long strides, trying to put as much distance between him and the ammunition crates as he could. He sped through the room with the burning blankets and entered the main corridor outside.

His ears filled with a mighty and terrible roar. The floor heaved like the deck of a ship in high seas, and dirt poured onto him. He dived down and the wall beside him caved in, covering him with dirt, which clogged his nostrils and got into his mouth.

149

Coughing and spitting, struggling wildly, Butsko clawed through the dirt and poked his head through the surface. Ammunition crates exploded in the storage room as the chain reaction continued and the awful thunder went on relentlessly. Butsko thought he was in the middle of the worst earthquake in history. On his knees, buried to his neck in dirt and stones, he tried to see in the darkness, but everything was pitch-black, adding to his panic.

His men shouted and screamed; he could make out their voices above the din. A clod of earth fell on Butsko's head and he was afraid that the entire roof would collapse, smothering him alive. Climbing frantically to the top of the pile of dirt, he pressed his hands against the ceiling, trying to hold it up there. *God*, he thought, *if you ever get me out of this one, I'll go to church every Sunday for the rest of my life.*

The shock waves traveled up the hill, and the ground shook under the feet of the soldiers milling about in the rubble of the mission station. They dropped to their stomachs, heard the explosions, and wondered what was going on. Walls off the fortress, already devastated by bombing and shelling, collapsed on soldiers. Colonel Stockton, who had set up his command post near one of the walls, dived to the ground at the first tremor, huddling against the wall, which proceeded to topple over him.

Bricks and stones fell onto him and some of his staff members, but the wall was only six feet high and no injuries were sustained. The explosions seemed to last an eternity but actually went on for about half a minute, and then everything settled down and the rumbling deep in the ground ended.

Colonel Stockton stood and brushed the dust off his uniform. Major Cobb arose next to him, his wire-rimmed eyeglasses crooked on his nose.

"Sounds like their ammo just blew," Major Cobb said, adjusting his eyeglasses. "I hope it didn't get any of our people."

"Find out and report to me."

Major Cobb walked away and Colonel Stockton rubbed his eyes. Much of his regiment was down in the tunnels, and he might have lost a large percentage of them. His victory could turn out to be a terrible defeat. *Oh, shit*, he thought, kicking a stone into the air.

THIRTEEN . . .

Butsko lowered his hands from the ceiling. The explosions had ended and no more dirt fell. An eerie stillness filled the tunnel, and the air was thick with dust.

"Anybody alive?" Butsko asked, and then choked on the foul air.

A chorus of coughing and spitting reverberated through the tunnel. The soldiers swore and snorted, climbing out of piles of dirt. One by one they spoke their names. After they'd all reported, Butsko realized that only Private Morehouse was missing.

"Delane, you still got that torch?" Butsko asked.

"I dropped it someplace."

"Good work." Butsko took out his Zippo and flicked the wheel. It lit on the first try, illuminating the faces of his men clambering over piles of dirt in the tunnel. No one could stand because so much dirt had fallen.

"Anybody got a flashlight?" Butsko asked.

Nobody said anything. Butsko's flashlight was in his pack, and his pack was back at the spot where they'd bivouacked the night before. He hadn't realized that he might get buried alive before noon. Butsko held up the lighter and moved on his hands and knees up the incline toward the top of the hill.

"Follow me," he said.

"I'm stuck!" shouted Private Pacillo.

"Somebody dig him out," Butsko replied.

Butsko crawled upward, holding his Zippo in front of him. He looked along the walls for another torch, but couldn't see any. Turning forward again, he saw something dark and ominous in front of him. He crawled closer to it, and his heart sank when he saw that it was a solid wall of dirt. The tunnel leading to the high ground was blocked off. But maybe there really wasn't that much dirt there.

He moved closer and shoveled dirt away with his hands, hoping the wall was thin and he could continue to move up the tunnel system toward the top of Kokengolo Hill. But the wall wasn't thin. He dug a foot and everything felt solid behind it.

"Is it blocked, Sarge?" asked Craig Delane.

"Yeah."

Butsko took his entrenching tool from its holster on his belt, adjusted the blade, and hacked the wall, but he couldn't break through. His Zippo, which he'd propped on a pile of dirt, went out, and everything was darkness again.

"Aw, shit," Butsko said wearily, going slack. He was on his knees, and he let his entrenching tool rest on the ground. He groped around for his lighter, closed the lid and dropped it into his pocket.

Sergeant Cameron's voice came through the darkness. "I got a piece of wood here. Maybe I can make a torch."

It was a piece of timber five feet long, part of a joist that held back a wall. Sergeant Cameron dropped it in front of him, aimed the flamethrower, and turned the nozzle slightly. A thin stream of jellied gasoline shot out and fell on the dirt, where it glowed phosphorescently as it burned. Sergeant Cameron prodded the timber into a gob of burning goo, and the timber caught fire.

"Now we're getting somewhere," Butsko said, wiping dirt off his face with his hand. "Let's see if we can dig out of here."

He ordered half his men to shovel through the wall, and the rest to find lengths of timber to use as torches. Then he leaned back, tempted to light a cigarette, but stopped himself because he didn't know how much air they had.

"No smoking," he said. "We need to save the air."

Two at a time, the soldiers hacked their entrenching tools against the dirt piled up in the blocked passage, and after five minutes they'd dug a four-foot tunnel, but the dirt was still a thick wall before them.

"Sarge," said Private Snead, the torch making shadows flicker on his dirty face, "I don't think we're gonna be able to dig through this. Maybe the whole tunnel has collapsed up ahead."

"Keep trying," Butsko said.

The men continued to dig, and Butsko became more worried. If the tunnel had truly collapsed, there was a strong possibility that he and his men were buried alive. He wondered if the Corps of Engineers would be able to dig them out.

Ten minutes later the dirt was still solid in front of the GIs. Butsko weighed the possibilities and decided it might be easier to search for another way out than dig through that wall. If they were blocked somewhere else, they could return there and keep digging. But how long would the air hold out?

"That's enough," Butsko said. "Let's try the other way."

"The other way only goes deeper," Sergeant Cameron said.

"Maybe there's a connection with a tunnel that goes up. Give the torch to Delane and keep your flamethrower ready, because there might be Japs down here."

They crawled on their hands and knees, because so little space was between the ceiling and piles of dirt on the floor. The men peered ahead at the shadows cast by the torch, fearful that they'd find a new wall of dirt, but the tunnel kept going downward.

The tunnel twisted like a snake, but Butsko tried to figure out where he was relative to the ammunition storage room. It was possible that it was near the tunnel that had caved in on them, because of all the turns they'd made. He hoped they'd soon reach a tunnel going up.

They passed the door of the room that had burning blankets on the floor, but now the blankets were piles of ash, and half the room was filled with dirt from floor to ceiling. That way led back to the ammunition storage room, but a section of the tunnel continued down past the outer door.

"Look—a torch!" shouted Private Ivey, pointing to the wall.

"Get it down," said Butsko. "Light it up. And you can smoke if you want to. It looks like we got enough air for that."

He took out a cigarette and flicked the wheel of his Zippo,

but only sparks shot into the air because he was out of fluid.

"Hold still," he said to Delane.

Butsko puffed his cigarette to life against Delane's torch, took a deep drag, and felt better immediately. He tried not to think that they all might be doomed underneath Kokengolo Hill.

"Let's go."

Holding their rifles ready, they walked down the corridor. Two soldiers lit the way with flaming torches, and shadows jiggled everywhere. They came to a bend; Butsko looked around it and couldn't see anything ahead. He moved into the open, turned the corner, and continued to walk, hoping that the tunnel would start inclining or that they'd come to another passage-way.

A BAR opened fire beside him, and Butsko dropped to the ground, pulling his rifle to his shoulder. All the other soldiers hit the dirt too. Nobody fired back at them. Butsko peered ahead and couldn't see anything.

"Who fired that BAR?" Butsko asked.

"I did," replied Private Briscoe, a tremor in his voice.

"What'd you fire at?"

"I saw something move."

"Go out there and see if you hit it."

"Alone?"

"Yeah."

Briscoe gulped and crawled forward, cradling his BAR in his arms. He was afraid Japs might be waiting for him in the shadows. He came to the place where his bullets had struck dirt, but no one was there.

"I can't see anything," he said.

"Keep going."

"All my myself!"

"We'll be right behind you." Butsko turned his head to the side. "Let's go," he said to the others.

They followed Briscoe as he crawled over the dirty floor. Slowly he covered another ten feet, then stopped again. "There's nothing here."

"Everybody up!" Butsko said.

They got to their feet and walked toward Briscoe, who was afraid that Butsko was going to punch him out—or worse.

Butsko walked up to him and slapped the back of his hand

lightly against Briscoe's stomach. "Relax."

Butsko motioned with his head toward the tunnel ahead. Craig Delane joined him, carrying the torch high in the air, and the others followed, their footsteps echoing from the walls and ceiling.

"Hey, Sarge," said Private Ivey, "you think we're gonna get out of here?"

"How should I know?" Butsko replied, because that was how he felt, but then he thought he ought to give his men some encouragement. It was better to have false hope than no hope at all. "Sooner or later we should come to a tunnel that'll get us out of here," he said. "Don't worry about it."

"What if this tunnel is a dead end?" asked Pfc. Temple.

"Then the Corps of Engineers'll have to dig us out. Stop worrying so much. You're like a bunch of whores in night court."

That shut them up, and they felt embarrassed for showing their fear. Hunching over behind their rifles, ready for anything, they advanced deeper into Kokengolo Hill. The torches sputtered and Craig Delane wondered if he was marching into his grave.

Butsko glimpsed a door up ahead. "Over here," he said, darting to the wall on the same side of the tunnel as the door.

The men huddled against the wall. Delane wished he wasn't carrying the torch, because if Japs were ahead, he'd be the first one they'd shoot at.

"There's another room up there," Butsko said.

"Shit," said Private Witherspoon.

"What was that?" Butsko asked.

"Nothing."

"If you don't have nothing to say, keep your mouth shut." Butsko peered down the tunnel, wondering if Japs were behind that door. There was only one way to find out. "Sergeant Cameron!"

"Yo."

"Follow me. The rest of you, trail behind Sergeant Cameron."

His back to the wall, Butsko tiptoed toward the door. Sergeant Cameron crept behind him, holding the nozzle of the flamethrower, and then came the rest of the recon platoon, their eyes darting around nervously, trying to be quiet. The flames from the torches made their eyes sparkle and cast sinister shadows on their faces, which were knotted with tension. They looked like a band of ghouls instead of a platoon of American GIs.

Butsko came to within ten yards of the door, then reached back and touched Sergeant Cameron. "Stay here," he whispered.

Sergeant Cameron nodded, and Butsko moved forward, pulling a grenade from his lapel. He yanked the pin, took a few more steps, then let the lever go and tossed the grenade in front of the door, where it plopped onto the dirt.

Butsko turned and ran back, and after a short distance he dived toward the floor. He held his helmet on his head and squinched his eyes, waiting for the grenade to detonate. He counted to three and then it blew, thundering through the tunnel, and Butsko felt the shock wave pass over him.

Sergeant Cameron charged the splintered door, his finger on the nozzle control. He rammed the nozzle into an opening and turned it on. Flames swooshed out and filled the room with a mighty roar. Butsko leaped to his feet and held his M 1 high.

"Follow me!" he yelled.

He galloped past Sergeant Cameron and busted through the shattered door, landing in a small room. It had a desk and chair against the far wall, and both were ablaze, filling the room with smoke. He could see no Japanese soldiers anywhere, but a closed door was in the middle of the wall on his right.

The rest of the recon platoon piled into the room behind him, tense and nervous, anxious to kill a Jap before he killed one of them. They bounced around on their toes and held their fingers against their triggers, their eyes sweeping the room frantically.

Butsko looked at the door and headed toward the wall beside it. "I'll blow down the door; the rest of you, follow me, Cameron in the lead. Got it?"

"Yo."

Butsko held his hand grenade and pulled the pin. He waited until the others were out of the way, then tossed the grenade in front of the door and turned quickly, dashing out the door, joining the others in the hall. They waited a few seconds and then the grenade exploded, making the walls tremble. A few chunks of earth dropped down from the ceiling.

Sergeant Cameron turned the corner and ran into the room, turning the flamethrower on as he aimed it through a wide crack in the door to the next room. Fire spat out the nozzle, and Sergeant Cameron saw it catch on to whatever was in the room.

He heard Butsko galloping like a stallion behind him and got out of the way. Butsko jumped into the air, crashed through the splintered door, and landed in the room, pulling the trigger of his M 1 rifle and putting a hole through the Jap sitting behind the desk, his body and head covered with a sheet of flame.

Butsko glanced around and saw that the burning figure behind the desk was the only Jap in the room, which evidently was an office, like the previous one. On the desk in front of the burning Jap was a picture in a frame, which was also on fire. The soldiers from the recon platoon crowded into the office behind Butsko, who spotted something long sticking out of the Jap's stomach.

"Jesus," said Butsko, "he must've just committed hara-kiri."

The figure behind the desk was Captain Hisahiro, and he hadn't just committed hara-kiri: He'd done it an hour before, when the American stormed the deeper recesses of the tunnel system. His troops had failed to hold the fortress, and there was nothing more for him to do except give his life for his Emperor.

Private Ubaldo pinched his nose with his fingers. "He stinks!"

Sergeant Cameron pointed the nozzle of his flamethrower toward a corner. "Isn't that chow over there?"

Butsko looked. The crates had the same markings as crates of food they'd captured in the past. "Have a look, Delane. Watch out for booby traps."

Delane approached the crates and felt around for wires but couldn't find any. He took out his bayonet and sliced into the crate. The round tops of tin cans stared back at him.

"It's chow!" he said.

"Haul that stuff out of here," Butsko said.

Soldiers heaved the crates onto their shoulders and carried them out of the room. Butsko kicked the smoldering Captain Hisahiro out of his way and pulled out a drawer of the desk. In it was a bottle of sake. "Bull's-eye!" he said. He pulled open another drawer and found a sheaf of papers, which he removed and handed to Private Ubaldo. In the bottom drawer

157

he found two more bottles of sake lying on their sides. "Well, whataya know," Butsko said, taking them out.

He searched through the rest of the desk as its front burned and crackled. The room was filling with smoke, and Butsko's eyes smarted. He took more papers from the other drawers, stepped over the charred body of Captain Hisahiro, and headed for the door.

"Let's get out of here," he said.

His men filed out of the room. Butsko was the last to leave. Behind, lying on the floor, Captain Hisahiro continued to smolder, his ritual hara-kiri knife sticking out of his stomach.

A tarpaulin had been set up on top of the ruined mission station to protect Colonel Stockton from the sun. He sat at his desk underneath it, enjoying a late lunch of hot C rations and hot coffee, which perked him up and made him feel even better than he already felt, because all resistance on Kokengolo Hill had ended, as far as he knew.

Elements of his regiment were sweeping through the jungle to the southwest of the hill, searching for Japanese stragglers. It was believed that a sizable contingent of Japs were on their way to Bairoko Harbor, where they expected to be evacuated; but if those Japs existed, they'd run into the Thirty-eighth Regiment's roadblock and be caught between it and Colonel Stockton's units moving up from the south. That should make short work of the final remnants of the Japanese army on New Georgia.

It had been a fine campaign, Colonel Stockton thought in retrospect. He'd lost a lot of men, but the Japanese had lost four to five times more, and the US Army had taken the island, a key to General MacArthur's Operation CARTWHEEL strategy. The next major objective would probably be Bougainville, the northernmost island in the Solomon chain, the stepping-stone to the principal Japanese stronghold in the southwest Pacific, Rabaul, on New Britain Island. According to intelligence reports, the Japanese had fortified Bougainville much more strongly than any other island in the Solomons, and the fight to capture it would be costly.

Lieutenant Harper approached Colonel Stockton and saluted. "As far as I can determine," Lieutenant Harper said, "the recon platoon was evidently trapped by that explosion we had awhile ago. I've been able to account for all our other units. Sergeant Clancy, here, from George Company saw the recon platoon before the explosion."

Colonel Stockton looked at Sergeant Clancy, who was lantern-jawed, redheaded, and as lean as a rail. "Where'd you see the recon platoon last?"

Sergeant Clancy shifted his feet nervously, because he was scared to death of high-ranking officers. "I seen Butsko and his men down in the tunnels. We came to a fork in the road; Butsko told me to go left, and he took his men right. About a half hour after that we heard the explosion, and part of our tunnel caved in, but we were able to make it back to the fork. We could see that the tunnel going to the right was completely caved in, and that was the direction where the big explosion came from."

Colonel Stockton thought for a few moments. "The recon platoon must have blown up a Jap ammo dump down there by mistake."

Sergeant Clancy nodded. "They had enough hand grenades to do it. They stole them from me and my men."

"What do you mean?" Colonel Stockton asked sharply.

Sergeant Clancy couldn't look Colonel Stockton in the eye. "Butsko pulled a gun on me and made us hand over our grenades."

"All your grenades?"

"One from every other man in my platoon."

"Did Sergeant Butsko ask first?"

"Yes, sir," Sergeant Clancy replied with a stutter.

"Why didn't you give them to him?"

"Because we needed them for ourselves."

"Was the recon platoon low on hand grenades."

Sergeant Clancy took a few moments to answer. "Yes, sir, I believe they were."

Colonel Stockton groaned with exasperation. "If he was low on hand grenades, you should have shared what you had with him."

"But we needed them grenades, sir."

"So did Sergeant Butsko. You should have given him some of your grenades. It's share and share alike in this man's Army, understand?"

"Yes, sir."

"If anything like this every happens again, you'd better share what you have. Is that clear?"

"Yes, sir."

"You're dismissed."

Sergeant Clancy saluted, did an about-face, and walked away. Lieutenant Harper lay a sheet of paper in front of Colonel Stockton.

"I've drawn a rough map of the tunnel system," Lieutenant Harper said, "based on what Sergeant Clancy told me. It appears that Butsko and the recon platoon are somewhere over here."

Colonel Stockton looked at where Lieutenant Harper was pointing. "Have Colonel McCawley report to me right away."

"You think the recon platoon might still be alive?" Lieutenant Harper asked.

"I have to assume that until I know otherwise. Get going."

"Yes, sir."

Lieutenant Harper walked away. Colonel Stockton stared at the map of the tunnel system, adjusting the reading glasses on his nose so that he could see better.

Click!

Colonel Stockton looked up and saw Lydia Kent-Taylor aiming her Leica at him. She lowered the camera, and he was surprised by how bedraggled she appeared. She'd lost her helmet somewhere and her hair was mussed up. Her face was dirty and her uniform torn. She sagged from fatigue.

"I think you'd better have a seat," he said. "Care for some coffee?"

"Coffee?" she asked dreamily. "I'd love some coffee."

"Private Bombasino!"

"Yes, sir!"

"Get some coffee for Miss Kent-Taylor!"

"Yes, sir!"

Lydia sat down next to Colonel Stockton and placed her Leica on the table, then took her haversack from her shoulder and laid it on the ground. This was the first time she sat down since Leo talked with her nearly two hours earlier.

"Get any good pictures?" Colonel Stockton asked disinterestedly, for he still was perusing the map.

"I think so."

"I imagine you'll be leaving us soon?"

160

"I don't know. Maybe."

"You look like you've had a hard day."

"Not as hard as the men who had to fight here."

He glanced up at her; her face was pale, her eyes half-closed. "Maybe you'd better lie down."

"I'm all right."

"You don't look well."

"As you said, it's been a hard day."

They heard the approach of footsteps and turned around. It was Lieutenant Colonel McCawley, a short, stout man with a round face and a mustache with the ends teased upward. He was commanding officer of the 271st Engineers, and he came to attention, saluting.

"At ease," said Colonel Stockton.

Lydia thought she should take a photograph of Colonel McCawley, but she didn't feel like lifting her camera again. She was tired of taking pictures. She just wanted to find someplace to relax.

"Have a seat," Colonel Stockton said. "Smoke if you like. Have you met Lydia Kent-Taylor yet?"

"I don't believe I've had the pleasure," Colonel McCawley said.

"Here she is."

"How do you do," Colonel McCawley said gallantly, because he considered himself a ladies' man.

Lydia could discern that from the prissy way he trimmed his mustache. "Hello."

Colonel Stockton cleared his throat. "Let's get down to business. Do you recall that explosion that took place a little while ago? Well, evidently it was set off by the recon platoon, and now they're trapped in a tunnel." He pointed to a spot on the map. "I want you to send some of your big boys down there with shovels to dig them out."

"May I have that map, sir?"

"Sure. If you have any other questions, refer them to my aide, Lieutenant Harper. He knows more about the situation than I do, and he has a sergeant who can lead you to the place where the cave-in is. Everything clear?"

Colonel McCawley picked up the map. "Yes, sir."

Colonel McCawley walked away, and Lydia stared at Colonel Stockton. "The recon platoon is trapped in this hill?"

Colonel Stockton nodded. "Evidently they blew up a Japanese ammo dump, and that made the tunnel system collapse."

"My goodness, are they all right?"

"I don't know, but it's a good thing you didn't stay with them."

Lydia looked away, astounded. The recon platoon was trapped underground. They might be dead. Perhaps Butsko had been killed. It was hard to imagine that such a man, full of vitality and malevolence, could be killed. She'd seen many dead men that day, but Butsko seemed deathless to her. You couldn't kill a man like that.

Colonel Stockton was surprised by the expression of concern on her face. He hadn't thought that she'd been that involved with the men from the recon platoon. "They're a very resourceful bunch, my recon platoon," he said. "If there's a way to get away, you can be sure they'll find it."

"But what if there isn't?"

"My military experience has taught me that there's always a way out of difficult situations, and often more than one way."

Major Cobb approached with a rolled-up map under his arm. "May I speak with you, sir?"

"Have a seat, Major."

Major Cobb sat on the other side of Colonel Stockton and rolled out his map, explaining that Japanese stragglers had been observed in the jungle to the southwest of Kokengolo Hill and that units of the Twenty-third Regiment were pursuing them. Private Bombasino placed a pot of coffee and three mugs on the table, and Lydia reached for hers, sipping it hot and black.

She was thinking about the recon platoon trapped underground and about stories she'd read in newspapers from time to time about coal miners being trapped by mine explosions in America. Sometimes they'd been found dead, but other times they'd walked out of the tunnels, and photographers had been there to catch the expressions of fatigue and relief on their blackened faces. Such photographs were sensational and appeared in newspapers all over the country. Sometimes the pictures even won awards.

She realized that if the recon platoon could be saved, she might be able to take such a picture, and it would have tremendous human interest because the men involved weren't mere coal miners but American GIs fighting the great Second

World War. The right picture capturing the right mood could give her career a tremendous boost.

The coffee enlivened her mind, and her visualization of the picture inspired her. She could almost see Butsko leading the recon platoon out of a hole in the ground, and they'd all have their rifles slung over their shoulders and their faces covered with dirt, hollowed-eyed and relieved to be saved. What a picture!

She gulped down the coffee and stood, slinging her camera bag over her shoulder. "Excuse me," she said, "but I've got to be going."

Colonel Stockton nodded and grunted, still conferring with Major Cobb, and Lydia ran off to find Leo Stern. He probably didn't know about the recon platoon's predicament; it'd be a hell of a story for him too. She looked around for him, and her eyes fell on a team of GIs loading dead Japanese soldiers into a truck. The light was behind them and in silhouette the scene was gruesome and macabre. She lifted her camera and focused in.

Click!

The Mosquito heard American soldiers moving toward him, and he opened his left eye to a slit. He saw American soldiers tossing dead Japanese soldiers onto a truck, and they were headed his way. His heart beat wildly, because he was afraid he'd be discovered. They might shoot him on the spot!

He became terrified. After lying in the hot sun for so many hours, with flies buzzing all over him, he might get shot anyway. He believed propaganda about American soldiers killing and torturing their prisoners. He still wanted to escape somehow and hide in the jungle until it was safe to surrender, maybe when the war was over. The jungle was full of coconuts and the streams loaded with fish. A man could survive if he was resourceful.

He decided to be calm and let the Americans load him onto the truck. Hopefully he'd land in a spot where he could get some air. He'd escape later. It'd be a good idea to get away from Kokengolo Hill anyway, because it was crawling with American soldiers and officers. If he were a fanatical Japanese soldier, he'd be able to kill an American officer without much trouble. Some high-ranking officers were seated at a table not

163

too far away from the Mosquito, and it'd be easy for him to jump up and throw a grenade over there or fire a few shots.

But he was no fanatic. He wanted desperately to live. Through the slit of his eye he saw the American soldiers come closer. There were eight of them, two to each team. One soldier would grab a dead Japanese soldier's arms and the other his ankles, they'd swing him side to side three times, and on the fourth swing they'd throw him onto the truck, his arms and legs wagging limply as he flew through the air.

Clouds of flies buzzed around the Mosquito and he could barely hear. The Americans came so close that he decided he'd better close his eye. He calmed himself and got ready for what he supposed would be the most difficult and dangerous part of his ordeal. Bodies were pulled away by American soldiers, and the Mosquito was jostled about. A GI boot came down painfully on the small of his back, and it was all he could do to keep from crying out. The American soldier stepped on him as he tugged another Japanese soldier loose from the pile. The Mosquito was afraid he'd be discovered, and beads of perspiration broke out on his forehead, which he was afraid the Americans would notice.

They were just a bunch of GIs on a shitty detail, and they weren't noticing anything. One picked up his hands, another his legs, and they carried him belly down toward the truck.

"This one's not too heavy," wheezed one of the GIs.

"Looks damn near starved to death."

The Mosquito thought his spine might crack in two. He tried to keep himself stiff, because rigor mortis should have set in somewhat. He hoped the Americans wouldn't notice how warm he was and that the one holding his hands wouldn't feel his pulse by mistake.

The American soldiers stopped, counted, and swung him back and forth. They tossed him into the air and he spun around, opening his eyes slightly, seeing the top of Kokengolo Hill and the bodies in the truck. He landed on the other bodies, somebody's elbow spearing his cheek, cutting it open, but he suppressed the cry of pain.

He lay on the other soldiers, and the stench of death filled his nostrils. It wasn't too strong yet, but it would be soon. That would be the worst part of his trip. But he would survive that too. Somehow he was going to pull through this.

164

He heard the American soldiers on both sides of the truck, and bodies came flying through the air. One landed on top of him, and another a few feet away. The Mosquito was hungry and thirsty and felt like vomiting, but he gritted his teeth and exerted his will.

That night, as soon as it was dark, he'd make his move. That wouldn't be too much longer, and then he'd be free from both the Imperial Army and the Americans.

Somehow I've got to hold on, he thought. *It'll only be a little while longer.*

FOURTEEN . . .

Deep in the ground, the remnants of the recon platoon trudged through a long dark tunnel. Butsko was in front, holding his M 1 in both hands, and Craig Delane carried the torch high in the air, lighting the way ahead.

They'd left the room with Captain Hisahiro a half hour before and had been moving through this tunnel ever since. They'd passed a few more rooms that contained no Japs, and now were hoping and praying that the tunnel through which they were passing would lead them to daylight pretty soon.

Every time they turned a corner they hoped to see daylight, but every time they'd been disappointed. Butsko was beginning to think that this tunnel might become his tomb. He'd always thought he'd die from a Japanese bullet or bayonet, but it looked as though he were facing a slow agonizing death from suffocation or starvation.

The tunnel angled downward, and the men became more discouraged with every step they took. There seemed to be no way out. They were going to be buried alive. They thought of their friends and relatives back home, and those who were married remembered their wives, the pleasure and pain they'd had in their marriages, and wondered how their wives would fare without them.

Craig Delane thought of his opulent life in New York, the private clubs to which he belonged, the debutante balls he'd attended, his apartment on Sixty-eighth Street between Madison and Park avenues. How awful that a man like him would die in a hole in the ground on an insect-infested island in the South Pacific. He wished that he'd never enlisted in the Army. He imagined that his father and mother would be able to feel like patriotic Americans for the rest of their lives, because they'd given a son in the war.

The soldiers became more demoralized with every step they took. They dragged their feet over the floor and bent forward, straining to see that ray of light that would mean safety and life. Their jaws hung open and their eyes bulged out. *Please, God,* thought Butsko, *if you get me out of this one, I won't drink anymore and I won't go to any more whorehouses.*

They turned a corner, but once again no light was in front of them, only endless blackness and gloom. It was damper and cooler at that depth, and the air smelled musty. The sides of the tunnel were damp, and somewhere in the distance they heard the drip of water.

Suddenly and shockingly, machine guns and rifles opened fire in front of them. Pfc. Pacelli was shot in the chest, Private Reardon stopped a bullet with his stomach, Private Farr caught one in the balls, and Private Marguilies was shot through the face.

Bullets whizzed all around Butsko as he dropped to the ground. Craig Delane landed next to him and rolled the torch in the dirt, trying to put it out, but a bullet slammed into his shoulder and knocked him unconscious. Butsko peered ahead and saw flashes of light, the muzzle blasts from Japanese guns that roared and thundered in the tunnel. Then he heard the sound of hand grenades landing in the dirt nearby. *Oh, my God,* he thought squinching his eyes shut. *This is it.*

The three grenades exploded violently, reverberating through the tunnel and loosening dirt from the walls and ceiling. Butsko felt the shock waves pass over him, and bits of shrapnel whizzed around him, one so close he could feel its heat against his cheek. He thought he was a dead man for sure, but when the sounds diminished he realized he was not only alive but unhurt.

Soldiers moaned nearby. Craig Delane was motionless to his right, and Private Shane, who carried a BAR, was on his back to Butsko's left, the top of his head blown off. Jap soldiers chattered up ahead and Butsko wondered how many of his men had lived through the blasts. He didn't want to say anything because he didn't want the Japs to think he was alive.

A fucking ambush, he thought. *They were waiting for us.* Well, he could play that game too. Lying on the floor, pretending to be dead, he made his plans. The Japs would come forward to see how many Americans they'd killed, and when they got close, Butsko would throw a grenade of his own at them, then roll to the side and pick up Private Shane's BAR so he could shoot the survivors.

Craig Delane's torch had blown to bits in the explosions. Butsko moved his hand toward his lapel, the darkness covering him. He pulled loose a grenade and was about to pull the pin when a flashlight came on.

He froze. The Japanese soldiers jabbered and stood up. Peeking over the dirt, Butsko could see that they were behind a barricade of crates, and he could count eight of them. They climbed over their barricade and advanced, holding flashlights and their rifles.

They approached cautiously, talking to each other. Butsko could see two flashlight rays scanning back and forth. The rays passed over him, making him feel naked and vulnerable. He tensed, ready to make his last stand.

The Japs drew closer. Butsko's heart pounded loudly. He wasn't sure he'd be able to kill all the Japs before they killed him. Death might claim him in the next few minutes, but he'd go down fighting. He'd be able to kill some of them before they got him.

The Japs came within range. Butsko yanked the pin and drew back his arm. The Japs shouted in alarm and dropped to the floor as Butsko threw the grenade.

They shrieked, trying to keep the grenade in the rays of their flashlights, but they couldn't follow it, and it dropped to the dirt in their midst. They scrambled like rats, trying to find it, and Butsko rolled over, getting into position behind Private Shane's BAR.

The grenade blasted apart, sending lightning and shards of steel in all directions. Some of the Japs were blown into the air, and many of the rest were wounded. Butsko was on his feet while the roaring still echoed throughout the tunnel, and he charged forward, firing the BAR from his waist at the Japanese soldiers lying on the floor. He raked the dead ones with the wounded and unharmed, and a few tried to get their weapons, but Butsko saw them in the light of their dropped flashlights and cut them down.

Pow—a bullet zipped past his ear, and he dropped to the ground amid the Japanese soldiers he'd shot. *Pow*—another bullet flew over his head. Now he knew that the Japs had a few soldiers left behind their barricade. A flashlight went on behind the barricade and Butsko fired a burst; the light went out.

Butsko knew that when you were attacking you had to keep going if you wanted to keep the enemy off-balance. He pulled his last grenade from his lapel, yanked the pin, and let it fly, getting ready to jump up and charge like a son of a bitch. He licked his lips and clicked his teeth, because this could be Butsko's Last Charge.

The grenade ripped apart in a golden flash, tearing Japs to pieces, and Butsko ran forward like a madman, hollering and screaming at the top of his lungs, firing the BAR at the crates in front of him. He leaped over them and crashed against a dirt wall he hadn't seen before, nearly knocking himself senseless. He fell to the ground amid some dead Japanese, hearing Sergeant Cameron's voice and shots.

Butsko was dazed, but he climbed to his feet anyway and held his BAR ready to bash anything that moved. Sergeant Cameron attacked, weird shadows on his face from the flashlights. Butsko saw a Japanese soldier on the floor lift his arm, so he aimed his BAR downward and gave him a burst in the back. Sergeant Cameron leaned over what was left of the barricade and fired shots at Japanese soldiers who already were dead. Butsko and Sergeant Cameron kept firing until they were sure they'd killed all the Japs, then they released their triggers and looked at each other.

Butsko reached out and touched the wall. "Looks like this is the end of the tunnel," he said.

Sergeant Cameron climbed over the wrecked crates and kicked a Japanese soldier. "I wonder if all these fuckers are dead." He pulled his trigger and shot a bullet into the Jap's head.

Butsko's chest heaved from exertion and anxiety. Somehow

he'd survived the Jap sneak attack, but now he was buried alive. He flinched as Sergeant Cameron shot another Jap.

Butsko kicked some wood slats lying in front of him and stepped away from the Japs on the floor. He took a cigarette out of his shirt pocket and tried to light it with his Zippo, forgetting that his Zippo was out of fuel. He passed the dead Japs whom he'd grenaded and shot earlier, and then came to the men from the recon platoon, lying on the floor.

Only one was making any sound, and that was Craig Delane. Butsko's unlit cigarette dangled out of the corner of his mouth as he knelt beside Delane and rolled him over. Delane was unconscious, moaning, his lips moving slightly as if talking in his sleep. His shoulder was bloody, and Butsko cut away his shirt, then took the bandage from the pouch on Delane's belt and applied it to his wound, wrapping it around and tying a knot. The blood was coagulating; probably the damage wasn't serious. Butsko reached into Delane's pocket, took out his Zippo, and lit his cigarette, dropping Delane's Zippo into his own pocket.

Sergeant Cameron approached from behind him, shining one of the Japanese flashlights. "He alive?"

"Yeah," replied Butsko, puffing his cigarette.

"Anybody else?"

"I haven't checked yet."

They crawled over the other soldiers, feeling their pulses, pulling back their eyelids, but they all were dead. Butsko and Sergeant Cameron stripped them of weapons and ammunition, took dog tags, and finally took their cigarettes.

"We might as well go back," Butsko said. "All we can do now is try to dig ourselves out of here."

"Fat chance of that."

"You got a better idea?"

Sergeant Cameron said nothing. He just puffed his cigarette and looked around grimly. The recon platoon had boiled down to him, Butsko, and Craig Delane. Butsko walked back and picked up one of the Japanese flashlights. He took batteries from the other flashlight and stuffed them into his pockets. Turning around, he returned to Sergeant Cameron.

"I'll carry him first," Butsko said, bending over to lift Craig Delane.

Sergeant Cameron took a drag on his cigarette as Butsko

heaved Delane onto his shoulder. He adjusted Delane's limp body, then headed up the incline toward the part of the tunnel that had caved in. Sergeant Cameron walked a few steps behind him, directing a flashlight beam straight ahead.

The truck rocked from side to side as it rumbled over the dirt road. The bodies bounced up and down and the Mosquito was climbing through them to reach the top of the pile. Pushing away stiffening bodies, trying not to think of the stench building around him, he finally made it to the top of the truck, where he could look around and see the tops of trees.

No GI guards were on top of the truck. The Mosquito moved cautiously toward the side and saw the jungle passing by slowly. No truck was ahead and none was behind. Nobody would see him. The Mosquito could jump off the truck now, and he decided to go while he had the chance. The road twisted and turned through the jungle, and another twist was up ahead. He'd jump just before the truck veered to the right.

Crawling over dead bodies, he made his way toward the rear of the cab. He reached the tailgate and placed his hand on the cold metal. The curve was only twenty feet ahead and the truck slowed down. He sniffed the clean jungle breeze and flexed his muscles, gazing down dispassionately at the face of Sergeant Suzuki beside him. Sergeant Suzuki had blood on his shirt and his eyes were closed. His face was drained of blood and his complexion was light yellow.

The truck turned to the right and the Mosquito jumped. He landed in the middle of the dirt road, fell to the side, and rolled over, getting onto his knees. Looking ahead, he saw the truck disappear around the curve in the road. With a broad smile on his face the Mosquito dashed into the jungle and in seconds could no longer be seen from the road.

He was free, running through the thick green foliage, waving his hands in the air. *I've done it!* he said to himself. *I've escaped the war!*

In the late afternoon all the American wounded were being tended by doctors and nurses, and combat medics like Private Joseph Gundy had time to rest. Gundy still was tormented by thoughts of the Japanese soldier he'd killed, and he made his way through the jungle to Captain Sheehy's tent.

Captain Sheehy was a Roman Catholic chaplain assigned to the Twenty-third Regiment, and he was in Headquarters Company. Private Gundy attended Captain Sheehy's masses whenever he could, and Captain Sheehy had become his confessor. Thus far, Private Gundy had found him extremely lenient.

He approached two pup tents pitched side by side, with a jeep parked nearby. Pfc. Schlee, the chaplain's assistant, sat in front of one of the tents, eating a can of pork and beans that he'd heated over a fire that now was burning embers beside him.

"Father Sheehy around?" Private Gundy asked.

"He's taking a leak in the jungle. He should be right back."

Pfc. Schlee had blond hair and had been a student at Catholic University in Washington, D.C., before he'd been drafted. He had gotten halfway to being ordained as a Catholic priest, so they'd made him a chaplain's assistant.

"You don't look so good," Schlee said. "Have a rough day?"

Gundy looked to the ground and pushed a pebble around with his toe. "I killed a Jap today," he said.

Schlee's face became serious. "Oh." He didn't know what to say, so he continued eating.

Gundy chewed his lower lip and rolled the pebble underneath his toe, trying to keep from trembling. He felt lightheaded and frightened, as if he weren't in control of his body. He had a constant headache, which he kept numbed through the constant use of APC tablets, which were mostly aspirin.

Father Sheehy, a skinny man with a bony freckled face and big ears, came out of the jungle, carrying a roll of toilet paper. He wore a yardbird hat and silver crosses on the lapels of his green shirt. He took one look at Gundy and knew something was up.

"Hello, Joe," Father Sheehy asked, trying to grin. "Whataya know?"

"I'd like to talk with you, Father, if it's all right."

"Sure it's all right." He lobbed the roll of toilet paper into his tent, then turned around and pointed to a tree at the other end of the jungle.

"Over there okay?"

"How about someplace where we could have some privacy."

"We'll go into the jungle, then."

They walked across the small sunlit clearing and entered

173

the thick, dark jungle, full of vines hanging down. Bushes and trees grew close-packed, and narrow trails crisscrossed around. Father Sheehy moved off the trail and they plunged into the leaves and branches, holding up their arms to protect their eyes. After a short distance they came to a tiny clearing.

"This okay?" asked Father Sheehy.

"It's fine."

They sat, each leaning his back against a tree. Father Sheehy took out a cigarette and lit it up. He didn't offer one to Gundy because he knew Gundy didn't smoke.

"Well," said Father Sheehy, smiling benevolently at Gundy, "what's the matter?"

"I killed a man today," Gundy replied in a low dull voice.

Father Sheehy looked at him. He knew Gundy's whole story, how he had left Saint Joseph's Abbey to become a combat medic, and that he was a conscientious objector. "How'd it happen?" Father Sheehy asked.

"There was a Japanese soldier near me, and I thought he was dead but he wasn't. He tried to shoot me, but I shot him first."

"Sounds like you shot him in self-defense."

Gundy nodded. "I suppose you could say that."

"Do you think there's something wrong with killing in self-defense? Is that what's bothering you?"

Gundy looked him in the eye. "Would Christ have killed in self-defense?"

Father Sheehy thought for a few moments. "I suppose not. But you're not Christ."

"Christianity tells me to be like Christ, and I failed. I shot that Japanese soldier in cold blood."

"Not really," said Father Sheehy. "He tried to shoot you first."

Gundy shook his head. "I still don't think I should have killed him."

Father Sheehy tried to figure out what to say. The hardest part of being an Army chaplain was justifying the war to soldiers like Gundy. "He's dead now," Father Sheehy said, trying to evade the issue. "We can't bring him back, so there's no use worrying about it."

"I'm not worrying. I just think I've committed an extremely serious act. The Ten Commandments ordered us not to kill, but I did."

"You're in the middle of a war," Father Sheehy said. "Killing happens. We Catholics believe this is a just war, so you did what you had to do."

"I don't know," Gundy replied. "I believe it's a just war, but I don't think I personally should kill anybody. I violated my principles. I'm a hypocrite." Gundy's voice broke and stuttered. "I think I'm going crazy."

"Have you prayed?"

"I haven't had time."

"Well, I think that's what you'd better do. I know how I feel about the war, but I'm not you. The Ten Commandments may say *'Thou Shall not kill'* but, as you know, there are many exceptions. We kill mosquitos all the time, for instance. We kill the plants we step on. We kill the plants we eat. We kill the chickens and pigs that we eat. And we kill the people who are trying to destroy us and civilization as well."

"Christ said to turn the other cheek," Gundy said.

Father Sheehy shrugged. "I'm not going to argue theology with you. I believe what I believe and you believe what you believe. Your training in theology is as good as mine and you're an intelligent young man. I don't believe I could convince you of anything that you didn't want to be convinced of. I suggest you pray for guidance. I think only God can clarify the confusion in your mind."

"Your're right. I'll try to pray."

"Maybe you ought to get a sedative from someone in your medical unit, to calm you down."

"I don't want any sedatives. I want to think clearly."

Father Sheehy wanted to remark that he didn't think Gundy was thinking so clearly without sedatives, but decided to keep his mouth shut. The young man was obviously distraught, and he didn't want to say anything that might send him over the edge.

"You can come back here and talk with me anytime you like," Father Sheehy said.

"Thank you, Father. I appreciate that."

Father Sheehy bent forward and touched Private Gundy on the shoulder. "Try to relax, all right?"

"Yes, Father."

"I'm going back to my tent. You can stay here as long as you like."

"Yes, Father."

Father Sheehy stood and walked into the jungle, disappearing in seconds. Private Gundy got onto his knees and clasped his hands together. He tried to pray, but all he could see before him was the bleeding body of the Japanese soldier he'd shot. He heard Father Sheehy moving away from him through the jungle. Then Father Sheehy's sounds stopped suddenly. There was silence for a few moments, then it sounded as if Father Sheehy was walking back toward him. Private Gundy moved to a sitting position and crossed his legs underneath him. Father Sheehy crashed through the jungle and poked his body through the leaves.

"I just thought of something," he said with a faint smile. "Mind if I tell you what I thought of?"

"Go ahead?"

"Well, I was thinking that if you let the Japanese soldier shoot you, you wouldn't be able to save the lives of wounded American soldiers anymore. When you shot the Japanese soldier, you only took one life, but if the Japanese soldier shot you, he might have killed ten or twenty, maybe even fifty, people indirectly."

Gundy sighed. "I don't want to be rude, Father, but I think that's just sophistry. The plain fact is that Christ wouldn't have shot anybody."

"Christ was never a combat medic, so we don't know what he'd have done in those circumstances."

"I know what he'd have done," Gundy said.

"I guess you're smarter than I am. Sorry to bother you. I won't bother you again."

Father Sheehy walked into the jungle again, and Private Gundy lowered his head, trying to pray.

FIFTEEN . . .

Deep in the tunnel system, Butsko carried the unconscious Craig Delane over his shoulders, while Sergeant Cameron pointed the flashlight straight ahead. The tunnel floor slanted upward and the air was fetid and damp. Butsko felt his morale slipping as the possibility of dying in the tunnel became more plausible.

The explosion of the Japanese ammunition dump had been a huge one, and it must have caved in much of the tunnel system. He'd never be able to dig out of there, but he'd have to try. Butsko wasn't the kind of man who would lie down and die.

"Shouldn't be much farther," Sergeant Cameron muttered.

"Yeah?"

"Think we'll get out of here, Butsko?"

"We've got a chance."

"We'll never get out of here," Sergeant Cameron said with resignation.

"We can try."

The tunnel twisted like an intestine through the bowels of the earth, and they trudged over the dirt floor, Butsko's shoulders drooping under the weight of Craig Delane. Butsko stopped for a moment, lit up a cigarette, and puffed it as he resumed walking. He felt frustrated and angry at the wall of dirt separating him from safety.

They turned a corner and Sergeant Cameron's flashlight shone on the part of the tunnel that had caved in. Dirt was halfway to the ceiling in spots, and then came the solid wall.

"Here we are," said Butsko. "You go first with the light."

Sergeant Cameron mumbled something unintelligible as he crawled forward over the piles of dirt. Butsko laid Craig Delane on his back and dragged him by the collar of his shirt. They came to the wall and Butsko pulled Craig Delane to the side, where he'd be out of the way.

"I'll take the first shift," Butsko said, pulling his entrenching tool from its sheath. "You can rest for a while."

Butsko adjusted the blade of the entrenching tool and hacked at the dirt, while Sergeant Cameron sat next to Craig Delane. Sergeant Cameron bent to the side, opened Craig Delane's eyelid with his thumb, and saw the white. *Looks like he ain't gonna make it,* Sergeant Cameron thought, taking out his package of cigarettes.

He lit one up and took a drag, watching Butsko leaning back and swinging his entrenching tool at the dirt wall. Butsko had broad shoulders and thick legs. The sinews of his arms were like ropes in the light of the flashlight Sergeant Cameron held. Sergeant Cameron felt weak and demoralized. He didn't see the point of digging, because he didn't think they could ever get through the tunnel. He was the kind of man who'd lie down and die.

Butsko slammed his entrenching tool into the wall, pulling away dirt, then hit it again. Perspiration trickled down his cheeks and he gritted his teeth as he worked in a frenzy. He wanted to believe that he could dig himself out of the tunnel. The harder he worked, the more he could convince himself that he was making progress. Straining, putting all of his considerable strength behind every blow, he gradually dug a tunnel into the wall. The tunnel was five feet high and a few feet across. If he had a pickax and shovel he could go a lot faster, but he had to be satisfied with his entrenching tool, whose small blade only removed a few handfuls at a time.

Butsko glanced at his watch. He wanted to work for an hour and then be replaced by Sergeant Cameron for an hour. Bending and shoveling, he gradually moved inside the narrow tunnel he was digging. The earth smelled fresh and moist—a farmer probably would love it—but to Butsko it was just the stuff that might make up his grave.

He thought of his wife Dolly, back in Honolulu. He'd had a reconciliation with her when he was on furlough two months earlier, after he'd beaten the shit out of her current boyfriend, a sergeant in the Marines. He'd been hoping they'd get together again when the war was over, but now it looked like he wasn't going to survive, and that thought made him shovel harder. She'd get a telegram that said he'd been killed in action. He wondered how she'd take it. She'd cry for a while, he imagined, but then she might feel relieved. She'd get his GI insurance, but she probably wouldn't hang on to it long. Dolly loved to spend money on clothes and booze and good times. Butsko wished he could have left a son behind, but he and Dolly hadn't been able to have children. He didn't know whether he or Dolly was the problem, but he suspected it was Dolly, since he was such a strong virile man.

His shirt plastered with sweat to his body, he whacked the blade of the entrenching tool into the dirt in front of him. Leaning back, whipping forward, he grunted as he struggled against the dirt, moving deeper into the hole he was digging. Sergeant Cameron couldn't see him anymore and decided to take a nap. He closed his eyes and drifted off into semiconsciousness, hearing the clang of Butsko's entrenching tool striking earth.

Butsko thought of his recon platoon and realized the battle for New Georgia hadn't been as big as the the the battle for Guadalcanal, but it had wiped out most of the recon platoon and would probably finish the job in the next two or three days. He figured that was how long he and Sergeant Cameron would last without food or water, and the air was getting bad already. He and Sergeant Cameron ought to stop smoking, but he'd rather not spend the last hours of his life on nicotine withdrawal.

He looked at his watch; his hour was just about up. He'd only dug into the wall about four feet, which wasn't very much. His chest heaving, he returned to the area where Sergeant Cameron was sleeping.

"Your turn," he said.

Sergeant Cameron opened his eyes. "I ain't digging."

179

"What do you mean, you ain't digging."

"What's the point?"

Butsko's shoulders sagged, because he was discouraged himself. "We ought to at least try."

"We'll never get through that wall."

"We ought to try," Butsko repeated, dropping down beside Craig Delane, feeling his pulse.

"Listen, Butsko," Sergeant Cameron said, his voice quavering, "we're going to die down here."

"Maybe not."

"Bullshit. You just don't wanna face the truth. This whole damned tunnel is caved in, and we're not gonna dig through it."

"How do you know?"

"I know."

Craig Delane's pulse was weak. Butsko removed his hand and took out a cigarette, lighting it with the Zippo he'd taken from Delane.

"Suit yourself," Butsko said. "I'm gonna keep digging."

"Do what you gotta do," Sergeant Cameron replied, "and I'll do what I gotta do. All I know is that we're not gonna get out of here, and I don't feel like digging anymore."

"You just wanna sit here and die?"

"That's right. What's wrong with that?"

"A man ought to try, at least."

Sergeant Cameron spat into the dirt. "Try what? I've worked hard enough in my life, and I don't feel like working anymore. Fuck it. I'm ready to die."

Butsko leaned his back against the cool dirt wall of the tunnel, smoking his cigarette. He had only three more. It looked like he was coming to the end of his road. Staring into the darkness, he thought of his childhood in McKeesport, Pennsylvania, where he'd quit school at the age of sixteen to work in the steel mill. Then the Depression came and he joined the Army, because the steel mill shut down. He met Dolly, got married, and then the war broke out. *Jesus, is this all my life has been? I was here for a while, I fucked around a little, and now I'm gonna die. What's it all for?*

He looked down at Craig Delane, who was breathing shallowly, lying on his back with his eyes closed. Delane had been rich before the war and could have bought anything he wanted, but he went crazy and enlisted after Pearl Harbor, and look what happened to him. *If only we all could have it to do over again. But what would I have done differently?* He thought about it and realized his life had been logical from start to finish and that he couldn't have done anything any differently.

The thoughts troubled him, and he decided to go back to work. Better to die trying to do something than sitting around feeling sorry for himself. He rose, stepped on his cigarette butt, and picked up his entrenching tool.

Sergeant Cameron glanced up at him. "What're you gonna do?"

"Dig some more."

"You're nuts, you know that?"

"Yeah."

Butsko carried the entrenching tool in his right hand and the flashlight in his left, and entered the tunnel he'd dug. He stepped inside it, repositioned the flashlight on the floor, and gripped the entrenching tool tightly, raising it. He tensed his muscles and was about to drive the entrenching tool forward into the dirt, when he heard something and stopped in mid-swing.

He wrinkled his nose and narrowed his eyes. *What the hell was that? Maybe only some water dripping someplace.* Pulling back the entrenching tool, he heard the sound again and stopped himself, frozen like a statue. The sound was extremely faint, but there it was again, and again. It was coming from the other side of the dirt. Butsko's face creased into a grim smile. Somebody was digging on the other end of the cave-in!

Butsko wanted to throw down his entrenching tool and jump for joy, but then he thought of something: The little tunnel he was in was acting like an echo chamber, amplifying the sound, but Sergeant Cameron probably couldn't hear it at all out there. Why not teach Sergeant Cameron a lesson about giving up too soon?

Butsko walked out of the little tunnel and saw Sergeant Cameron dozing against the wall. "Hey, wake up!" Butsko said, kicking Sergeant Cameron's boot.

"Huh—what happened?"

"I understand you're a betting man," Butsko said, kneeling beside Sergeant Cameron.

"I was, but now I just wanna die in peace."

"I wanna make a bet with you."

Sergeant Cameron opened his eyes wider. *"Now?"*

"Yeah."

"Leave me alone. I never mentioned it to you before, but everybody thinks you're crazy and so do I, now more than ever. Let me die in peace, will you?"

"I'll bet you a hundred dollars that we get out of here," Butsko said.

"Get the fuck away from me," Sergeant Cameron replied with a wave of his hand.

"If you don't think we're gonna get out of here, put your money where your mouth is."

"What money, you crazy bastard!"

"I'll write you an IOU if I lose."

"What the fuck good is that gonna do me? Get away from me!"

"Make the bet and I'll leave you alone," Butsko said, anxious to seal the deal before Sergeant Cameron heard anything.

Sergeant Cameron held out his filthy hand. "Okay—it's a bet."

Butsko shook his hand and laughed. "You just lost a hundred bananas, you stupid son of a bitch!"

"Whataya mean?"

"Come with me."

"Where?"

Butsko pointed to the tunnel he was digging. "In there."

"What's in there?"

"You'll be able to hear somebody digging us out."

Sergeant Cameron's jaw dropped open. *"Digging us out?"*

"That's right, shithead. They're digging us out right now."

"I don't believe it!"

"Come on and hear for yourself."

Butsko rose and walked hunched over toward the tunnel he'd been digging. Sergeant Cameron followed with an incredulous expression on his face. They entered the tunnel and Butsko looked at Sergeant Cameron. The sound of the digging on the other side was more distinct. Sergeant Cameron scowled.

"You son of a bitch," he said.

Butsko laughed and gave him the finger. "Up your ass!"

"You cheated me!"

"Fuck you."

Butsko walked out of the tunnel and picked up his M 1 rifle, opening the bolt to make sure bullets were inside.

"C'mon, let's let 'em know we're alive," he said.

He aimed backward into the depths of the main tunnel system and pulled the trigger of his M 1. It fired, echoing back and forth through the passageways, and he pulled the trigger two more times in rapid succession, the beginning of an SOS signal.

Sergeant Cameron watched, a disgusted expression on his face. Although he was going to be saved, he had something new to worry about: the hundred dollars he owed Butsko.

"You cheated me, you son of a bitch!" he said. "You took advantage of me!"

Butsko chortled, feeding a fresh clip into his M 1. "That'll teach you to pay attention to your old sarge. C'mon, fire your rifle. Let's tell 'em they're not digging for nothing."

Colonel Stockton was having lunch under his tarpaulin on Kokengolo Hill. More tables had been set up so that his staff officers could dine with him, and Lydia Kent-Taylor was there with Leo Stern, enjoying the Spam and dehydrated potatoes as if it were a steak with all the trimmings at a fancy restaurant in New York City.

Lieutenant Harper came running toward the table, stopping next to Colonel Stockton and saluting. "Sir, Colonel McCawley reports that somebody's firing rifles in the tunnel on the other side of the wall where his men are digging!"

Colonel Stockton looked up, a smile spreading over his face. "It must be the recon platoon!" Then he realized that Japs might be firing down there, and his smile vanished. "You'd better have some armed men down there, just in case."

"Colonel McCawley's got his combat engineers ready."

Lydia Kent-Taylor stood and picked up her camera bag.

"Where are you going?" Colonel Stockton asked.

"Into the tunnel to take some pictures."

"You'd better stay up here. There might be Japs down there." He looked at Lieutenant Harper again. "Did Colonel McCawley say how long he thought it'd be before he gets through the dirt?"

"About another hour or two."

"Go down there and let me know when he breaks through."

"Yes, sir."

Lieutenant Harper saluted, turned, and ran back toward the tunnel, the holster on his hip slapping up and down. Colonel Stockton cut into his chunk of Spam.

"I'll bet it's Butsko," he murmured.

Some of the officers thought that was wishful thinking, because Colonel Stockton was so fond of Butsko and the recon platoon. Lydia leaned toward Leo Stern.

"I hope it's them," she said softly.

"If it is, it'll be one helluva story, and we'll be right on top of it."

Lydia pushed away her half-eaten meal and opened her camera bag to check her equipment one more time. If she could get the right picture, *Life* magazine might even buy it for the cover. She'd had her photographs published in *Life* before, but she'd never had a cover. Unscrewing the fifty-millimeter lens from the camera, blowing a speck of dust from the rear element, she thought about Butsko and wondered if he was alive or dead. She already knew that the Twenty-third had taken an unusual number of casualties inside Kokengolo Hill, and hoped he hadn't been one of them. *I'll be glad to see him again,* she admitted to herself. *I don't know what I'll do, but I hope he survives.*

Butsko sat with his back against the wall, smoking his last cigarette and listening to the sound of digging nearby. It was clear that there wasn't much dirt between him and the people who were digging. He even could distinguish between the pick-axs and the shovels. A lot of men were out there, and they were digging like sons of bitches.

Sergeant Cameron had gotten over his anger about the bet and now was looking forward to being rescued. He puffed his cigarette, humming a little tune. He'd thought he was going to be buried alive, but now he was going to live. The battle for New Georgia was over. He'd be able to rest, maybe even get a furlough back to the States.

Butsko blew a smoke ring into the air. "You wanna know what I'm gonna do with your hundred dollars? I'm gonna spend it all in a whorehouse! Every fucking penny!"

"I hope you get syphilis, you bastard."

"That's a helluva thing to wish on your old sarge."

184

"I hope you get the clap too."

Dirt fell down from the wall in front of them, and a shovel gleamed in the ray of the flashlight.

"Anybody there?" asked a voice through the hole.

"You're damned straight somebody's here!" Butsko replied, getting to his feet. "About time you showed up!" He walked toward the hole, bent down, and saw a face with a growth of beard. "Who're you?"

"Pfc. Drake, Two-Seventy-first Engineers."

Butsko extended his hand. "Sergeant Butsko, recon platoon, Twenty-third Infantry. Hurry up and make this hole bigger, because I want to get the hell out of here!"

The engineers dug out the hole, and Butsko lifted Craig Delane, draping him over his shoulder. He entered the smaller tunnel and saw that the hole was big enough for him to pass through. Lowering his head, he stepped through it, and Delane's head brushed against the dirt.

"Is there a medic around here?" Butsko asked.

"I'm a medic," said a voice in the shadows.

"This guy's been shot, but he's still alive."

"Put him down over here."

A stretcher was laid out on the ground, and Butsko set Craig Delane down on top of it. "A bullet's in his shoulder," Butsko said.

"You all right?"

"Yeah."

The medic looked at Sergeant Cameron. "How about you?"

"I'm okay."

Lieutenant Colonel McCawley walked up to Butsko. "Anybody else alive in there?"

"I don't think so, but you might want to check."

"Very well, Sergeant. Good to see you." He shook Butsko's hand. "Colonel Stockton is waiting for you topside. Can you make it okay?"

"We're fine," Butsko said. "We can make it on our own."

Lieutenant Harper ran ahead to notify Colonel Stockton that Butsko and Sergeant Cameron were on their way. The two GIs followed, walking slowly, weary and glad that they'd been saved. They turned the corners and saw the rooms where they'd fought earlier in the day, climbing steadily until they could see a shaft of sunlight ahead. The tunnel became lighter as they approached the opening, and they had to squint because they'd become accustomed to the darkness.

"We made it," Butsko said.

"For a while down there I never thought we'd get out."

"There were times I thought we'd never get out too."

"Are you still gonna make me pay you that hundred bucks?"

"A bet is a bet."

Colonel Stockton, his staff, Lydia Kent-Taylor, and Leo Stern were among the crowd waiting at the entrance to the tunnel. Butsko and Sergeant Cameron emerged, and Lydia had her camera ready. She filled the frame with Butsko, the cigarette hanging from the corner of his mouth, his eyes squinting, rifle slung over his shoulder, dried blood showing on nicks and scratches on his face.

Click!

Colonel Stockton stepped forward and shook Butsko's hand. "Nice to see you again, Sergeant."

"Nice to see you, sir."

Colonel Stockton shook Sergeant Cameron's hand. "Glad you made it."

"Not as glad as I am, sir."

Lydia stepped forward and waved her hand. "Can I get a shot of the three of you together?"

"Sure," said Colonel Stockton. "Line up with me, will you, boys?"

Lydia got down on one knee so she could shoot upward, altering the angle. "Let's have a smile, gentlemen," she said, holding her finger poised on the button.

Colonel Stockton smiled his best officer's smile; Sergeant Cameron scowled, because he was thinking of the hundred dollars he had to pay Butsko; and Butsko didn't feel like smiling, because nearly his entire platoon had been killed or wounded that day.

"C'mon, Sergeant Butsko," Lydia said. "Let's give us a smile."

Butsko didn't feel up to it. All he could do was pull back his gums and bare his teeth like an angry dog. Lydia realized that that was the best she'd get, so she pressed the button.

Click!

SIXTEEN . . .

The molten sun was sunk halfway below the horizon, and the Mosquito tiptoed through the jungle, stopping behind a tree every several paces to look and listen, then proceeding again.

The Mosquito had become a nervous wreck, because he'd been bumping into GI patrols, bivouacs, mess tents, and every other GI formation imaginable throughout the afternoon. Everyplace he went he kept bumping into GIs. They seemed to be everywhere. He'd thought it'd be easy to break into open jungle, but evidently he'd jumped out of that truck when it was far inside the American lines. Now all he could do was head in a westerly direction, following the setting sun, and hope everything would get easier when it was dark.

He passed silently between two bushes and dropped to his knees behind a tree. He was exhausted, had no water, and was nearly starved to death. Little puddles were all over the jungle, but he was afraid to drink the water and he had no means to boil it first. He was beginning to wonder whether or not he'd get away. He'd thought of surrendering, but was afraid the Americans would shoot him.

He heard the engine of a vehicle, and dropped lower behind the tree. Drawing his bayonet, the only weapon he had, he figured the direction of the sound and put the tree behind him and it. The vehicle came closer and the Mosquito peeked out from behind the tree. He saw a truck with a red cross on its side about twenty yards away, moving from right to left in front of him. Ducking behind the tree quickly, his heart beating like a machine gun, he hoped no one had seen him. He hadn't realized he was so close to a road.

How am I going to get out of here? he wondered as the sound of the truck receded into the distance. He had no idea of where he was, but he had to keep moving, because he had no other choice. Rising carefully from the ground, he crawled toward the road on his belly. When he reached the shoulder, he peered through a bush to make sure no GIs were marching on the road. He was relieved to see that no one was there.

Taking a deep breath, he jumped up and ran across the road, diving into the bushes on the other side and lying still for several moments, listening and looking around, before getting to his feet and continuing his long meandering trek to safety.

Private Gundy was in the regimental medical headquarters, helping with the wounded, although it wasn't his job. His praying had brought him no answers, and he'd gone there because he didn't know what to do with himself.

He was in a section of the tent where soldiers were being prepared to surgery, and he knelt next to Corporal Bannon, who'd go under the knife soon. At one end of the tent was a spot where two flaps joined, and a bright light shone on the other side. Through the crack Gundy could see doctors and nurses bustling about, operating on soldiers. Orderlies continually carried soldiers in and out on stretchers. The ones going in had dirty bandages, and the ones coming out were swathed in clean white strips, but some were without arms and legs, and some came out in rubber bags, having died on the operating table.

Gundy looked down at Corporal Bannon, who had so many bandages wrapped around his head, it looked like he was wearing a turban. Bannon was pale and his breath shallow. They'd pumped him full of morphine and he had a faint smile on his face.

Gundy placed his hand on Bannon's, because he'd liked Bannon. He couldn't imagine the recon platoon without Bannon. Bannon had been through much war on Guadalcanal, but this was the first time he'd been wounded badly. The doctor said Bannon would recover, but they'd have to put a steel plate in his head.

Butsko entered the tent, and Gundy spotted him immediately. "Hey, Sarge!" he said, waving his hand.

Butsko saw him and walked over, carrying his helmet under his arm and his M 1 slung on his shoulder. He stepped over the bodies of GIs and spotted Bannon lying next to Gundy.

"Just the guy I was looking for," Butsko said, kneeling beside Gundy. "How is he?"

"His skull's fractured pretty badly. They'll have to put a steel plate in his head."

"He'll probably get sent back to the States with a wound like that."

"I don't know. Maybe."

Butsko looked down at Bannon. "Poor son of a bitch."

"It was an artillery shell. I saw it blow him into the air."

"He's lucky it didn't kill him, but he's always had a hard fucking head." Butsko sniffed and wiped his nose with the back of his hand. "I hope the doctor's right. Bannon saved my life once on Guadalcanal." Butsko looked at Gundy. "You look a little green around the gills, kid. You all right?"

Gundy groaned and shook his head. "I'm not feeling so good myself."

"Maybe you'd better lie down."

"Naw, I don't want to lie down."

"What's eating you?"

"Oh, I'm sure you got enough to worry about without listening to my baloney."

Butsko shrugged. "I don't have anything to worry about. My whole platoon's been wiped out. Even Lieutenant Breckenridge is in here someplace. I've just got myself to take care of now. You see any of the other guys in here?"

"I saw Craig Delane and Frankie La Barbara. The orderlies told me Lieutenant Breckenridge was evacuated to Guadalcanal on a plane. He needed a special operation, and the only doctor who can do it is on Guadalcanal."

Butsko narrowed his eyes and looked Gundy over. "You sure you're okay?"

"I never said I'm okay. I'm going nuts."

"Shit, Gundy, you were nuts long before you ever came into the Army." Butsko grinned and slapped Gundy on the shoulder.

"That's true," Gundy said, "but I killed a man today."

"Congratulations. I hope it was a Jap."

"It was a Jap. I shot him."

"Good for you. A dead Jap is a good Jap, I always say."

"But, Sarge, I didn't join the Army to kill people."

Butsko nodded. "I know, you're a conscientious objector. Is that what's bothering you—you killed a Jap?"

"Yes."

Butsko squeezed Gundy's shoulder. "Listen, people always have to do things they don't like to do in a war. We got no choice. A war is a bloody, shitty mess and everybody has to make the best of it that they can."

"I know," Gundy said, "but I never wanted to kill anybody. I think that's wrong."

"The whole war is wrong. Life is wrong. It's kill or be killed out here. This ain't no John Wayne movie, you know."

"But God said *Thou shalt not kill*."

"Fuck God. If He doesn't want us to kill, let Him stop the war. You talk to the chaplain about this?"

"Yes."

"It didn't do any good?"

"No."

"Which one you talk to?"

"Father Sheehy."

"He's a nice guy, but he's a windbag, just like all the rest of them. You know what your problem is, Gundy? You worry too much. You're always afraid you'll do something wrong and God will send you to hell. Well, look around you, birdbrain. You think you're not in hell already? You think hell could be any worse than this?"

"Yes," Gundy said.

An expression of boredom came over Butsko's face. "Listen, if there is a hell, I don't think a person could get sent there for shooting somebody who was going to shoot him first. Somehow that don't make sense to me."

"But Christ told us to turn the other cheek."

"Fuck that," Butsko said. "That's bullshit." He placed his hand on Bannon's cheek. "Poor son of a bitch. I hope he pulls through." Butsko looked at his watch. "I'm gonna go look for some of the other guys, then I'll come back. Where'd you say Craig Delane was?"

"In that tent over there."

Butsko stood and stretched. "I'll see you later. And for Chrissakes, stop worrying so much. Don't be a shithead all your life."

Butsko turned and walked away, stepping over soldiers waiting to go into the operating room, dodging orderlies carrying soldiers on stretchers. He walked out of the tent. Gundy knew that beneath Butsko's tough exterior was a sensitive man, always concerned about his soldiers. Butsko could be sleeping right now, after a hard day of fighting and being trapped underground, but instead he was checking on his men. He was okay despite his rough edges.

Gundy felt tired. His eyes drooped and his mind was losing its snap. *Maybe I really do worry too much,* he thought. *If I had more faith in God, I wouldn't worry so much. I'd just let God take care of everything, and all I'd do is the best I can, just like Butsko said.*

He looked up as two orderlies approached with a stretcher. Their green fatigues were splattered with blood, and they laid the stretcher down beside Bannon.

"We're taking him in now," one of them said to Gundy.

Gundy got out of the way, and they rolled Bannon onto the stretcher. Then they lifted the poles and carried him toward the operating room, disappearing into the bright light, the tent flap closing behind them.

Gundy stood and wondered what to do with himself. *Maybe I should go pray for Bannon,* he thought. *I'm always worried about myself; maybe I should worry about somebody else for a change.*

Exhausted, his head feeling as though it were filled with lead, he stumbled out of the hospital tent, fingering the crucifix that hung around his neck with his dog tags.

SEVENTEEN . . .

Lydia Kent-Taylor stood beside Craig Delane, who lay on a hospital cot, his upper torso all bandaged. Delane was awake but heavily medicated: In other words, he was stoned out of his mind on morphine.

"Hey, look!" said Craig. "Here comes Butsko!"

Lydia spun around, and sure enough Butsko walked toward them through the aisle between the cots.

"Well, looka here," Butsko said, a roguish grin on his face, "we got a famous lady photographer and a doggie who zigged when he shoulda zagged." He bent down and winked at Delane. "How're you feeling, kid?"

"Okay, Sarge."

"They treating you all right?"

"Just fine."

Butsko straightened and looked at Lydia Kent-Taylor, who calmly crossed her arms under her breasts and returned his gaze. She'd seen so much blood and death within the past fourteen hours that Butsko didn't faze her anymore.

"How's the lady photographer?" he asked.

"Not bad. How's the sergeant who likes to scare people?"

"Still trying to scare people."

"Hey, Sarge," Delane said, "Gundy was here awhile ago and he said the whole platoon got wiped out today."

"It did. About half are dead and the rest wounded."

"Gee," said Delane.

"Me and Sergeant Cameron are the only ones still walking around," Butsko said.

"That's because you two are the toughest," Delane replied.

"Naw, just the luckiest."

"And the nastiest," Lydia added.

Butsko chuckled and pointed to Delane. "Nice guys usually wind up like that."

"C'mon, Sarge," Delane said, insulted, "I'm not that nice."

"No," he agreed, "you're not *that* nice. You're not as nice as the famous lady photographer here, for instance."

"She's not that nice either," Delane said.

"*Craig!*" she replied.

Delane laughed in a silly drugged way.

Butsko looked at his watch. "Well, I'm glad to see you're okay, kid. I wanna check on some of the other guys now, and I'll stop by again tomorrow if they let me come over here."

"Thanks for coming, Sarge. Hey, how're you getting back?"

"I'll hitch a ride with somebody."

Delane looked at Lydia. "Why don't you drive him back? You're going that way, aren't you?"

Lydia became flustered. "Why, yes...I...ah..."

"Good, you can give Butsko a lift."

Butsko smiled at her. "That'd be real nice of you, ma'am. I'll see you outside in about a half hour?"

"All right, Sergeant."

Butsko patted Delane on the head. "Take it easy, kid. See you later."

Butsko turned and walked away, his gait unsteady from fatigue.

Craig Delane watched him go. "He's a terrific guy."

"To each his own," she replied dryly. "I wish you hadn't volunteered me to drive him back."

"Why don't you want to drive him back?"

Lydia didn't know what to say, because she didn't want to admit the truth: She was starting to feel turned on by Butsko again. And Leo wasn't around to chaperone; he was back with the Twenty-third Regiment, typing his big story about the attack on Kokengolo Hill.

"I just asked you a question," Delane said.

"I've got enough to do without having to operate a taxi service for your platoon sergeant."

"But you're going back the same way he is."

"I know it," she said testily.

Delane laughed.

"What was that for?" she asked.

"I was just thinking that what you probably need most right now is a good screw, Lydia."

"What?"

Delane laughed again. "You heard me."

She balled up her fists. "If you weren't wounded, I'd punch you right in the nose!"

"If I weren't wounded, I'd probably try to get you myself."

"Craig!"

Craig Delane closed his eyes, a big smile on his face. Lydia ran her fingers through her hair and tried to think. *It must be all the drugs they've given him,* she thought. *He doesn't know what he's saying. He'd never say anything like that if his mind were clear.*

The smile vanished on Craig Delane's face as he dropped into slumber. Lydia looked at her watch. *Maybe I'd better get going,* she thought. *I need some sleep myself. I can always come back tomorrow.*

She slung her camera bag over her shoulder and headed for the door. The tent was full of wounded soldiers lying in rows, and it'd make a good picture, but she didn't feel like taking any more pictures.

I hope Butsko doesn't show up, she thought. *I really don't feel like dealing with him right now.*

Butsko did show up. Lydia sat behind the wheel of her jeep, waiting for him, and he stepped out of the tent, pausing and lighting a cigarette, the flames from his lighter flashing over his face. He looked around, spotted her, and strolled toward her.

"Move over," he said. "I'll drive."

"That's all right," she said, not moving. "I know the way."

"At night?"

"More or less."

"I don't feel like getting lost. Move over."

"Don't give orders. I'm not in your platoon."

"Listen, lady," Butsko told her, the tent behind him leaking shafts of light, "there's Japs still wandering around out there, looking for somebody to kill, and I don't feel like taking any chances."

"Oh, all right."

She shifted to the passenger seat, and Butsko got behind the wheel. He tossed his helmet onto the backseat, and his black hair sprawled in all directions. He needed a haircut badly—also a shave and bath.

"You stink," she said.

"Fuck you," he replied.

Butsko reached forward and turned on the ignition switch, while Lydia boiled and fumed. She didn't know whether to slap Butsko in the face, tell him what a lowlife he was, or call the MPs.

"Relax," he said, shifting into reverse and backing up. He turned the wheel, shifted into first, and pressed the accelerator. The jeep jumped forward and rolled onto the dirt road.

A full moon shone high in the sky, and the breeze felt good against Lydia's face as Butsko accelerated. The sound of the engine made conversation impossible, which was all right with her. She didn't want to talk with Butsko or have anything to do with him. He was just a brute, a pig, a beast. She glanced sideways at him and saw his profile in the moonlight. Clean him up a little and straighten his broken nose, and he might not be too bad-looking. His shirt was unbuttoned halfway to his waist and she could see the hair on his chest, his bulging shoulders and biceps, and farther down his muscular legs. Despite the breeze, she began to feel warm again.

Lydia started to get that old horny feeling. She looked away from Butsko, took out a cigarette, held her head below the dash, and lit it up. She felt troubled and angry, because she didn't want to be attracted to him. He definitely wasn't the sort of man for her, and she didn't like sex that much anyway. It was too animalistic and embarrassing, an unwarranted invasion of her privacy. But if she believed that, why did she keep glancing at Butsko? Why was her mind spinning out sex fantasies about him, despite her attempts to think about other things? Why did she want to reach over and squeeze that big bulge between his legs?

She looked to her right, into the jungle whizzing by. They

196

passed a company of soldiers in a column of twos, and Butsko steered to the side of the road so a deuce-and-a-half truck could get by. The night was clear and the full moon provided excellent visibility. As soon as she returned to the Twenty-third Regiment she'd pack her bags, round up Leo, and get the hell out of there.

They drove for a half hour, and then Butsko turned to the left. Ahead was the Pacific Ocean, and the full moon made a long golden line across it. Butsko drove onto the sand, turned to the right, continued for twenty yards, and stopped.

"What are you stopping here for?" she asked.

"I thought it'd be a good place to fuck," Butsko replied.

She couldn't believe her ears. "What was that again?"

"I said I thought this'd be a good place to fuck." He pointed to the sky with his hand. "We got the moon, we got the stars, we got the ocean—what could be better?" He reached forward and turned off the ignition switch, then pulled up the emergency brake.

She wrinkled her nose and forehead in alarm. "Are you crazy?"

"That's what everybody says."

She still couldn't believe it. "You mean you're going to rape me?"

"Something like that."

"I'll scream!"

"No one will hear you."

She looked at him and tried to smile. "C'mon, be a nice guy, okay? Drive me back to the Twenty-third Regiment, and I promise I won't mention this to anybody."

"What do I care who you mention it to?"

Butsko swung his feet around, stood, and walked to her side of the jeep. Lydia didn't know whether to shit or go blind.

"Now, see here . . . !" she said.

He stopped in front of her and grinned. "Let's stop fooling around. You want to fuck me and I want to fuck you, so let's do it and get it over with."

"What!"

He grabbed her wrist and pulled her out of the jeep. She scrambled down, trying to work her hand loose.

"Let me go!"

"Cut out the bullshit!"

197

He dragged her across the sand and into the jungle, while she struggled to get loose.

"You can't do this to me!" she screamed.

"You wanna bet?"

They came to a little clearing, and he let her wrist go. "This looks like a good spot," he said, unbuttoning his shirt. "Take your clothes off."

"I will not!"

"If you don't take them off, I'll take them off for you."

She turned to run, but he tackled her and they fell to the ground. He rolled her onto her back and lay on top of her.

"I thought I told you to cut out the bullshit," he said hoarsely. "You know you're going to give in eventually, so why don't you do it now and save both of us some trouble."

She gritted her teeth and her eyes sparkled in the moonlight. "Let me go!"

"C'mon, you know you want to fuck me."

"I do not!"

"Sure you do. I been around long enough to know how a woman acts when she wants my cock, so I thought I'd do you a favor and give it to you. I don't know why I'm taking the trouble, because women like you are usually lousy fucks anyway."

"What!"

He lowered his head and touched his lips to hers. His great weight pressed against her and he pinned her wrists to the sand. She could feel something huge against her stomach, and realized it was his dick. He was a big, smelly, muscular man and he was overpowering her. She hated herself because somehow, perversely, she was becoming aroused.

He kissed her lips so gently that it surprised her. "C'mon," he said, "don't be such a bitch."

"Please let me go," she whispered, trying to avoid his mouth.

"You really don't want me to let you go, do you?" He kissed her again and let her wrists go, taking her face in his hands. "You're a real doll, and you've got a real nice ass for a woman your age."

"Woman my age? How dare—"

Before she could spit the words out, he covered her mouth with his and licked her lips with his tongue. Her hands were loose and she thought she should pull his hair or gouge out his eyes, but what she really wanted to do was hug all that strength and virility, so that's what she did, reaching around him and squeezing.

"That's better," he said, unbuttoning her shirt.

"I don't know why I'm doing this," she murmured.

"I do," he replied, lowering his head and kissing the valley between her breasts.

She reached up and ran her fingers through his shaggy hair, while he pulled her brassiere down and touched his tongue to her left nipple. Lydia felt electricity up and down her spine, and he took her nipple into his mouth, sucking rhythmically, squeezing her breast with his hand. She closed her eyes and thought: What the hell, there really wasn't any harm in a little sex, and he wasn't hurting her; he was being very nice. His big monstrous thing throbbed against her stomach, and she squirmed so she could feel it better.

"I don't know what I was afraid of," she whispered to the man in the moon.

"You're a nervous wreck," Butsko replied, "but I've got just what you need." He rolled to the side, lay on his back, and unbuttoned his pants, taking out his primary weapon, which he wagged back and forth. "This."

"You're a bastard," she said.

"That's true, but I'm your bastard," he replied, rolling onto her again.

They made love for nearly three hours, in all the positions, rolling around on the jungle floor, going down on each other, having numerous orgasms. The breeze from the ocean kept the insects away from them and made the air briny as they hugged and kissed and humped like wild animals. It was the greatest sexual experience of Lydia's life, and a few times she thought she'd died and gone to heaven, but for Butsko it was just business as usual; this was the way he loved all his women.

Lydia never had sucked a cock in her life, and never thought she would, but she sucked Butsko's for long periods of time and with great relish, and he even came in her mouth once. Nobody had ever gone down on her in her life, but Butsko did, chewing and nibbling, licking and slurping, and she thought she'd get so far out she'd never come back again; but she did come back, after she came against his lips and tongue.

He told her to get on all fours, and he screwed her like a dog. He laid on his back and she sat on his joint, bouncing happily up and down. They lay side by side, facing each other, and did it that way for a while; then she rolled over so that her back was to his front, and he slid it in from that direction, which she thought was really lovely.

But no one can do it forever, not even a sexual degenerate like Butsko. Finally he was dry and she was sore. All they could do was collapse and fall asleep. The moon rose higher in the sky, and waves gently lapped the white sand of New Georgia as they snored in each other's arms.

The Mosquito moved through the shadowy jungle, weak from hunger and dizzy with thirst. He'd heard the ocean and smelled the salt air and now headed toward it, hoping to catch a fish so he cold eat its flesh and drink its blood.

The bright moonlight was a mixed blessing, because it permitted him to see more easily, but it would also make it easier for someone to see him. He walked hunched over, hiding behind bushes and trees, stopping frequently to look and listen for Americans.

He knew the ocean was close: He could hear its waves rush against the shore. He didn't know exactly how he'd do it, but he couldn't wait to catch a fish and eat it raw. Maybe he could find clams and mussels too. Perhaps there'd even be coconuts and he could have a feast.

If he found some food quickly, he could survive. He needed strength to carry him deep into the jungle and away from the Americans. But he had little strength left after his grueling day and night. His hands trembled and his eyes played tricks on him. His knees wobbled and sometimes he thought he'd faint.

He had survived in the back alleys of Tokyo since he was six years old, against all the odds, and had a strong will. Resolutely he pushed his legs forward, gulping air, grinding his teeth together, pressing on. *Somehow I'll make it,* he thought. *I know I can do it.*

He entered a small clearing and couldn't believe what was in front of him. It looked like a man and woman, Americans, lying on the ground, embracing each other, fast asleep. He thought he might be hallucinating, the scene was so preposterous and sudden. Stepping backward to get away, his foot came down on a dry twig.

Butsko heard the twig snap and reached for his M 1 rifle. Blinking in the moonlight, he saw a Japanese soldier in front of him, waving his arms and screaming. Butsko, on his knees, rammed a round into the chamber and fired, holding the rifle butt to his waist. He couldn't understand that the Mosquito was saying "I surrender" in Japanese. Butsko thought the Japanese soldier was coming to slit his throat.

His M 1 fired and he pulled the trigger again. Lydia shrieked in horror, holding her fists to her cheeks, seeing the bullets send the Japanese soldier flying backward into the bushes. Butsko jumped to his feet and charged, naked as a jaybird, firing his M 1 from the waist. He rushed toward the Japanese soldier bleeding on the ground, stopped, aimed down, and blew the Japanese soldier's head apart.

Butsko crouched and looked around, swinging his M 1 from side to side, expecting more Japs to attack, but no one came and the jungle was quiet.

"What is it?" Lydia cried.

"It's all right!" Butsko replied. "C'mere!"

Lydia put on her shirt, covering scratches, black-and-blue marks, and sucker bites made by Butsko, and tiptoed into the bushes. She saw Butsko standing bareassed in the moonlight over the bleeding body of a Japanese soldier whose head was partially missing.

"My God," she said, pressing her fingers to her lips.

"He was sneaking up on us," Butsko replied. "Another few seconds and he would've had us. Wanna take his picture?"

She looked away. "No, I don't think so."

"We'd better get out of here. There might be more Japs around."

"Really!"

"You never know."

"You brought me here and there are Japs around!"

"Calm down. Put your clothes on. Jesus Christ, you're a nervous wreck, you know that? You're even worse than some of the guys in my platoon."

Lydia returned to the clearing and put on her clothes. Butsko joined her and got dressed too. She sat on the ground and laced her boots. A thought occurred to her.

"Maybe he was trying to surrender," she said.

"Don't be an asshole all your life. Jap's don't surrender. They fight until they're dead. You almost ready?"

"Just a few more seconds."

"Let's get out of here."

Butsko held his rifle in both hands, glancing around furtively, his body tensed for action. Lydia tied her bootlaces and stood.

"I'm ready."

"Let's go."

They turned and walked swiftly out of the jungle, heading toward the jeep parked near the treeline. In the jungle clearing the Mosquito's lifeless body leaked blood onto the ground. A rat crawled out of a hole nearby and chewed on the Japanese soldier's finger. Blood glistened in the moonlight as the jeep started up and drove away, heading toward the safety of the Twenty-third Regiment bivouac.

Look for

DO OR DIE

next novel in the new RAT BASTARDS series from Jove

coming in November!